ORPHANS OF WONDERLAND

GREG F. GIFUNE

JOURNALSTONE
YOUR LINK TO ARTIST TALENT

JournalStone books may be ordered through booksellers or by contacting:

JournalStone

www.journalstone.com

ISBN: 978-1-947654-42-6 (sc)
ISBN: 978-1-947654-43-3 (ebook)

JournalStone rev. date: July 27, 2018
2nd Edition

Library of Congress Control Number: 2018947242

Printed in the United States of America

Cover Design: Claudia Sperl / labelschmiede.com / 99designs
Life after death – stock image © exile7 / depositphotos.com
Interior Layout: Jess Landry

Proofread by Scarlett R. Algee

ORPHANS OF WONDERLAND

For that orphaned part of me I'm still looking for.

CHAPTER ONE

There was something wrong.

Lonnie Scott knew this to be true. He could no longer deny it. In fact, it was the last thing on his mind just before everything went dark.

Night had fallen earlier, but there was something different about this darkness, something unnatural, malevolent and wise. Something familiar. And the deeper he looked into it, something profound began to emerge: a basic instinct to survive, and the primal fear that accompanied it.

A feeling of light-headedness from somewhere behind his eyes slowly bled out across his skull, and Lonnie feared he might pass out. He closed his eyes, trading one kind of darkness for another. A moment later, he opened his eyes.

The sensation had passed.

Unnoticed, the night around him moved, swirling like liquid.

Lonnie adjusted his position in the recliner, searched around beneath the blanket covering his legs for the television remote, and finally found it tucked beneath the back of his calf. Pulling it free, he aimed the remote at the TV in the corner, which was displaying nothing but snow, and switched it off.

The apartment fell into darkness. As his eyes adjusted, the moonlight, though sparse, was sufficient enough to help him focus somewhat, and his surroundings gradually became clearer. Had he fallen asleep? What the hell time was it?

Lonnie checked his watch, bringing it close to his face. It was a little after three in the morning. Last thing he remembered was having a few drinks, then watching a documentary on TV. Something on one of the nature channels about the migration of monarch butterflies, but he couldn't recall much else. A disposable lighter, an empty glass, and a bottle of whiskey with a third left in it sat on the coffee table, alongside a plastic ashtray and a cheap cigar smoked down to a stub.

Yes, he—he'd been dreaming. Just now, he was sure of it. Traces of it still lingered just beyond his reach. The car…the big black car…that's what he'd dreamed of, that goddamn monstrosity from all those years before, slithering down the street like a living thing, a demon serpent come to devour him and the others. Those awful memories—blurred and vague and unimaginably horrifying—now consigned to his nightmares, had never left him, and he knew they never would. It wasn't possible.

His tongue swirled around inside his mouth, tasted the harsh remnants of smoke and booze. Stifling a yawn, he rubbed his eyes and looked to the barred windows of his first-floor apartment. Heavy snow blew against them, spattering on the glass. Just beyond, on the sidewalk, thick flakes fell across a pool of pale light carved onto an otherwise black canvas of night. It wasn't moonlight guiding him after all, but a beam cast from the streetlight closest to the windows.

The city was quiet—unusually so—and everything was still. It should've seemed peaceful, but didn't. In fact, Lonnie felt anything but. He couldn't shake the feeling that something was horribly wrong. And he knew all too well what that could mean.

A peculiar sound echoed through the small apartment, startling him. He adjusted his position, reached for the lever on the recliner with his free hand, and pulled the footrest down. Now in a sitting position, he listened a moment.

There it was again.

A drip. The faucet in the adjacent bathroom was dripping, that was all. Lonnie drew a deep breath, let it out slowly and shook his head. Damn thing dripped all the time, not like he'd never heard it before. Why was it spooking him so? There was only one answer, and it whispered to him from the blackest corners of his mind.

No.

Lonnie put the remote aside, then rubbed his eyes. He'd nodded off a while ago and had been asleep for hours. Maybe he'd been dreaming again, having the nightmares that came to him so often. But he'd escaped sleep; why was he still so jumpy?

The feeling of dread tightened, wrapping around him like a funereal shroud.

With a muffled grunt, he struggled to his feet. His whole body hurt. This kind of weather made his joints and muscles ache even more than usual, and since he'd turned fifty, it had gotten worse. Every insignificant or nagging injury he'd ever sustained was exaggerated in winter, every ache and pain underscored.

Shadows drifted through the tiny apartment.

Shuffling along in his slippers, Lonnie made his way to the windows and looked out at the street. No one out there, no cars moving, everything draped in white, already a good four or five inches on the ground. The weather reports had called for more than ten inches by the time the storm was finished with them, and at the rate the flakes were falling, it looked like those predictions were dead-on.

His stomach gurgled. He blamed the Chinese delivery he'd eaten earlier, but he knew better. As if to illustrate the point, something across the street, at the very edge of the light's reach, separated from the darkness.

A form…a human form. Or was it? He squinted, hoping for a better look.

A dark figure, perhaps someone dressed entirely in black, stood across the street, staring at Lonnie's building. While it wasn't unheard of to see people walking about at all hours—this was a city, after all—it was unusual this late, and especially in this kind of inhospitable weather.

Lonnie was waiting, watching to see what the figure might do, when a second form stepped from the darkness and took up position next to the first. Then there came another, and another still, until four silhouettes stood in a row in what he now realized was the middle of the street. Snow fell all around them, but they seemed unconcerned. Like dark statues unmoving in the storm, they watched the building,.

The feeling of trepidation increased. Lonnie ran a hand along the stubble on his cheeks and chin and continued peering out into the night. Why were these phantoms paying such obvious attention to his building in particular? Lonnie had lived in his apartment about a year, but kept mostly to himself and knew only one of his fellow tenants well. Still, he knew enough to realize that no one of any importance lived there. The apartments above him, four units in all, housed three elderly retired couples and one middle-aged woman, a widowed postal worker.

But the others weren't here for any of them. They were here for him.

Lonnie crouched down and opened a small set of doors in a storage unit below the windows. Rummaging around quickly in the dark, he retrieved a small case that held his 9mm handgun. He placed it carefully on the coffee table, opened it and pulled the gun free. As he slid the safety off, he glanced at the cordless phone, but there was no point in concerning himself with that. A call to 911 couldn't help him.

No one could.

His eyes darted around the dark apartment until they came to rest on the door. He went to it quickly and made sure it was locked. When he realized it was, he fell against it, his head spinning and heart pounding.

Looking back at the windows, he realized they were quickly becoming so badly caked with snow and ice that within minutes he'd no longer be able to see the street beyond, so he hurried back over to them for another look.

The dark figures were moving along the street just beyond the windows. He crouched lower, so as not to be seen, as they walked in single file, slowly passing beneath the streetlight. If they'd seen him, they gave no indication. But God help him, he'd seen them, and they didn't look right. They didn't look right at all. They looked impossibly, horribly wrong. Wearing what appeared to be strange and intricate headpieces of some kind, all four were otherwise nude.

And covered from head to toe in blood.

Something scratched at the door, slowly scraping its way across it.

Lonnie spun around, his terror so great his body shook with a level of violence he couldn't control. He raised the gun, hands shaking.

Something was seeping beneath the door.

Blood…a river of it forming a growing crimson puddle on the floor.

"Please…"

And then, suddenly as it began, it stopped.

Lonnie blinked rapidly, trying to keep everything in focus.

The blood he'd seen on the floor was gone.

Quietly, he crept closer to the door. Leaning in, he pressed his ear against it and listened.

Silence.

Still trembling, Lonnie looked back at the windows, but they'd become covered with snow and ice and offered nothing more. Locked inside his dark little cocoon, he had no choice but to ride out the storm, wait out the night and pray for morning.

He wanted so desperately for this to be a bad dream. But it wasn't.

It wasn't a dream at all. It was an omen.

The beginning of the end…

CHAPTER TWO

Standing in the bathroom, Joel Walker sighed and stared at his reflection in the mirror above the sink. He looked pale, needed some sun. His closely cropped beard was dark but he'd need to dye it again soon, as flecks of gray had begun to pepper it. His brown hair, a bit long, was disheveled and needed a trim. Tired, he thought. I look tired. Or is it just old?

It was the second day of a two-week vacation, but because he and his wife Taylor hadn't been able to coordinate their vacation times, he had no particular plans for the time off. Of course there were always things to do around the house. He'd been promising Taylor for months he'd straighten out the garage. And with the recent dump of snow, there was plenty of shoveling to do. Then again, it was a damp and dreary day, might rain later; maybe he'd curl up on the couch and have a movie marathon instead. Maybe even sneak in a nap or two.

Two hours later he found himself cleaning off their vehicles and shoveling the front walk. It hadn't rained yet, but the cloudy sky was still threatening it. Joel convinced himself that once he had the walk cleared, he'd jump in the shower, then settle onto the couch for the day for some serious relaxation.

Taylor appeared on the front steps in a heavy bathrobe, a cordless phone in one hand, the other pressed strategically over the mouthpiece. She mouthed the word work, and gave a questioning stare.

Joel stabbed the shovel into the snow, pulled his gloves off and joined her near the steps. "Billy?" he asked quietly.

She nodded. "Sounds strange."

"Doesn't he always?"

"More so. Sounds concerned."

He nodded and motioned for the phone.

Taylor handed it over. "I have to get dressed, running late."

"Okay," he said, pressing the phone to his ear. "Hello?"

"Joel, it's Billy," his boss said with his usual lisp, a speech impediment he'd struggled with since childhood.

Although technically, as editor in chief, Billy Gill was Joel's boss, over the years they had also become good friends. "Hey. What's up?"

"Sorry to bother you on vacation, but figured I'd better give you a heads-up. Couple minutes ago there was a woman in here asking for you. When I told her you were on vacation, she said she needed to get in touch with you, said it was urgent. She wanted your home address, but I told her we couldn't give out information like that, offered to take a message instead. She said her name was Katelyn Burrows and she needed to speak with you ASAP."

"About what?"

"Wouldn't say, just that it was personal business."

It wasn't unusual for people to stop by the paper and request to speak to one of the reporters on staff, but he was relatively sure the name meant nothing to him. "What was the name again?"

"Katelyn Burrows."

"Never heard of her."

"Well, she knows you, and she didn't strike me as the patient type, if you get my drift. It's easy enough to find your home address on the Web. Wouldn't surprise me if she comes looking for you. Just wanted you to know."

A light wind rustled the trees, blowing some snow back onto the walk. Joel turned and looked out at the street. No walkers, no approaching cars. "Thanks, appreciate it," he said softly. "She didn't say anything else? Nothing at all?"

"She didn't look like the sales type, but I asked if she was selling something anyway. When she said no, I asked if it was newspaper business. She said it was personal."

"Huh. How old was she?"

"I'd guess early twenties. None of my business if it's personal, but—for my own peace of mind here—is there anything going on I need to know about?"

"Not that I'm aware of."

"You in some kind of trouble?"

"I don't see why I would be."

"Any money problems? Miss a couple car payments or something?"

"There's nothing like that happening."

"You got a honey on the side?"

"Three, actually."

"Maybe she's a long-lost daughter you didn't know about." He chuckled.

"Don't even joke."

"Come to think of it, she did kind of look like you."

"I can only hope not, for her sake."

"Anyway, just wanted to let you know. I got to go, got a paper to run."

"If you hear from her again, give her my cell."

"Will do. We still on for dinner tonight?"

"Definitely."

"All right, tell Taylor I'll bring the wine. See you then."

"Will do. Later." Joel disconnected the call and thought a moment, rifling through his mental Rolodex. Nothing. Still, he couldn't help but be concerned. One never knew, especially in his business. But he hadn't worked for a paper of any importance or standing in decades, much less written anything of real significance. Theirs was a quaint and quiet little town of about eight thousand people in central Maine. Now and then he encountered someone upset by one of his articles on local politics, but they tended to be from the same crowd, and over the years he'd come to know most of them, if not by name then by sight. He could think of no one fitting the description given, and the very

16

idea that Billy would take the time to call him with this indicated he believed there was something unusual about it. He rarely did things like that, and although Billy was single, hopelessly lonely, and had ample amounts of time in his personal life, professionally he acted like he ran *The Washington Post* rather than a small-town rag in the middle of who-gives-a-shit.

Another gusting breeze sent snow snaking across the pavement in front of his house. A twinge of fear scurried through him, a whisper from a long-dead past, perhaps, reminding him that no matter how deeply he buried them, some things would never completely leave him.

Back in the house, he climbed the stairs to the bedroom, then ventured into the master bath to find Taylor putting the finishing touches on her makeup. Her reflection in the large mirror over the double sinks glanced at him as she carefully applied the last of her eyeliner. "Everything all right?"

"Yeah," he said absently. "Some woman was at the paper looking for me."

"And?"

"That's it." He folded his arms and leaned against the counter next to her. "Not sure what it's about."

"Well, be careful. You never know today. If she comes by here—"

"I doubt she will," he said. "If she does, I'll handle it. I'm sure it's nothing."

Taylor finished up, straightened her business suit, and stepped into a pair of heels she'd left just inside the bathroom door. Her dark hair was short and styled in a purposely mussed pixie cut, and as she slid her eyeglasses on, her big brown eyes grew larger still behind the lenses. "Well?"

Joel gave her a thumbs-up. He vaguely remembered something about a meeting with new clients she had scheduled in Portland later that day. As the vice president of a small advertising agency in Bangor, Taylor was often charged with handling and ushering in new clients. "You look great. Smart, sexy, professional."

"Thank you." She leaned in, gave him a quick peck on the lips. "Smell good too."

"Crazy day, but I'll be home in time for dinner."

"Yeah, don't forget, we invited Billy over tonight. He's bringing the wine."

"Super. He always makes such *interesting* choices when it comes to wine."

"He does his best, honey. This is Billy we're talking about. Anyway, think I'll bake a chicken with stuffing and potatoes, maybe green beans or a salad, cool?"

"Sure, sounds good."

As Joel followed her into the bedroom, Taylor scooped her briefcase off a small desk on the far wall, then whirled around to face him. She cocked her head, as if she'd heard something in the distance, but her eyes never left him. "Are you sure you're all right?"

"I'm good."

"I just—"

"Taylor, I'm good. I promise."

"If this business with this woman is anything important, call me, okay?"

"Of course. You worry about your meeting. I'm going to finish up shoveling. I plan to spend the rest of the day watching movies and baking chickens."

She nodded but didn't seem convinced. "I love you."

"Love you too."

"See you tonight."

With a wink, she descended the stairs and was gone. A moment later the front door opened, then closed, and the house fell silent. Outside, the breeze had become a wind. The house shifted, settled. Joel went to the window and looked down at the driveway. Taylor pulled out, turned at the end of the street and drove from sight.

Joel returned to the bathroom and stared at the medicine cabinet a while. Eventually he opened it and rummaged around inside until he found the old pill holder he'd once depended on. Segregated into days of the week, each little box still held two pills. He hadn't needed them on a regular basis for years, but he did take one now and then, and in some ways, just knowing they were there if he absolutely needed them often prevented him from taking them. But now that he had the container in his hands and could see the little pills through the thin blue plastic, he remembered why he'd needed them in the first place, and his heart began to race. That awful feeling of losing control surged through him. He returned the container to the cabinet, forcing it way into the back where he'd found it, then swung the door shut and headed out to finish his shoveling.

He'd been at it less than ten minutes when a small car pulled up in front of the house. A woman in a coat and a white knit hat with a pom-pom on top stepped out and slowly approached him.

Well, Joel thought, *that didn't take long*. He dropped his shovel and moved down the walkway to meet her halfway. It wasn't until he'd gotten closer that he realized just how young the woman looked. Billy had said early twenties, and he was likely right, but she had a baby face that could've belonged to a high school kid.

She crossed onto the stone walk leading to the front door. "Mr. Walker?"

"Yes. Can I help you?"

"I hope so." She smiled pleasantly, but it looked as if it took great effort for her to do so. "I'm Katelyn Burrows."

"What can I do for you, Miss Burrows?"

"I went by the newspaper," she explained. "I'd hoped to find you there."

"Yes. I got a call that you'd stopped by looking for me."

"Your boss said you were on vacation, but wasn't very helpful beyond that."

"He was trying to protect my privacy. He assumed, I'm guessing correctly, that you were able to find my address online anyway."

"Amazing what you can do with a phone these days."

"It certainly is. I'm sorry, but do we know each other?"

Her full cheeks were rose-red, her complexion flawless as a child's and her hazel eyes slightly watery in the chilly air. A short woman, she was just over five feet and a bit chubby. Sprigs of dirty-blonde hair coiled out from beneath the knit hat on her head and looked like they needed a good brushing. "Not exactly, no."

"Then again, what is it I can do for you?"

"I was hoping we could speak privately."

"Far as I can tell, we're alone." Joel motioned to the street and the yard in a slow, sweeping motion. "Knock yourself out."

"If you're not comfortable inviting me in, maybe we could go somewhere and sit, have a cup of coffee or something. It's awfully cold out and I'd like to—"

"Look, Miss Burrows, I don't mean to be rude, but I don't know who you are or what you want. Why don't you start there and we'll see where it leads?"

She blushed on top of her already red cheeks. "It's *Mrs.*, actually."

"All right then. *Mrs.* Burrows."

She held up her left hand so he could see her wedding band and diamond, the way newlyweds often did. "My maiden name's Scott. You're an old friend of my father's. Lonnie Scott."

"Lonnie? You—you're Lonnie's daughter?"

"Yes, sir."

"Well, I—hello—I'm sorry, I—I wasn't expecting this. I haven't seen Lonnie in years. How is he?"

Brow knit, she swallowed hard and cleared her throat. "He's dead."

CHAPTER THREE

Joel returned from the kitchen with a cup of tea to find Katelyn Burrows exactly where he'd left her, sitting on the couch in the living room with her purse in her lap. She was still wearing her coat and knit hat. He'd offered to take them for her but she'd declined, explaining she was perpetually cold. Odd, since the house was quite warm. He carefully placed the teacup on the coffee table between them, then sat in a comfortable chair across from the couch. "I hope green tea's all right," he said. "It's all we have."

"It's fine, thank you."

"My wife's the tea drinker. I've always been more a coffee guy."

"I don't care for coffee, never developed a taste for it." Katelyn raised the cup to her lips and took a delicate sip. She didn't look the part, but spoke and carried herself in a very refined manner. Despite her young age, she struck Joel as an old soul, like someone plucked from an earlier, more formal time. "Oh, that's delicious."

Snow blowing about and riding the wind beyond the bay window caught Joel's eye, mesmerizing him a moment.

"You have a lovely home," Katelyn told him.

Her voice broke the spell and returned his attention to her. "Thank you."

She looked to a nearby wall, which was covered in framed photographs showcasing Joel and Taylor throughout their lives together. In addition, there were several pictures of them in various stages of childhood, along with some older photographs of parents, grandparents and other relations. "And a beautiful wife. You both look so happy."

"Thank you, I'm very fortunate. It's a nice quiet life."

"No children of your own?"

Joel shook his head. "No, never really thought I was cut out for parenthood."

"That kind of honesty is refreshing." She sipped more tea. "It seems so many people today have children out of some sense of duty or something. It shouldn't be like that. I think people should only have children when they absolutely cannot live without them."

"Agreed."

"My husband and I hope to have one or two at some point, but not quite yet."

"Katelyn," Joel said, awkwardly clearing his throat, "can you tell me what happened to your father? Was he ill or..."

She looked down into her tea. "He was murdered."

"Murdered?" Joel's face twisted into a bleak grimace. "My God. What happened?"

Upset, it took her a moment to answer. "He was shot in the head. Executed in the street."

"But why? By who?"

"No one seems to have any idea."

"When did this happen?"

"Twelve days ago."

Joel wondered why she hadn't contacted him sooner, and why she hadn't simply called him with the news rather than come all this way to tell him in person. He and Lonnie had been close friends years before, but they hadn't even spoken to each other in nearly twentyfive years. There had to be more to this visit, but rather than ask her directly, he said, "Was it some sort of botched robbery or something?"

"He wasn't robbed, so it doesn't appear so. But the police have said one theory is that my father may have resisted and the perpetrator shot him, then panicked, and realizing what he'd done, fled without completing the robbery."

"Could be."

"Except that there were no signs of struggle or other injuries on the body. According to the autopsy, the only injuries were from the gunshot wound to his…" She drew a deep breath. "To his temple, and the bruises and scrapes he sustained when his body collapsed to the pavement."

"And the police don't have any leads on who might have done this?"

"They rounded up several locals but came up empty. With the exception of the first few days, the police have been useless."

"Surely they must have some—"

"Useless," she said again, this time more adamantly.

Unsure of what else to do, Joel refrained from further comment.

"As you can tell, I don't have a lot of faith in the local police."

"I'm sure they're doing their best," he said.

"Yes…well…I apologize for just showing up like this and springing such horrible news on you, but I needed to talk with you."

Somewhere within the fabric of normal everyday sounds, in that strange and sad moment, Joel could've sworn he heard something inhuman say his name, its voice muffled, distorted and lingering at the very edge of his range of hearing. "There's certainly no reason to apologize," he said through a heavy sigh. "I'm just so sorry to hear about this. Your dad and I were good friends for many years when we were younger."

"He mentioned you quite a bit."

"That's nice. I was always sorry we'd lost touch. Our lives went in different directions and we just sort of drifted apart."

"These things happen." She drank some more tea, then set the cup down on the coffee table. "At any rate, I hope you don't think I'm here to disrupt your life, Mr. Walker, I—"

"Joel, please."

"All right. I just want you to know that I'm not here to cause any trouble."

"Well, that's a plus." He forced a smile and leaned back in an attempt to portray a more relaxed demeanor. "I'm a bit confused, though. Why exactly *are* you here? As I said, your dad and I were good friends, but that was many years ago."

"He always referred to you as the smartest friend he'd ever had. He said of all his old buddies, you were the best man in the bunch."

"I don't know about that, but it was kind of him to say."

"He thought very highly of you."

An image of Lonnie flashed in his mind; a much younger and carefree version, he was sure, than the woman sitting across from him had known. "Your father was a good man."

"He had…problems. Especially later in his life."

"We all do of one sort or another."

She smiled politely. "I read your book."

"Really?" Though surprised, Joel did his best to appear non-chalant. "It's been out of print for years."

"My father had a copy, a paperback he'd saved. I found it with his things." She retrieved her cup and saucer from the coffee table and had another sip of tea. "Disturbing subject matter but a compelling read. You were certainly willing to dig deeper than anyone else did into that case, regardless of how awful and evil it was."

"I wrote that book twenty-five years ago. I was only a couple years out of college, a cub reporter for *The Boston Globe*, and the story sort of fell into my lap. In all honesty, at the time, no one thought it would amount to much. It was a bizarre, disturbing homicide, to say the least. They gave it to the new kid because everyone else was busy that day. That's literally how I got it. I was the only one at my desk when it came in. The story turned into something no one thought it ever would, including me. But I haven't been involved in that or anything similar in decades. It's not who I am anymore. It's not what I do. I walked away from all that years ago."

"You didn't exactly *walk* away, though, did you?" Her tone sounded almost confrontational. "I heard you suffered a nervous breakdown. Is that true?"

Unsure what to make of her or her question, he said, "And where did you hear that?"

"I'm sorry," she said, considerably softening her tone. "That wasn't very tactful, was it? I didn't mean to be disrespectful. My father told me. He said he'd heard the story got to you and you eventually broke."

"I'm truly sorry about Lonnie's death, I really am. But what's this all about?"

"The woman's death you investigated in your book—"

"Cindy Mello," he said. He hadn't spoken her name in years, and doing so rattled him more than he'd suspected it might. "Her name was Cindy Mello."

"Although her murder remains *officially* unsolved to this day, you did everything you could to get to the truth. In fact, you're the only one who did."

"That's not entirely true. The police—"

"Were like everyone else. Terrified. Maybe on some level even complicit."

"If you're asking me to investigate Lonnie's death, I don't do that anymore."

"I want to know the truth about my father's murder."

"Of course you do, but…" He ran a hand through his hair as horrible images and bloody flashes ripped through his mind, unlocked and set free from places he thought he'd never have to deal with again in the light of day. He forced the memories away and bit his lip. "Katelyn, listen, here's all I can tell you. A long time ago, I covered the murder you read about in my book, okay? The circumstances surrounding her murder—the entire topic— exploded back then in the 1980s. I was at the right place at the right time, and my articles picked up steam and took off. All of a sudden I was doing national TV interviews and the whole thing became bigger than anyone could've imagined. I decided to cash in—I admit it—and I wrote a book. It became a bestseller and I made the talk show circuit at the time. Tabloid TV was in its infancy back then, but already huge. During my investigation I found things no one else had seen, or, more importantly, *wanted* to see. I went into areas I never should've gone, because once you've been there you can't get back out, you can never wash yourself clean, do you understand? Some things happened and I walked away. I had a hard time for a while, yes, and I got out of the game altogether for a few years. I moved up here, took a nice little job at a nice little newspaper. I'm not an investigative journalist anymore, haven't been in years. I write about school committee meetings and public park ordinances now. Let me tell you, riveting stuff. My life's quiet and uneventful, and that's exactly the way I want it."

Katelyn Burrows looked back at the bay window and street beyond as if she expected to see someone coming. "I just want the truth. I have a right to it."

"Yes, you do, but I'm not the one to get it for you."

"My father was brutally executed in broad daylight on a street corner in Fall River, and no one is doing anything about it. There were news reports at first, and the police assured us they'd get to the bottom of it, but it's simply gone away. Everything has stopped, and—"

"Sometimes it seems that way with police investigations, but they're actually doing quite a bit of work behind the scenes."

"That's not the case here."

"How can you be sure?"

"There's something bigger at play, like there was with the case in your book."

"What happened to Cindy was a tragedy, a horrible crime, but—"

"A crime against man," she said evenly. "Against God."

Joel changed positions, unable to remain comfortable. "There were bad people involved, evil people who—"

"There was a bigger conspiracy than the police wanted to admit. They still won't admit it all these years later. But you got it right, didn't you?"

"I'd like to think I did, yes."

"*Once the Devil takes you, he doesn't give you back.* Isn't that what you wrote in your book?"

"There's no such thing as the Devil."

"You didn't seem so sure back then."

Joel looked away.

"Your book was a lie, then?"

"I got swept up in the hype and hysteria of the times," he explained, "made some mistakes and made some connections where there probably weren't any."

"Everyone knows the satanic scare business from the eighties was mostly nonsense. But there was some truth in there too, wasn't there?" she pressed. "You know better than most that it wasn't *all* hysteria, don't you?"

He offered a vague nod. It was all he was willing to give her.

"Ms. Mello was sacrificed as part of a satanic ritual."

"She may have been, yes."

"And it involved a cult that may have stretched as far as—"

"I'm familiar with the case," he said, immediately regretting his tone.

"My point is that what you uncovered in your book wasn't hysteria or hype," she continued, unfazed. "It was fact. Fact people didn't want to see—especially the authorities—and you made the case, put the pieces together when no one else was willing to stick their necks out to find the truth."

"It was a long time ago. Trust me, it wasn't quite that noble."

"My parents were never married," she said abruptly. "And for a variety of reasons I won't get into here, I wasn't at all close to my mother." She took another swallow of tea. "My father raised me and took care of me on his own. He never made a lot of money or had a fancy job. He worked security most of his life, he was a mall cop. He sometimes drank a little more than he should've, and he smoked these awful cigars, but—" Katelyn nearly laughed, but caught herself before it escaped her. Her eyes glistened. "He worked his entire life, sacrificed for me and went without so I'd want for nothing, and I never once heard my father complain. I worked hard, studied and got scholarships so I could go to college. I'm a schoolteacher now. Well, I will be soon as I have my certification."

"That's great," Joel said, hoping it sounded as sincere as he'd intended. "Congratulations, I'm sure you'll make a wonderful teacher. Your father would be very proud."

"Thank you. I'd like to think so, because if it weren't for my father, I'd be nothing. He was a good and decent man, and he didn't deserve to die like some thug in the street."

Joel plucked a tissue from a box on the coffee table and handed it to her. "No, he certainly didn't."

"I'm sorry," she said, delicately wiping her eyes and nose. "I promised myself I'd stay composed and not get emotional."

"Katelyn, you loved your father, and obviously he loved you

too. He did his best, and in the end a terrible thing happened. Horrible things happen to good people every day. Terrible, senseless things that—"

"A few months ago, my father changed. Something happened to him, something profound. Something I could tell he wanted to explain to me, but for some reason couldn't. He began acting differently, told me something bad was going to happen to him, that there were people after him. He was terrified."

"You told the police this?"

"Of course. They allegedly looked into it, but found nothing."

"Could he have been suffering from some sort of emotional or mental issue?"

"If he was, it was a result of what he was talking about, not some figment of his imagination." She placed her tea on the coffee table again. "I need your help, Mr. Walker—*Joel*. Won't you help me? Please?"

"Help you how? What do you want me to do?"

"Investigate my father's murder."

"I told you, I don't do that kind of work anymore."

"If you don't do it, no one else will."

"I know this isn't what you want to hear, but maybe that's best. Besides, even if I wanted to, which I don't, I—for God's sake—I wrote a book twenty-five years ago, all right? If you want someone to look into your dad's death, I'd suggest hiring a private detective that specializes in this kind of thing."

She shook her head. "In your book you talked about how, whenever people were faced with things beneath the surface, outside of their comfort levels and what they wanted and needed to be true, they shut down and in some cases even turned and looked the other way, because it was preferable to knowing the truth and how awful it might actually be. You wrote that—"

"I wrote a lot of things in the book. Much of it was speculation, and I made that abundantly clear." He tried to collect his thoughts and remain calm. "Katelyn, my book was a sensationalistic true crime thriller, nothing more, do you understand?"

"That's not true, and you know it. Even it were, it still showed a gifted journalist determined to find the truth, no matter what that truth was."

He forced himself to look into her eyes again, and for the

first time he saw fear. It was something he knew well, because he'd experienced it himself, on levels she couldn't even begin to imagine. "I became obsessed with the story, and because of that, I allowed it to take me to depths I almost didn't make it back from. These things, they get in your head and they play tricks on you. If you buy into it, if you give it any credence whatsoever, it starts to grow stronger and more involved, and before you know it, you're seeing demons behind every tree, devils under your bed and monsters in your closets. It doesn't end. It just gets worse, stronger, and eventually it drives you down into places you do not want to go. Dark, black, bleak places you can never forget. I damn near lost my mind."

"*Once the Devil takes you, he doesn't give you back,*" she said, quoting his book a second time.

"He never had me."

"But he was close, wasn't he?" she asked without irony.

He stared at her, this time seeing traces of Lonnie in her eyes.

"A few days ago I came across an old video on YouTube of you and some others," she said when he offered no reply. "It was a clip from one of those awful eighties tabloid TV shows where all the guests—*experts* so called—were talking about satanic crime and related topics. There was something different about you, though. I could tell the others were either trying to push some slanted religious or political agenda or simply selling the hype and making money from people's ignorance and fear. But you weren't like that. You were sincere. Haunted. Troubled. It showed in your writing, and it showed in your appearance on television."

"This isn't the same thing."

"You look all right now," she said. "Despite your *difficulties* in the past."

"I am all right."

"Are you?"

"Yes."

"But it still haunts you, doesn't it?"

"What's your point?"

"There's still a part of you that needs truth, just like I do. Somewhere deep down, that investigative reporter is still there. I'm asking you to resurrect him and to help me find out what happened to my father, to your friend."

Joel rose to his feet, unable to remain seated any longer. "Look, you read my book and it gave you this idea that I'm something I'm not, okay? I'm not capable of doing what you're asking. And not to be rude, but you have no right to ask me to do it in the first place. I'm sincerely sorry about what happened to Lonnie, but it has nothing to do with me. I just want to live my life in peace. Please, let me do that."

"He told me strange things were happening," she said, as if she hadn't heard a word he'd said. "He said people were following him. Or what he *hoped* were people. Whoever—or whatever—they were, they drove my father insane and then they killed him."

"And you don't think the police would want to know this?"

"They certainly didn't behave as if they did." She took a moment to collect herself. "And there was something else. He had a strange tattoo—well, not exactly a tattoo but more of a *brand*, really—on the back of his left shoulder. He had no idea what it was or how it had gotten there. It's a symbol of some kind, I'd never seen anything quite like it before."

"Did you research it at all?"

"Yes. I thought it might be a satanic or occult symbol of some kind—you'd mentioned in your book that kind of thing was common when it came to these subjects—but I couldn't find anything. When I did a regular search it came back as something called a *triskele*. Apparently it's an ancient Celtic representation that symbolizes the power of life and rebirth. It combines spirals with the number three. Beyond that, I have no idea what it means or how it was burned into my father's skin without his knowledge."

"Lonnie claimed he had no idea how he got it?"

"None. And it frightened him."

"I'd imagine so. That's bizarre, for sure, but it doesn't necessarily mean—"

"Not long before his murder, he kept talking about…*demons*. He said he thought that's what might be after him."

"Demons don't exist, Katelyn." He pointed to his temple. "Only in here."

"Maybe that's enough. Or maybe we choose not to see them, because if we do, the only thing it leads to is madness." Katelyn straightened her posture, and a cool detachment slowly overtook her. "I never believed in these kinds of things before. But my father wasn't a drunk or a drug addict. He wasn't mentally ill. He was experiencing something, and I believe it led to his murder."

Joel folded his hands and placed them in front of him so Katelyn wouldn't see them shaking. "The human mind is complex."

"So is evil."

"No, in my experience it's actually pretty straightforward."

"I want to know what happened to my father."

"He was murdered by a person, possibly persons, who haven't been caught yet. And while I certainly hope this isn't the case, it's possible they never will be. It's not like on TV, where homicides are solved in sixty minutes every week. In the real world thousands of murders go unsolved, and stay that way. It's tragic, and I'm terribly sorry this happened to Lonnie. I always will be. But your father's gone, and no amount of investigation is ever going to bring him back. Let the police do their job. If you're not satisfied with their conclusions, or lack thereof, hire a private investigator or try to get an investigative journalist on it. But I'm not your guy on this. I'm sorry. I'm out of the game, and I plan to stay that way."

"I've come a long way, drove over four hours to see you. There's more I can tell you, but it seems pointless if you have no intention of getting involved. Isn't there anything I can do or say that will convince you to help me?"

"I can't do this. I'm sorry."

She opened her purse, retrieved a computer disk from it and placed it on the coffee table. "I've put everything I have, all the information and documentation regarding his murder, on this disk, along with my contact information. Maybe you could just take a look at it when you have a moment. If you change your mind, contact me soon as possible. My husband is an accountant and I'm not working yet, so we don't have a lot of money, but of course I'd be willing to pay for your services. There was an insurance policy. Ten thousand. Most went toward funeral—"

"This isn't about money," he told her.

"No," she said, rising from the couch. "It isn't."

"Katelyn—"

"Thank you for seeing me." She extended her hand. "And for the tea."

Joel shook her hand. Her palm was warm. "I'm very sorry for your loss, and I wish I could be more help to you."

With a curt nod, she crossed the room and slipped out the front door. It closed behind her with a dull thud.

He went to the bay window and watched as she followed the walkway to her car. Once there, she hesitated and looked back at the house.

Joel stepped away from the window.

When he looked again, Katelyn Burrows was gone.

CHAPTER FOUR

After another hour of shoveling, Joel spent the next two tidying up the house and readying things for dinner that evening. The disk Katelyn had left on the coffee table in the living room taunted him the entire time. He passed by it several times, assuring himself he'd grab it, put it away somewhere and, at one point or another down the road, take a look at it. Until then, he'd do his best to forget about the disk, because if Taylor learned what this was about or who and why Katelyn had come to see him, she'd hit the ceiling. And who could blame her? That was the last thing he needed. But he felt terrible about Lonnie, and kept picturing his old friend in his mind. They'd been so close once—all those years before—he and Lonnie and the other guys in their little circle, Sal, Dorsey and Trent, buddies since junior high, and though they'd drifted apart and gone their separate ways as they got older, it still seemed impossible that one of them could be dead. Whenever Joel thought of them—or even himself in that context—they were frozen in time, forever young, not middle-aged men of fifty, some with children as old as they'd been when they were friends, and certainly not murder victims. Why hadn't he stayed in touch? Sure, he'd had his dark times—they all had to one extent or another—but was it really so hard to pick up a phone every once in a while and check in, or to fire off a quick email? Then again, he didn't even know Lonnie's number, much less his email address. In fact, he'd lost his contact info for the other guys too.

Shame on me, Joel thought. *Shame on all of us.*

In a way, his separation from them was not only inevitable, it was also necessary; another casualty of what he'd been through, collateral damage from walking away from that life, that time and those memories. Lonnie and the others were irrevocably tied to Joel's past, and in order to recover, he'd needed to start fresh elsewhere. His healing depended on acquiring an entirely new life, and that's exactly what he and Taylor had built after leaving Massachusetts and reestablishing themselves in Maine. But how long had he been all right now? A long time—several years—so there was no excuse for not getting back in touch, or at least making an effort, and he knew it.

Still, they'd been through an ordeal together when they were younger, something no one outside their circle knew about because they'd never told.

The black car…

Joel's hands began to shake. He hadn't thought about that in a very long time, but it was always there, in the shadows and fog, in his dreams and nightmares.

He pushed that aside and refocused on Lonnie. He wondered if the others knew, and if they'd attended Lonnie's funeral. Had they wondered where he was, why he wasn't there? As far as he knew, they all still lived in Massachusetts. Joel was the only one who'd left the state. But then, he'd always been the pioneer of their group. He was the one who went to college, who made that first step away from the group and out of town. He was the one who broke free, became something more than a townie with a nowhere job and a house full of kids. But it had cost him, and cost him dearly. It had worked out in the end though, hadn't it? He'd been through hell and survived. And he had Taylor—always Taylor—the great love of his life. She'd saved him, and with the sheer power of her love and dedication, prevented him from forever burning in those horrible flames.

With a plethora of emotions throttling him, Joel took a shower, got dressed, then wandered back downstairs to the living room. Standing over the coffee table, he stared at the disk for several minutes, trying to convince himself he could take a quick look, then put it aside. But he knew the truth. Once he looked, there'd be no turning back. Not for him. He simply wasn't wired that way. He could already feel it rising in him, this need to investigate and get to the bottom of what happened to Lonnie. Maybe there could be a redemptive quality to looking into this and possibly even solving it. Last time he'd been buried, drowned in the madness, but maybe this time could be different. Or maybe it would end him, finish the job once and for all and send him plunging off the edge of the cliff he'd been hanging from for so long.

A memory of Lonnie came to him, one from just after high school. He was laughing that big, booming laugh of his, eyes alive and mischievous as ever. Could that rambunctious kid really be the same person who would later father Katelyn Burrows? How could Joel have ever imagined that in some bizarre and distant future, Lonnie's child would seek him out to help solve his murder? Like so many other things from Joel's past, it all seemed impossibly beyond belief.

But there it was.

"Fuck it." He grabbed the disk, hurried across the room to the hallway and ducked into their home office. Heart racing, he dropped into the chair and fired up the computer. While it booted, Joel opened the clear plastic case, popped the disk free and fed it into the tray before he could change his mind.

A box appeared on the screen with a list of items, files and photographs contained on the disk.

The first several files were either links to newspaper articles online or actual newspaper reports that had been scanned and enlarged, then saved to the disk. In all but two, a photograph of Lonnie dominated the page, along with the headline describing his murder. Words like *senseless* and *random* appeared liberally throughout. LOCAL MAN VICTIM OF APPARENT RANDOM SHOOTING... VICTIM OF SENSELESS SHOOTING IDENTIFIED... MOTIVE IN LOCAL SHOOTING LIKELY ROBBERY, COPS SAY... NO CLUES IN MURDER OF MAN SLAIN IN STREET...

Despite the lurid headlines, Joel's eyes kept returning to the photograph. It was one they'd obviously obtained from the family, a head shot of Lonnie smiling that had been cropped to remove whoever else had been in the picture with him. It looked fairly recent, as he was much older than the last time Joel had seen him, but it was hard to tell exactly how old he'd been when it was taken. Joel guessed middle forties.

"What the hell did you get yourself into?" he asked the photograph.

Even with the articles and photos in front of him, none of it seemed real. How could Lonnie be dead? Although Joel didn't read every article thoroughly, he scanned them enough to know the authorities had no leads or clues as to why Lonnie had been executed or who might have done it.

Oddly, the more Joel looked through the articles, the more vaguely familiar the whole thing sounded, and he began to wonder if he'd somehow heard about the case without realizing Lonnie was the victim. Perhaps he'd caught the tail end of a news report on TV, or had seen the story come over the wire at work. Sadly, homicides weren't exactly big news these days, and one out of state in a city like Fall River was hardly headline news in Maine, so unless he'd heard Lonnie's name or there were specifics of the murder that caused it to stand out, he wouldn't have paid much attention.

Moving the mouse, Joel closed the articles file and double-clicked the next choice. A drawing of the brand Katelyn had told him about appeared, along with a note that read: *This is a sketch of the brand my father had on the back of his shoulder. It was quite small, no more than an inch in height and width, and at first glance looked like a mole or possibly a birthmark. When I made this sketch, I was careful to draw it exactly as it appeared. The lines weren't as clean as they are in the sketch, but the basic design was the same as below.*

Joel minimized the disk window and opened a new one for his browser.

A quick Google search returned examples and information on the symbol. As Katelyn said, it was a Celtic symbol known as a triskele or triskelion. It apparently symbolized life and rebirth, as she'd told him, with the use of spirals, which illustrated the cycle of life, and of the number three, a sacred number that referred to the phases of the Triple Goddess, three female deities who, in many different versions and incarnations, were worshipped by numerous cultures and appeared in several mythologies, including the Celtic, Norse and Greek traditions. Although the versions of these goddesses varied somewhat from culture to culture, there was a consistency as well, along with the basic meanings and powers of the number three in various forms of magic and numerology.

What any of that had to do with Lonnie Scott was anyone's guess, but how the hell could someone be branded and not know it?

Joel closed the browser and returned his attention to the disk.

In addition to the newspaper reports, Katelyn had included some links to television news stories the three major Boston stations had done on Lonnie's murder. Joel hit each link, listening to the reports showing Lonnie's apartment building, as he'd been killed only a block from his home; the crime scene; and more stock photos of Lonnie. Several featured brief interviews with local detectives working the case, as well as interviews with Katelyn speaking about justice for her father's murder. But there wasn't anything new in the reports, or much of anything he could use. Everyone seemed perplexed by what in the end seemed little more than a senseless crime of violence. Just the same, he grabbed a pad and pen from his middle desk drawer and jotted down the names of the detectives and the reporters and their station affiliations, then did the same with those who had penned the newspaper and online stories.

Only one file remained, a JPEG. Joel double-clicked it and an old photograph appeared on his monitor screen. He recognized it immediately.

Taken in 1982, the year after they'd all graduated high school, it showed Joel with Lonnie and the rest of their circle of friends: Sal Valano, Trent Pierce, and Dorsey Hill. They stood side by side near a stone jetty at the beach, laughing and mugging for the camera, arms slung over each other's shoulders. He and Lonnie with their long hair, Sal with his mullet, Trent with his Mohawk, and Dorsey with what they all affectionately referred to as his "big-ass 'fro."

Happy. Young. Carefree. Yet there was something else there too, just beneath the surface. Something dark that tied them all together, bound them, forever. And when Joel looked hard enough, he could still see it.

My God, Joel thought, *look at us.*

He remembered the day it was taken. Dorsey's girlfriend at the time had snapped it just as Sal had made one of his typical wisecracks. Joel stared at the photo, letting the memories wash over him. He could almost hear their laughter.

Clearly the photograph was one Katelyn had found among her father's things, and had included on the disk for the sole purpose of playing Joel's heartstrings. And it was working. If something like this didn't elicit the emotions needed to convince him to help her, then nothing would.

"Kid's good," he muttered.

Joel's eyes came to rest on Lonnie. None of them—least of all Lonnie—had any idea what was waiting for them out in the world. He thought about it a moment, did the math.

They were all nineteen in the photograph, which meant that when it was taken, Lonnie had thirty-one years to live. Sounded like a long time, but it really wasn't. Most of it had come and gone in what felt like the blink of an eye.

Gone. So many years just…gone.

Hey, what are you gonna do? Lonnie's favorite expression; he could almost hear him saying it across all these years.

You're gonna die in the street, that's what you're gonna do.

Joel clicked the photograph closed, spun his chair away, and forced himself to his feet, wanting—needing—to get away from it. His emotions were getting the better of him, replaying a conversation he'd had with Lonnie a few months before that photograph was taken. Joel's girlfriend and high school sweetheart had dumped him, and Lonnie, even more than the other guys, was right there to let him know everything would be all right.

What are you gonna do? The hell with her, bro, plenty of babes out there. You'll meet somebody else, somebody better, and before you know it you won't even remember that bitch's name.

What they hadn't realized was that in an even shorter span of time their lives would lead them in different directions, and they'd no longer play the integral parts in each other's day-to-day existences they'd all been so sure they would. Everything was about to change, and nothing would ever be the same again.

Time was coming for them. Life was coming for them.

And Death was hitching a ride.

CHAPTER FIVE

Dinner over, the dining room table sat empty but for the remnants of what had been a delicious and very pleasant meal. Before Billy arrived, Joel had filled Taylor in on who Katelyn Burrows was and what she wanted. The result was more than a little tension throughout dinner, but both managed to keep it under control. Before Billy got there, Joel filled him in over the phone, hoping this would cause Billy to stay quiet and not bring up anything that might open the door to discussing the situation. They'd kept it light, but Joel knew what was coming.

An older REM tune played from the stereo, and as Taylor excused herself, then went to the kitchen and began straightening up, Joel and Billy stepped out onto the patio off the living room so Billy could have a cigarette.

It was a cold and clear evening, the sky starless. Joel pulled his jacket in tight around him, buried his hands in his pockets and shuffled his feet as Billy, who always seemed oblivious to the cold, lit his cigarette. "Too chilly for you?" he asked, exhaling a cloud of smoke that mingled with their plumes of breath.

"Yeah, it's freezing. What's wrong with you?"

"How much time you got?" Billy chuckled. "Think Taylor liked the wine?"

"For future reference, if it comes in a box, don't get it."

"Fine, nothing but cans from now on." A short, portly, and balding man in his early fifties, Billy Gill had a penchant for inexpensive polyester slacks, ill-fitting sportcoats and comfortable shoes. He almost always wore a tie, and tonight was no exception, but they always hung loose and sloppily around his neck, which fit in well with the rest of his perpetually wrinkled and slightly stained clothing. Never married, Billy lived alone in a small condominium complex near Bangor with his two cats, Woodward and Bernstein. He rarely dated, and when he did, things never went well. As a result, his was a rather lonely existence, and the small newspaper he ran had become his life. He'd worked there since graduating college, and had climbed his way up to editor in chief several years before. Once a week he and Joel and a few other guys got together for poker night, but other than that, Billy Gill's evenings were uneventful and spent alone, so Joel and Taylor tried to have him over for dinner at least a few times each month. Although he'd hem and haw and act like he couldn't possibly fit dinner into his busy social calendar, he always found a way to make it. "But wine's about the last thing you've got to worry about tonight, pal."

Joel nodded. "We didn't get much of a chance to talk about it, but suffice to say, Taylor's not pleased."

"Can you blame her?"

"No, of course not. But..."

Billy took another puff. "You sure this is something you want to do?"

"If it was about wanting to, I wouldn't be going. I need to do it. I owe Lonnie that much."

Billy stabbed the cigarette between his lips for emphasis and left it there, letting it dangle. He still didn't look cool. It probably wasn't possible. "You don't owe anybody a damn thing."

"We were tight once, went through a lot together. That matters."

Billy suddenly looked unusually serious. "Yeah," he admitted softly, "it does."

"I just don't want it to cause any major problems."

"What do you think it's all about?"

"I've got no idea. I don't think it's anything like…before…but there's strange aspects to it for sure."

"I mean, this business with the brand you were talking about, what the hell's that about? And he didn't know he had it? How is that even possible?"

"I don't know. Maybe he wasn't conscious when it was done."

"What kind of person *brands* a human being?"

"What kind of person brands any living being?"

"I don't mean to badmouth your friend or his memory, but odds are he was into some bad shit or pissed off the wrong kind of folks. People don't get shot in the head on the street for no reason. You know that. Could it be a random thing? Sure, it's possible. But how often does that really happen?"

"Maybe it was a mistake." Joel shrugged. "Shooter got the wrong guy."

"That's the problem—you don't know much of anything at this point."

"No, I don't. I have no idea what the hell I'm walking into."

"That's never wise, my friend."

"Sometimes it's necessary. I'm guessing it won't amount to much."

"Guessing or hoping?"

"Little of both. Either way, I've been out of the game a long time, Billy."

"You're still a reporter. It's not like you're selling furniture or something."

Joel stared at him. "My last story was about the school lunch program and how pizza is still being featured. Hard-hitting investigative journalism at its best. I don't want to come off arrogant or anything, but I'm thinking Pulitzer."

"Once a reporter, always a reporter."

"I thought that was priests."

"Fine. Them too."

"My point is the last real investigative work I did was twenty years ago, and I haven't stepped foot in that part of Massachusetts in all that time. My old stomping grounds probably don't even exist anymore, and any connections I had back then are likely long gone. So I figure I knock the rust off as best I can, go poke around a little, see if I can come up with anything or make some sense of things. If I come up empty—which is probably exactly what'll happen—I come home none the worse for wear and able to live with myself, because at least I'll know I gave it an honest shot."

Billy smoked his cigarette a while, thinking. "I realize we didn't know each other back when all that other stuff went down and you had those problems, but I know enough to realize that's not something you need to get anywhere near again."

"You think I don't know that?"

Flashes of memories blinked before Joel's eyes. Photos of the Catholic church...the altar on which Cindy Mello had been slaughtered and sacrificed...the symbols and sacrilegious writings in her blood and fecal matter smeared across the walls and floors...the desecration...the madness and evil falling through his mind like black rain...

He forced them away. It had been years since such things had tormented him or come to him so vividly.

"It's not like I didn't read your book," Billy said. "I do know something about what happened and—"

"It was a long time ago."

"But it also nearly killed you. You almost didn't recover."

He and Billy had never really talked in-depth about those days, and Joel had no intention of starting now. "It was a completely different time, a different case and an entirely different situation. This has nothing to do with that sort of thing."

"That you know of."

"Look, man, I appreciate your concern, okay? But I'm fine, and I'll be fine."

"You've got a good life here, Joel. A damn fine woman, a nice home, a badass best friend." He grinned, then grew serious again. "Don't fuck it up. Some people would kill for what you have. And by some people I mean me."

Joel gave a quiet, obligatory laugh, but both he and Billy knew there really wasn't anything funny about any of this. As an awkward silence fell over them, a chilly but gentle breeze slipped through the trees at the edge of the backyard. A set of wind chimes hanging off the back of the house swayed into motion, their ethereal song dancing through the darkness.

"It's not only a totally different situation," Joel finally said. "I'm a totally different person now."

"Just tread carefully, my man. If you feel a sense of duty to look into this for your friend or his kid or whatever, I get it—I do—but it's not worth losing what you have. It's not worth losing Taylor. It's not worth losing *you*. No matter what happens, you remember that. Then get back here safe and sound. And don't be gone longer than your vacation. I don't want to have to fire your sorry ass, but I will because I'm an insufferable douche. Besides, we've got work to do, dinners to have, poker games to play, you hear me?"

"With your softly melodic voice it's virtually impossible not to."

"Side-splitting. Anyway, if you need anything—"

"You'll be the first one I call. And seriously, thanks."

Billy clamped a beefy hand on Joel's shoulder. "You know Taylor still expects me to talk you out of this, right?"

"I'm sure she's hoping."

"Lie and tell her I did my best, okay?"

"Sure." Joel felt himself smile. "There's a good chance she'll corner you before the night's over, though, probably try to get you to take another run at me."

"I'll be ready. I'm not afraid of her." Billy took another hard drag on his cigarette, dropped it to the ground and stepped on it. "Actually, yes I am."

"Come on," Joel said, cocking his head toward the house. "We better get back in there before she thinks we're out here scheming."

"Yeah, I don't want her drinking the rest of my wine."

"Trust me, that wine could not possibly be in less danger."

"Hey, what's sexier than a big ole gallon box of three-dollar wine?"

"Literally every other thing in the universe."

Laughing, they returned to the house, and much as Joel tried to convince himself to enjoy the evening—as he knew it would be the last time he'd have the opportunity to do so for some time—he realized he was simply whistling past a graveyard. For now, he'd escape the night for the warmth, safety, and clarifying light of their home.

But the darkness was rising, and soon, he'd be walking right into it.

CHAPTER SIX

In the quiet house he'd called home for so long, memories crashed like waves, reminding him that the life he'd built and worked so hard to obtain had saved him, cleansed him from the madness and the wolves that even then crouched drooling just outside his door, biding their time until more flesh could be ripped from bone. The slaughter, that's what they lived for, the thrill of the hunt and the joy of the kill. For Joel, existence was far more complicated.

Survival was only the beginning.

All those years before, sitting in the Mello's home, he watches as her parents—a devastated middle-aged couple—huddle together in the limited light of their small apartment. On the television a VHS tape plays. In broken English, Cindy's father explains he had it transferred from film not long before her death. It shows a little girl, his little girl, the little girl their daughter Cindy used to be.

"This was our first summer after we left Portugal," he explains, the words catching in his throat as his bloodshot eyes fill with tears. "You have to see, you—you have to see who my little girl was. My... my baby..."

Joel nods, frozen in place in the corner of the room.

A little girl runs along wet beach sand in her bare feet, a small plastic bucket in one hand. All pigtails and big brown eyes, Cindy joins her father at the sand castle they're building together. It's nothing spectacular, as her father clearly has no real talent when it comes to such things, but far as he and his daughter are concerned, it is the most beautiful and magical castle ever made.

Her father shows her where to put the last bucketful of wet, formed sand, and Cindy carefully dumps it out. He packs sand around it, shaping it a bit with a plastic shovel, then sits back on his heels and smiles. "What do you think?" he says to the camera, to his wife who is filming them.

Cindy smiles wide and bright. "What do you think?" she echoes.

"Wonderful!" her mother says off-camera.

Even then Joel knows he must remember this moment. He must let it burn into his mind, because unlike the countless photographs he has seen from a number of sources, this is his first—and perhaps only—opportunity to see Cindy alive, moving, talking and laughing. And while there will be other poignant moments, because she is such a small child in the film, so innocent and gleeful and unaware of what life has in store for her, none will be as special as this one. Joel will never be able to reproduce this exact experience, the chance to look in on this dead woman's joyful childhood. It will only happen this one time, and just like her makeshift sand castle, once it's gone, none of them will ever get it back.

Except in memory.

Cindy watches the coming tide, the waves gently gliding closer and closer along the beach. "Will the water come this far, Daddy?"

"It will soon, yes."

"Will it wreck our sandcastle?"

He nods, makes a face he hopes is funny.

"But why?" Cindy asks.

"It's all right; it's not meant to last. It's only here for a short while and then it's gone. That's what makes it special."

The sun blinds them a moment, so bright and warm, and Cindy becomes a phantom, a blur at the very edge of the film, like a dream, really, a figment of their collective imaginations. Her father reaches for her...

And then she too is gone, lost in the sand, sunshine, and glistening ocean.

Later, in the sand castles of his tormented dreams, Joel reaches for the little girl she'd once been too, finds only wet sand, and begins to weep.

"What are you thinking about?"

The sound of Taylor's voice dragged him from that darkness and the depths of its sorrow to one more immediate, its shadows nearly filling their bedroom as it drifted through them like the spirit it was. It was late, and the moon was high, creeping through the bedroom windows and splitting the room into two separate worlds. Beyond the reach of moonlight, Joel lay on his back, nude, eyes trained on the night sky. He didn't want to tell her about the things going through his mind, but saw no way around it. "The home movie Cindy Mello's parents showed me of her when she was a little girl."

"I remember that in your book. It was very powerful."

"She was this little tiny peanut, so innocent and happy, you know?"

Lying next to him on her stomach, legs bent and crossed at the ankles, Taylor was nude as well, but partially wrapped in a sheet. "Your depiction of her parents was absolutely heartbreaking."

Their pain, coupled with Joel's realization that there were things in this world that could conspire to hurt and maim and torture and kill something as precious as the Mello's daughter, had been a determining factor as to why he and Taylor had never had children of their own. He'd used his breakdown as an excuse, just as Taylor liked to blame her career. But when it was just the two of them in the dark, both knew the truth. "They were the most thoroughly destroyed human beings I'd ever seen," he said softly, "and all I kept thinking about was what was coming for that little girl, the horror waiting on her, that she had no idea, no way of knowing what was on its way to her. I remember wishing I could step into that movie and warn her. I couldn't, of course, so I did the only thing I could do. I told her parents I'd find justice for their daughter. I told them I'd find out what happened to their precious little girl, and who'd done such terrible things to her."

"Joel, don't do this to yourself."

Rather than reply, he listened to Taylor's slow and steady breathing a while, and admired the small gold-and-black butterfly tattoo on her ankle he'd always found so sexy and mesmerizing. Not long after Billy left, they'd gone to bed, made love, and had since lain there quietly, trying to figure out how to approach something neither wanted to think about, much less discuss.

Earlier, before Taylor got home and Billy arrived for dinner, Joel had gone into their cellar and rummaged around until he located a dusty old suitcase he'd packed away years before. Sitting on an overturned crate, he laid the suitcase across his lap but didn't open it for several minutes.

Once he finally convinced himself to look inside, he found one hardcover and two paperback copies of his book, *Chasing Down the Night*. All were pristine and had never been read. After digging deeper, he located another paperback copy, this one with a badly cracked spine and dog-eared pages covered in highlighter markings and various notes he'd scribbled in the margins in pen. In addition to numerous newspaper clippings, a few old VHS tapes, a portable cassette player, a handheld microphone and a small stack of audiocassettes in plastic cases, there were several old notebooks too, creased and aged and full of notes from years before. He next found a manila envelope containing several photographs, but couldn't bring himself to go through them. Everything was there, just as he'd left it. He'd saved everything. Like a damn time capsule, he thought.

And damned it was.

A twenty-year-old college girl had gone missing, only to be found two days later, what remained of her massacred body sprawled across the altar of a local Catholic church. A story Joel would follow and eventually link to a large, wildly violent, but shadowy satanic cult operating in the area at the time, a cult that had possible nationwide ties and more power and influence than anyone had previously imagined possible. And the deeper he looked, the worse it got. His proof, even in the end, was largely circumstantial, but juries had convicted people for less. He knew some names, had identified certain members, but could prove nothing. Like the dark master they believed in and claimed to serve, these types and their activities existed largely in shadow, glimpses and rumor, like fleeting trails of smoke, whispers in the night. There, then gone, leaving one to wonder if they'd ever really been there at all.

He wrote the book, it took off, and he reaped the benefits and tried his best to forget what he'd seen and experienced. What he'd learned.

But by then, the Devil already had hold of him.

Or maybe he was just weak, his mind and spirit not strong enough to fight off the things that had begun to course through his head, haunt his dreams and stalk his waking hours. The strange phone calls, the people following him and watching, the odd things left at his doorstep—talismans made of sticks and animal bone, warnings—the severed heads of dogs and a litter of dead kittens, their little heads twisted, necks snapped. Just nut jobs who had read his book, believed his nonsense and were sick themselves, everyone assured him. As if they had any fucking idea what they were talking about.

What the types who said such things didn't know was how it all crawled into Joel's mind and nested there. How it festered and slowly began to cripple him.

No one was willing or able to help. The *Globe* let him go, and colleagues who had once considered him a young investigative journalist with tremendous potential now shunned him as a charlatan and an embarrassment. He was a pariah with the police as well, as he'd been highly critical of them and their investigation in his book and on numerous television appearances, and had implied that a handful of them might have even been involved.

And then came the backlash.

The entire satanic scare of the 1980s lumped everything— even legitimate cases like the one he'd been involved with—into a single mass of nonsense and hysteria. There was no proof, people said, no hard evidence, and even the small amount that did exist simply wasn't enough. It was all a bunch of lunatics and religious fanatics, people making accusations and telling stories with nothing to back them up, resulting in innocent people going to prison and having their lives ruined for the sake of sensationalism. *You're a hack, Joel Walker*, people said, *a liar more interested in sensationalism and making money and being on television and selling books than the truth.*

In the end, Cindy Mello was still dead. She'd been slaughtered.

Not by some devil cult like in the movies, everyone claimed. Just one or perhaps two very sick individuals who were never caught. And the satanic symbolism and writings in her blood found all over that church in New Bedford—the areas in the nearby Freetown State Forest he'd found where ceremonies had obviously taken place, where dogs had been sacrificed and possibly even other human beings—it was all coincidental, they said. It was just a few crazies, or drugged-out kids playing cult in the woods. None of it was what he'd claimed, because that sort of thing didn't exist, and if it did, then why couldn't he prove it?

More smoke…more whispers in the night…

All he'd wanted to do was find out who had killed that poor young girl and help bring them to justice. Not only had he failed, but the attempt had cost him his career and, for a while, his sanity. They hadn't seen the things he'd seen, the broken souls he'd met or the stomping grounds they inhabited. They didn't hear the growls, the whispers, or feel the evil moving within them, trying to control them and take over, to grind them down into insanity…or worse.

The rest of society knew nothing of the world behind the world, the one that existed beyond the veil few were even aware of. But Joel knew the truth, and that truth had almost killed him.

Do you believe the Devil is talking to you, Mr. Walker?

After three months in a psychiatric hospital, he came to believe the same as they did. He turned his back on what he knew because he knew he'd never leave that place unless he did.

Do you believe he's inside you right now?

The Devil's not real.

Even now, he told others that. He told himself that. And he believed it.

But was it true? Did it matter either way? If those who serve a god and its doctrine are real, does it matter if the deity actually exists?

With all those old memories and experiences flooding back into his mind, Joel had transferred everything into a newer nylon duffel bag and thrown it in the back of his closet. There would be a time and place to look through these things, to bring them back to life again like toys thrown long ago into boxes and forgotten, but that time had not yet come. Maybe one day.

"Lonnie's daughter should've left you the hell alone," Taylor said.

"But she didn't."

"You don't have to do this. It took you years to get to where you are now. Where *we* are now. We have everything we ever wanted. Why risk ruining that?"

His eyes found her in the moonlight. "What can I do?"

"Stay here with me."

"You have no idea how badly I wish I could."

"Then do it."

"I don't know if I can."

"You don't know if you will. There's a difference."

Joel touched her face, gently ran his fingers across her cheek. "I'll just go back and check some things out, see what I can see. That's all. It doesn't have to rule our lives or become a big—"

"Don't lie to me, Joel." She pressed her palm against his chest. "There are more than enough lies in this life already, enough cruelty and deception and fear and uncertainty. We don't need it between us. It's just you and me now." She delicately stroked the hair in the center of his chest, traced it with her fingertip down along his stomach, where it encircled his navel. "I've spent forever watching and helping you put yourself back together. I know firsthand what this did to you last time. That was bad enough."

"This isn't the same thing. Different time, different story, different me."

"It could very well lead to some of the same things; you know that. Lonnie told his daughter he was being stalked by *demons*, for God's sake."

"Katelyn also told me he had issues. Besides, we're talking ancient history when it comes to the other case."

"Are we?" Taylor's beautiful eyes blinked at him slowly. "You were just replaying the home movie you watched with Cindy Mello's parents in your head."

"So what?"

"So *that's* what you were thinking about, Joel, not Lonnie or what may have happened to him, but that woman and her murder."

The wind blew snow from the trees, spraying it against the windows.

"Even if it had any similarities to what happened back then," he eventually answered, "which it doesn't, all those old trails will be long cold anyway. This has nothing to do with cults or any of the satanic crap that was taking place back then. There's a strong possibility Lonnie got himself into something he should've stayed clear of, got in over his head or crossed the wrong kind of people or something along those lines. But we're not talking about the types involved in Cindy Mello's murder. Lonnie had nothing to do with that kind of thing. It's not him. He wouldn't have been anywhere around that sort of stuff."

She searched his eyes. He could feel her fear.

"It's coming back to you though, isn't it? It's already seeping back into your mind, those things from all those years ago. Frightening things. Things the doctors warned you needed to—"

"Taylor…"

She sighed. "I know if you've already made up your mind, you'll go no matter what I say."

Joel stretched his legs out a bit, pushed his feet under the blankets they'd kicked off earlier. "Katelyn was right about one thing," he said. "Deep down I am still an investigative journalist. It's still a part of me."

"You were a gifted journalist—"

"Exactly, past tense."

"No, you still are, and you could be doing any number of more fulfilling things than you're doing now, but that doesn't mean you have to go back to something that nearly destroyed you."

"I was a flash in the pan, a one-trick pony. That story was all I ever had. It made me and broke me all at the same time." He lay there a moment, thinking. "Part of me wants—*needs*—to prove I can do this and not stumble like last time. Maybe I'll get lucky and actually find something out and be able to give Katelyn some closure and peace, something I was never able to do with Cindy's family. Maybe then I'll be able to leave this darkness and all those demons behind once and for all."

Taylor looked away, as if something in the shadows had caught her attention. "I thought you already had."

"So did I, baby. Believe me, so did I."

"All that evil and horror and darkness and violence is dead and buried. Why do you want to dig it up again? What do you possibly hope to accomplish after all this time?"

"That's the problem, isn't it? It's not dead, and it's not buried as deep as I thought it was." He took her chin in his hand and raised it up until she was looking at him again. "Those old ghosts are still rattling their chains, Taylor, and they're never going to let me go unless and until I cut them loose myself. I know that now. And I'm afraid, okay? I am, I admit it. I can't go through what I did before, not again. I won't survive it. But I can't let fear stop me either. Not this time. Not ever again."

She licked her lips. "What do you want me to say?"

"That you believe me. That you believe *in* me."

Taylor's eyes sparkled in the moonlight. "Always."

"I love you. More than you'll ever know, I love you."

"Go do what you have to do." She took his hand in hers, held it against the side of her face and kissed it. "Then come back to me."

Joel closed his eyes, snuggled closer to his wife and listened to the wind just outside the windows, distracting him, if only for a while, from the horrible whispers creeping through in his head.

CHAPTER SEVEN

Joel stood in his room before the partially pulled curtain, watching occasional cars rush along the nearby highway. Though only five foot ten, at first glance his wiry build made him appear taller than he actually was. Trim and in reasonably good shape, his body resembled that of a swimmer, though he rarely swam, his build understated in clothes but a bit less subtle in his present state: a pair of boxers. His was the kind of unremarkable look and manner that often made it easy to blend into a crowd or go unnoticed, something that had served him well back when such things could be relevant in his line of work.

The room was dark, the parking lot and areas surrounding the roadside motel dimly lit. Every now and then headlights from passing cars reminded him he was not alone in the night, but it was late, too late to be up. Undeterred, the thoughts storming through his head had prevented him from sleeping, and there seemed little point in going back to bed, at least not yet. They'd begun so nicely, with visions of him and Taylor making love or walking hand in hand along some of their favorite wooded paths not far from the house. But they soon morphed into memories of

Taylor waving goodbye, standing in the doorway of their home as Joel backed out of the driveway. She looked beautiful as ever, but even that did little to mask her sadness, which left him riddled with nearly unbearable guilt.

Joel glanced at his watch. Nearly two o'clock. He'd called home earlier and they'd said good night, but by now Taylor was long asleep, snuggled up in bed, the TV next to the bed probably still on, flashing ghost lights across the otherwise dark walls while some self-proclaimed entrepreneur extraordinaire prattled on about the virtues of his real estate seminar and how it was guaranteed to make attendees wealthy beyond their wildest dreams.

Wishing he were there with her, Joel moved from the window to a nearby table. Taylor faded from his mind, lost in misty shadows and darkness. On the table he found his iPod and a pair of in-ear headphones. He pushed one bud into his right ear but left the other dangling, as was his habit when alone, and, using the lighted face of the iPod to guide him, located *Kind of Blue* on his playlist, his favorite Miles Davis album. He selected the cut "All Blues," then sank down into one of the chairs.

Joel sat back in the dark, put his feet up and let the sultry sounds entangle him like creeping vines of smoke. And as his head slowly bobbed with the beat, he closed his eyes and drifted back to his memories of earlier in the day, and the events that had landed him in this lonely little motel so far from home...

It was a dreary, overcast day, the kind that threatened rainstorms but rarely delivered much besides the occasional mist or insipid, icy trickle. The drive from Maine to Massachusetts had been tedious and uneventful, and by the time he'd reached the city of Fall River, his initial thought was that it hadn't changed much in the last twenty years. Joel hadn't been back in all that time, but the city looked much the same as it had when he'd last seen it.

Originally an outpost of the Plymouth Colony, Fall River had rather modest beginnings, but by the nineteenth century it had become the largest textile-producing city in the nation. The death of that industry had ravaged the city, but Fall River had always survived and found alternate ways to thrive and survive. A city of nearly 90,000 people located along the shore of Mount Hope Bay, at the mouth of the Taunton River, it was not only famous for its textile history, but also for Lizzie Borden, for Portuguese culture (due to the large Portuguese population), and for being the home of the USS *Massachusetts* and a large assembly of World War II naval vessels, an area known as Battleship Cove.

Although the city had its share of ups and downs over the years, in the 1980s there was a considerable amount of new development and revitalization, including the infusion of a vibrant mix of cultures from around the world. But in 2010, Fall River had also been ranked one of the most dangerous cities in the United States, largely because of a heroin epidemic with ties to the shipping ports in nearby New Bedford. Still, as Joel negotiated the streets and made his way to the address Katelyn Burrows had given him, the city appeared to be on the rise and to have rebounded in most neighborhoods, as the higher crime still seemed to be mostly limited to certain specific areas.

It was still early in the day, late morning, when Joel's directions led him to an enclave of single-family townhouses. Complete with small, identical front yards, the neighborhood had less of a city feel and more closely resembled the kind of development one might find in a smaller town.

Following the circular layout of streets, he soon located the correct unit and pulled over, parking on the street so as not to block the driveway. He turned the car off, then studied the property a moment.

The units looked reasonably new and had a suburban, middle-class look. A small SUV and a compact car he recognized as the same one Katelyn had driven to Maine were parked in the driveway. Both were well cared for, as were the front lawn, manicured shrubs and chipped stone path leading to the front door.

Joel gathered the case containing his laptop and notebooks from the passenger seat, then stepped out of the car. He hadn't quite reached the front door when it opened and a lanky man in his twenties emerged. Joel assumed this was Katelyn's husband, as he sported a buzz cut and was dressed in an inexpensive suit, tie and black wingtips. He looked exactly like the accountant she said he was. Waiting for Joel to get closer, the man lingered on the front steps awkwardly before he extended his hand and asked, "Mr. Walker?"

"Yes—call me Joel—it's Joel."

"Adam Burrows. Nice to meet you, sir."

"Pleasure," Joel said, taking his hand. There hadn't been any snowfall beyond southern Maine, but it was just as bitterly cold here, and Joel couldn't help but wonder why, once their hand-shake had concluded, they were still on the steps and not already inside. "Everything all right?" Joel finally asked.

"Yes, my apologies," Burrows said, apparently as formal and stiff as his wife but far less comfortable with verbal interaction. "I just wanted to thank you for doing this. It means the world to Katelyn, and to me too. When you called and told her you'd agreed to check things out, she was so happy, I—well—I want you to know how much it's appreciated."

"Like I told Katelyn, I can't promise any results, but I'll do what I can."

"That's all we can ask. Of course we expect to pay you for—"

"Don't worry about it. If things become complicated, which I'm not anticipating at this point, I might need some expenses covered, but that's it. I'm not doing this for money, Adam."

"That's very kind. Please, come in," Joel said, finally escorting him inside.

Joel stepped directly into a modest living room that opened up into a kitchen. Katelyn was standing at a bar in the kitchen area, drinking a bottle of water. When their eyes met, she offered a reserved smile.

"Hello again," Joel said.

"Please, come in." Katelyn motioned to a stool opposite her. "I hope the directions were effective?"

"Yes, perfect."

"And how was your drive?"

"Long. Boring. The usual." He forced a smile, but it felt as awkward as the ones Katelyn and Adam threw back. After re-moving his coat and giving it to Adam, who placed it on the back of a nearby couch, Joel slid onto the nearest stool and put his case on the bar between them.

Their townhouse looked as formal as they were, almost sterile: all-white walls, counters and appliances, understated furniture and a few random pieces of inexpensive minimalist artwork scat-tered throughout. *Cold*, Joel thought.

Katelyn, dressed in moccasin slippers and a pink sweat suit, her dirty-blonde hair pulled back into a sloppy ponytail, motioned toward her refrigerator with the flair of a spokesmodel. "Something to drink?" she asked. "Some hot cocoa, maybe? Or water, soda, maybe a beer? Something stronger?"

"Thank you, I'm fine." Joel opened his case, removed a notebook and a pen.

Adam sat on a stool to Joel's right. "Old school," he said, attempting humor.

"Old guy." Joel chuckled and then turned back to Katelyn. "When you were at my house, you said you had some other things to tell me, but if you don't mind, I have a few questions I need to ask first. Some may be a bit uncomfortable for you, but they're necessary."

"I understand," Katelyn said. "I'll answer anything I can."

"Great. Ready to start?" When she responded with a nod, Joel referred to his pad and some earlier notes he'd made. "Was your dad on any medications?"

"He took a pill for high cholesterol. He'd been on that one for about four or five years, I think. He had some pain issues too—his legs and back mostly, from all those years on his feet—but didn't take prescription drugs for that, mostly Tylenol, that kind of thing. He also self-medicated with liquor now and then."

"But no other prescription drugs?"

"Not that I know of. There was something else, though. He had a strange bottle of pills in his medicine cabinet. It was the typical kind of pill bottle you get from a pharmacy, but there was no label on it, which I found odd."

"Do you remember what the pills looked like?"

"Small," she said. "White."

"Did they have any markings or numbers on them?"

"No. They looked a little like aspirin, but I don't think that's what they were."

"You don't still have them by any chance, do you?"

"No. The police took them when they went through his apartment as part of their
investigation. I was told they planned to get them tested, but apparently the bottle was lost."

Joel arched an eyebrow. "Lost?"

"*Misplaced* was the word the detective used. He said these

things sometimes happen, things are filed or catalogued incorrectly, but that they'd likely turn up at some point. He didn't seem the least bit concerned about it, frankly. As far as I know they still haven't found them, and never identified what they were."

"Okay," Joel said, making a note. "Should you get further information on that, let me know soon as you can, all right?"

"Of course."

"What about other drugs?"

"Like?"

"Like illegal drugs, was Lonnie doing anything along those lines?"

"Not that I'm aware of. As I mentioned, my father was a bit of a drinker. I'm sure back when you knew him, in his younger days, he experimented or partied like most everyone else, but I never knew him to do drugs."

Adam held a hand up like a child in a classroom.

Joel turned to him. "Yes?"

"I think, maybe, he smoked marijuana."

Joel did his best not to laugh. This guy was the squarest and stiffest twentysomething he'd ever encountered. He and Katelyn were about as hip as bingo night at the local nursing home. "And why do you say that?"

Adam glanced quickly at his wife, who was frowning her disapproval at his interruption. "Well, we found a package of rolling papers in his dresser drawer. Remember, honey? Remember when we found a package of rolling papers in his dresser drawer?"

Katelyn's hazel eyes shifted from her husband to Joel. "He may have smoked pot now and then, but I don't believe it was something he did regularly."

"Okay," Joel said. "So there wouldn't have been any issues with that then. Was he ever treated for mental illness or emotional disorders—problems with depression, suicidal tendencies or attempts—that kind of thing?"

"No," Katelyn answered evenly, "there was never any of that."

"Well, he was depressed a lot," Adam interjected. "And then not long before he died, he—"

"He could be brooding at times," Katelyn said, glaring in her husband's general direction. "But I wouldn't say he suffered from depression to the point that it was a problem, or something that needed to be medicated or monitored by a professional." Katelyn became very still and quiet for a moment, but it was obvious she had more to say. Eventually, she continued. "My father didn't have the easiest life. Of course he was depressed or down at times. He worked hard his entire life and never really had anything to show for it."

"He had you," Joel reminded her.

Katelyn smiled, and it was the most genuine expression she'd shown since he'd arrived. "Thank you," she said softly, her eyes glistening with tears.

Adam dropped from his stool, hurried over to a nearby coffee table and came back with a small box of tissues. He handed them to his wife, then returned to his seat at the bar.

"Katelyn, I don't want to belabor this point, but it's important. You told me that in the months prior to his murder, Lonnie changed quite a bit, that he was claiming something bad was going to happen and that there were people after him."

"Yes," she said with some reluctance. "That's true."

"Well, then is it safe to say he may have developed some mental or emotional issues but never sought formal treatment for them?"

"You asked me if my father had ever been treated for mental illness or attempted suicide. The answer is no. I also do not believe my father was mentally ill, even in the months before his death. Troubled, yes. Insane, no."

"Fair enough," Joel said. "But you also told me he was terrified, said that strange things were happening. People—or what he hoped were people—were following him. Later, he spoke of demons. Surely you can see where…"

Katelyn nodded.

"Could he have developed some sort of paranoid, delusional—"

"I'm not a psychiatrist, but I knew my father very well, and I'm telling you the fear he had was genuine. It was neither imagined nor the result of the onset of some sudden mental illness or paranoid delusion. He was afraid because something was happening to him. Something real."

"Adam," Joel asked, "do you agree?"

Clearly in a panic at being asked, Adam did his best to avoid eye contact with his wife as he drew a series of slow deep breaths, then finally said, "Yes, I do."

"All right, let's move on. Did Lonnie have any problems with the law?"

"No," Katelyn replied. "Few traffic and parking tickets, that's about it."

"Did he gamble at all?"

"He'd go to Foxwoods or Mohegan Sun, maybe Twin Rivers now and then, but it was recreational and very rarely. Once every few years, I guess. He certainly never gave any indication that he had a gambling problem or addiction or anything even close to that sort of thing, if that's what you're asking."

"Any significant debt?"

"No. He only had one major credit card and a couple department store ones. None of them had large balances."

"No mortgages, anything like that?"

"His apartment was a rental. Sadly, he never owned his own home."

Joel nodded and made more notes. Although it was brutally cold outside, the heat here was so strong and dry it was becoming uncomfortable. "Actually, could I bother you for a bottle of that water after all?" he asked.

"I'll get it," Adam said, quickly heading for the refrigerator.

"Were there any relatively new people in his life?" Joel asked. "Maybe new friends or acquaintances that came into the picture not long before he died?"

"Not that I'm aware of."

"Was he seeing anyone? A girlfriend or anyone special?"

"He dated from time to time, but he hadn't had a serious re-lationship or what I'd call an actual girlfriend in several years," Katelyn explained.

"He'd become kind of a solitary guy," Adam offered, appearing at his side with the bottled water.

"Thanks." Joel took the bottle and had a long drink. "Do you know why?"

"No," Katelyn said. "He'd never had a huge group of friends. He led a very quiet and simple life, for the most part. He was friendly with a couple guys he knew from work, and he still saw Sal and Dorsey now and then—more Sal than Dorsey—but they stayed in touch, got together maybe a couple times a year."

"So Sal and Dorsey are still in the area?"

"Sal's still in Westport. In the same house he grew up in, in fact. Dorsey lives in New Bedford with his girlfriend."

"Were they at the funeral?"

"Dorsey was. Sal wasn't."

"Much of a tough guy as Sal could be," Joel said, mostly thinking aloud, "he never did handle things like that well."

Katelyn shrugged.

"What about Trent Pierce?"

"He's fallen off the radar. Sal said no one's sure where he is."

"When did this happen?"

"Several years ago. Sal said he was somewhere out west, but no one's heard from him in quite some time, as I understand it. Sal said Trent went through some hard times, a bad divorce and some other things, then just sort of fell off the grid."

That didn't strike Joel as that surprising or odd, since at least in their circle of friends, Trent had been the most rebellious one, the least establishment and the most likely to have issues with society in general. As he knew all too well, things changed. People changed. Nothing—no one—stayed the same. But it sounded as if Trent had only gotten worse in that regard. "Katelyn," he said, "can I ask why you didn't tell me about the funeral? Why didn't you contact me until afterwards?"

Looking physically uncomfortable with the question, she said, "I should've called you, and I'm sorry I didn't. My father talked about you a lot. He missed you, missed your friendship. But he also felt bad for you, because he knew you'd been through hell with that other business. He told me that if anything ever happened to him to leave you alone, to let you know after the fact because you'd been through enough. I honored his wishes. Until I realized that, under the circumstances, you were the first person I should've contacted, not the last."

"It's fine," Joel assured her, giving her hand a quick pat. "You mentioned he was friendly with a couple guys he worked with."

"They weren't terribly close, but he socialized with them now and then."

"In our last conversation you said he was still working in the security field."

"Yes, mall security. He was with the same company for years. He worked his way up to senior officer, a supervisory position. The company has contracts with several area malls, so he moved between them a lot."

Joel turned his notebook to a blank page, then handed it to Katelyn along with his pen. "Jot down their names and the company they work for, please." He turned to Adam. "Were there any people he knew you'd call suspicious?"

"Suspicious?"

"Any friends with unsavory contacts or associations, troubled pasts, that kind of thing."

"Not that we know of," Katelyn answered for him.

"You mean like a criminal element?" Adam asked.

Joel nodded.

"I don't know; that Sal character is a little scary," he said, laughing lightly.

"He could be intimidating for sure, and was always was a little rough around the edges," Joel said, tossing out some brief obligatory laughter. "But far as I know, Sal was never a criminal."

"No, of course he isn't." Finished, Katelyn slid the pen and notebook back. "My father didn't associate with criminals. People make jokes about mall cops and all that, but he cared about people and their safety. He was a good man, he liked helping people and the businesses he protected, he took pride in keeping them safe."

"You said he had very little credit card debt, but did he owe anyone else money? Personal loans or things like that?"

Katelyn shook her head.

"Did he have any enemies to speak of? People he'd had problems with or who were vocal about disliking him for some reason, maybe someone he had a disagreement with or had issues with through his job? A person he might have caught shoplifting or had a prior confrontation with, for example? Someone who may have had a vendetta against him and just taken it too far, or maybe a neighbor with some sort of gripe that got out hand?"

Katelyn and Adam exchanged quick glances. "Sorry, the police asked these same questions. Far as I know there was nothing like that going on. He had problems with people at work at times, as you say, shoplifters or rowdy kids or whatever, but none of that ever translated to his personal life. He was careful to keep all that separate so he wouldn't have problems with those sorts outside work. And on the personal front, as I said, his was a very small circle of friends and acquaintances, and within that circle he was well liked and respected."

Joel referred to the notebook briefly, then folded it closed. "You told me your mother and Lonnie were never married, and you lived with your father growing up."

"That's correct."

"Can you elaborate on that?"

"My mother had struggles with drugs and alcohol most of her life. She was out of the picture from the time I was a very little girl. She served time in jail on occasion and ran with a rough crowd—bikers and whatnot—so I rarely saw her. Now and then she'd appear as if from nowhere, and my father would let her see me for a few minutes, maybe an afternoon, and then she was gone and I wouldn't see her again for months, sometimes years. I never really considered her my mother, to be honest. She was just some strange woman who made me uncomfortable and smelled like cheap booze and cigarettes." Katelyn sighed heavily and wiped away more tears with a fresh tissue. "My father loved her—or did at one time—and I'm not sure he was ever the same after she left him. But it did bring us closer together. He was a wonderful parent. He did his best."

"So is your relationship with your mother still strained?"

"She died four years ago of a heroin overdose."

Joel was surprised it had taken her so long to mention this, but it also struck him how difficult it must have been for her to lose both parents at such a young age. "I'm sorry," he said.

"I barely knew the woman, but thank you. She was living somewhere in New Jersey when she died. I hadn't seen or spoken to her in about five or six years, and neither had my father."

Joel had another drink of water, hoping a brief silence might ease the tension in the room. "You mentioned a brand on the back of Lonnie's shoulder. What else can you tell me about that?"

"He implied *they* had marked him. Whoever *they* were."

"Marked," Joel said. "Interesting way to put it."

"That's the word he used. But he had no memory of when or how it had been done, and had no idea why."

"And you're certain he was telling you the truth?"

Katelyn's eyes, red from tears, locked on his. "My father didn't lie to me."

"No, of course not, I—I'm sorry, I didn't mean it like that." This time it was Joel's turn to sigh heavily. "Can either of you think of any reason why anyone would want to hurt Lonnie?"

"No," Katelyn answered.

Adam shook his head. "No, sir, I can't."

"All right. If I have more questions I'll be in touch." Joel finished off his water. "Now, Katelyn, you said you had more to tell me. I'm ready to hear it."

She tensed up again, and rather than lean against the bar counter as she had since Joel arrived, Katelyn gathered his and her empty water bottles, walked to a bin in the corner marked RECYCLABLES and dropped them inside. "My father wasn't the type who scared easily," she said with her back to them. "Or much at all, for that matter. When I thought about it, I couldn't come up with a single time, not even one memory, of ever seeing my father afraid." Slowly, she turned around. "Until the last months of his life. He was terrified. I'd never seen anyone so frightened. Maybe a child, but not an adult, and certainly not my father."

"I understand."

"No, I don't think you do."

The dark memories lingering at the back of Joel's mind begged to differ, but he saw no sense in arguing the point. "Did he say anything specific about the people he thought were following him and had marked him, or expound at all on his fear that something bad was going to happen?"

"On more than one occasion I asked him to elaborate, but he kept saying he didn't want me to know what he knew, what he'd seen. I got the impression he was more concerned with protecting me from whatever he was dealing with, and telling me anything more or giving me any details would have the opposite effect."

"And this sort of behavior went on for months?"

"It was a gradual thing," Adam said, and then, realizing his wife was less than pleased that he'd interrupted, added, "wouldn't you say so, honey?"

Katelyn nodded. "It began with a change in his behavior, then progressively got worse, yes." She moved closer to the counter. "There's something I haven't told the police." She hesitated, as if she expected Joel to say something. When he didn't, she continued. "A few days before my father was killed, he asked me to meet him at a diner not far from his apartment. When I did, he gave me something." She looked to Adam, and this time gave him a quick nod. He immediately hurried off, disappearing into the other room. "He told me not to tell anyone about it—he was adamant about that—and that if anything happened to him, I was to destroy it."

Adam returned carrying a small, wrinkled paper bag. He handed it across the counter to his wife without comment, then sat back down.

Katelyn removed a thick notebook from the bag. With shaking hands, she placed it carefully on the counter between them. "This is what he gave me."

Joel watched as she slid it over to him. There seemed nothing remarkable about it, just a standard four-subject spiral notebook one might find at any number of stores. He opened it.

Written on each line were a series of numbers that repeated again and again, all the way down the first page. "What is this?" he asked.

"Keep going," she said softly.

He turned the page. The second page was identical to the first. The numbers were the same, all of them written in the same intense, somewhat hurried hand. Joel drew a breath and went to the third page. It was the same. Unsettled, he flipped quickly through the notebook. Every page was filled with the exact same number sequences, repeated again and again throughout the entire notebook.

"Jesus." Certain all the blood had drained from his face Joel slowly ran a hand up over his forehead and through his hair. "Did Lonnie do this?"

"It's his handwriting, yes."

"What does it mean?"

Katelyn swallowed so hard it was audible. "I have no idea."

"He didn't say anything about it?"

"Only that I was to destroy it if anything happened to him."

"But you didn't. Why?"

"Because I felt that if you agreed to help us, you needed to see it."

"Why didn't you show it to the police?"

"They already think my father was out of his mind. A notebook full of the same numbers scribbled thousands of times wouldn't exactly help to convince them otherwise."

Joel nodded. "Yeah, I can see what you mean there. But you have to agree that it's not normal to have something like this. It's not normal to do something like this."

"For some reason, it had importance to him."

"Regardless of his mental state or what he may or may not have been suffering from, Lonnie was still murdered; there's no disputing that. You need to show this to the police, Katelyn."

"Turn to the last page," she said.

He flipped through until he'd reached the final sheet. Drawn across it in pencil were a haphazard series of stick figure sketches of extremely disturbing humanoid beings with distorted limbs, and several lines scribbled across and hanging from their bodies and heads.

"He claimed that's what they looked like," Katelyn said. "The demons."

Joel pointed to the odd lines hanging from the bodies. "What is this supposed to be, clothing of some sort hanging from them?"

"Not hanging. Dripping and running. It's blood."

He slammed the notebook shut. "You have to turn this over to—"

"I don't trust the police."

"The sketches are very disturbing, but they could mean something. And the numbers are likely a code of some sort. If it is, they have people who can—"

"I'm giving it to you, not the police."

"Katelyn, listen to me. You need to give it to them. I know you're upset with the cops right now, but your father's murder is less than two weeks old. It's still a fresh wound for you, and I'm not sure you're thinking clearly about this. You're frustrated, and I don't blame you, but investigations like this can take time to—"

"If you don't want it, I'll follow through with his wishes and destroy it," she said evenly. "But I'm not giving it to the police."

Joel looked to Adam for help, but soon realized none was forthcoming. After a moment, he took the notebook and tucked it into his case. "I'll see what I can come up with on it. Is there anything else?"

"I think we've covered it."

"His apartment, have you broken it down and vacated it yet?"

"No. The landlord gave us until the end of the month." Katelyn wiped her eyes again but seemed to have evened out emotionally. "We've been meaning to get to it, but it's difficult. I can't spend much time there. It's too upsetting."

"I'll need to borrow a set of keys. I'm sure you and the police have been through his place thoroughly, but I'd like to take a look too."

"His address is listed on the disk I gave you, but I can show where it is if—"

"That's not necessary. I'll find it."

Katelyn moved to a drawer next to the sink, pulled out a set of keys on a metal ring and handed them to him. "The gold one unlocks his front door."

"I assume he had a car?"

"A blue Chevy pickup truck, actually. We plan to sell it, but it's still parked on the street across from his apartment." She pointed to the key ring. "The black one."

Joel retrieved his coat from the couch and slipped it on. "I'll be in touch."

"Thanks again," Adam said, offering his hand.

"I've only got a few days to dedicate to this," Joel explained as he shook first Adam's hand, and then Katelyn's. "But soon as I have anything—assuming I do—I'll let you know. If either of you remember anything else you think might be useful, or hear anything more from the police or anyone else with further developments, let me know right away. This lists my cell number." From his wallet, he removed a business card he had for his position at the newspaper, and placed it on the counter. "I know this is a very difficult time. Try to hang in there. I'll do my best for you."

"I believe you," Katelyn said, though in a tone that could only be described as noncommittal. "I have all the faith in the world that you'll get to the bottom of this."

Joel opened his eyes and focused on the window and night beyond. The sultry jazz continued in his earphone, relaxing him as much as could be expected. Except for the light from his iPod, the motel room was draped in darkness. The highway outside was less traveled now at this even later hour, though the occasional pair of headlights still streaked past now and then.

Somewhere not so very far from there, Lonnie lay dead in his grave, already a memory. Suddenly. Irreversibly. Joel tried to remember the last time he'd seen him.

Not long after Joel graduated from college and landed the job at *The Boston Globe*, they'd run into each other at a local eatery in Westport, the town they'd grown up in. Although Joel was already living in Boston, he'd returned to visit his father for the weekend. It was the first time in more than a year that he'd seen or spoken to Lonnie, or any of the guys for that matter, and although it had been a pleasant exchange, there was a degree of awkwardness between them that had never existed before. Their lives had already gone in different directions, and they had far less to talk about than they once had. Still, when their conversation had run its course, Joel had told him how nice it was to see him, and he'd meant it, and Lonnie had said, "You take care of yourself, man."

Those were the last words Lonnie ever said to him.

Nothing, it seemed, had quite worked out the way they'd hoped.

Joel pushed the memories away. It was very late but he still didn't want to go bed. It had been a long time since he'd slept apart from Taylor, and he wasn't looking forward to it, but exhaustion was winning out. Besides, he had a long day coming up; the last thing he needed was to be falling asleep at the wheel. He needed to be alert and on the clock. He had work to do.

Not only did he have plans to check out Lonnie's apartment in the morning, he'd likely have a sit-down with the police at some point too. Earlier, he'd called the lead detective on Lonnie's murder case, a man named Michael Rossi, and explained he was a friend of the family, had a few questions and wanted to meet with him whenever it was convenient. Rossi explained he had a full schedule but might be able to meet with him briefly the following afternoon. He took Joel's name and number and promised to call him back. Pleasant enough over the phone, though cautious and all business. Joel knew that odds were the detective would look into him before their get-together. He could only hope Rossi didn't realize who he was, because if he did, there'd be nothing but hostility coming Joel's way. Hopefully, after all these years, it didn't matter anymore, as most of the cops he'd dealt with years ago in New Bedford, Fall River and many of the surrounding towns had been older back then. Many were likely no longer alive, or long since retired.

He wondered if those who had died knew more now than they had then. Had they gained truths in death they'd never been able to grasp or comprehend in life? Did they know all the answers now, or was it the other way around? Maybe the truth was here with the living, but just like faith, it was elusive as a whisper, mysterious as a slow spiral of smoke. There, then gone before you could be sure.

Katelyn's voice lingered in his mind.

I have all the faith in the world that you'll get to the bottom of this.

Funny thing, faith: it could cure or kill. All depended on who was wielding it.

And why.

CHAPTER EIGHT

The new day brought sunshine, but the cold temperatures remained. Up and out early, Joel hit the road, activated his GPS and headed for Lonnie's apartment.

He was still a few blocks away when he noticed a car following him.

At first Joel thought he was being paranoid, but the same car had been behind him for the last several minutes, and he'd been followed enough times years before to know what to look for, and to recognize when the authorities or others were following him. The black four-door sedan, a Crown Victoria with Rhode Island plates, screamed unmarked cop car, and while the driver was male, due to glare and distance it was very difficult to see any detail beyond that. The car had been there since Joel first noticed it in his rearview mirror more than five full minutes prior, but was never directly behind him; there were always one or more cars between them. Whoever the tail was, he knew what he was doing. But why would the police be following him? If the car had had Massachusetts plates, it might make some sense that Rossi ordered the tail after their phone call, assuming he'd known exactly where to find him that morning (which was, at best, unlikely). But the car clearly had Rhode Island plates, and Joel had no history or connection, professionally or personally, in that state. So why would cops from Rhode Island be following him? It made no sense. Perhaps they weren't cops at all. But then who the hell were they?

It took a few minutes, but eventually Joel was able to make out the entire license plate. He grabbed his cell and dialed Billy's number. Billy had friends at the police department back home, and could easily get a plate run.

"Billy Gill."

"Hey, it's me. Can you do me a quick favor?"

"Hi—yeah, sure—you get down there okay? Everything all right?"

"Everything's fine, just pressed for time. Got a license plate I need run ASAP."

"Hit me."

"Rhode Island plate," Joel said, reciting it to him. "Got it?"

Billy read it back.

"That's it."

"I'll call you back."

Joel hung up and, ignoring the GPS, took a few unnecessary turns just to be sure. Each time, within seconds, the Crown Vic appeared in his rearview. "I'll be a sonofabitch," he muttered.

Remaining calm, he went back to following the GPS instructions and turned at the next corner. He drove into a congested intersection, which he went straight through, and a few minutes later arrived at the correct street. Rolling slowly along the avenue, he searched for the right number. The neighborhood, not nearly as nice as Adam and Katelyn's, was much deeper into the city proper, and although there were a couple nearby commercial properties—a dry cleaner, and a liquor mart that advertised check-cashing services—the street was otherwise residential, comprised of aged, gloomy, timeworn tenements and a few large old houses that had long ago been converted into two-family homes. Small and unimaginative, Lonnie's was a boxy three-story apartment building about halfway up the first block. Joel pulled over into the first space he could find, then checked his rearview.

The Crown Vic slipped along the cross street behind him and vanished.

He stepped out of the car and looked around. There was no one else on the street, and the neighborhood, at least this time of day, was relatively quiet. It made Joel sad to think that this was where Lonnie wound up, in such a drab little apartment in a run-down area like this. He'd never been wealthy, having been born into a lower middle-class family in the nearby town of Westport, but had grown up in a nice, modest house in a decent neighborhood, just like Joel and the rest of the guys. But at the end of Lonnie's life, he had a worse standard of living than when he'd started. Maybe Katelyn was right after all: despite the years of hard work her father had logged, when it was all said and done, he had very little to show for it.

Joel scanned the cars parked on either side of the street until he spotted Lonnie's pickup truck. He decided to check that out first, as it would allow him to kill some time to see if the Crown Vic returned. If it did, he wanted to be on the street, where he could get a better look at the driver.

Using the key Katelyn gave him, he opened the truck's driver's side door and slid behind the wheel. The truck was immaculate, except for loose change in the cup holder and a crumpled McDonald's bag on the passenger's side. Joel leaned over and grabbed it. An empty Big Mac box and what was left of some fries. He closed the bag, tossed it back on the seat, then popped open the glove compartment. Nothing out of the ordinary: the owner's manual, the truck's registration, a folder from a local Midas shop with a warranty for a replaced muffler and exhaust system, some paper napkins, a ballpoint pen and paperwork regarding the truck's last inspection, which it had passed several months ago. Joel slapped the glove box closed, checked under both visors, found nothing, then opened the center console, which folded down in the center of the bench seat. Empty. Either Lonnie had kept very little in the truck or the police had picked it clean.

Joel watched the cross streets at the top and bottom of the block, alternating between them every few seconds. A steady stream of vehicles moved along both, but not his tail, so he vacated the truck, locked it and headed for Lonnie's apartment.

Before he reached the steps, he grabbed his cell and dialed Katelyn's number. There were a few questions he'd wanted to ask her, but not until he was on the street and could get a feel for the area. "I'm sorry to bother you," he told her when she answered. "Just need to ask you a couple other things. I have the address of the corner where Lonnie was killed, but I need to know where it is in relation to his apartment."

"If you come out of his building and go down the steps," Katelyn explained, "then go to the right and walk straight for five blocks, you'll eventually come to an intersection. The corner you'll be standing on looks directly across the street at a large convenience store. That corner, where the store is, that's where he was…" She exhaled loudly into the phone. "Shot."

"I'm sorry, I know this is difficult. Almost done. According to the reports, the shooting took place on a Sunday morning at approximately ten o'clock."

"That's correct."

"Any idea what he was doing?"

"No."

"Could he have gone out to grab a Sunday paper or maybe something at that convenience store?"

"He had paper delivery, and if he needed something at the store, he drove."

"Maybe he just went for a walk?"

"As I said yesterday, he often had pain in his legs and feet. He didn't walk anywhere unless he had to."

Joel watched the street, looking in the direction Lonnie had walked on the last morning of his life. This was a city with a heavily religious population, lots of Catholics and churchgoers of different denominations. Most would be at masses or services at that hour of the morning on a Sunday. Good day and time to commit a murder on the street; there'd likely be fewer witnesses. "Do the police have any clue as to why he was there?"

"If they have any theories on that, they haven't shared them with me."

"Did your dad have a cell phone?"

"Yes. It was archaic, but he had one."

"What about a computer?"

"He had a laptop, a very basic model. He wasn't very computer savvy. The police have it, along with his cell. I'm supposed to get both back at some point."

"Okay. Do you know if the convenience store was open when the shooting took place?"

"I asked the detectives that and they said it was, and that they'd spoken to the clerk on duty that morning. He was the one who called 911. He heard the shot but didn't see anything. By the time he got outside, whoever had done it was gone."

Joel's phone beeped, signaling an incoming call. The ID read BILLY.

"Thanks, Katelyn, I'll be in touch." He switched to the other call. "What've you got for me?"

"No such plate, kemosabe. It doesn't exist. Sure it was a Rhode Island tag?"

"Positive."

"Maybe you took the down the wrong info."

"No, it was accurate."

"Then they're using fake tags, counterfeit plates."

"Okay, thanks. Talk to you soon." Joel hung up, slid his phone back into his coat pocket and slowly climbed the steps to Lonnie's apartment building. He took a quick look up and down the street one more time, but the Crown Vic was nowhere to be seen.

As he reached the front door, the black iron bars on Lonnie's first-floor apartment windows caught his attention. Not surprising, he supposed, given the neighborhood. But as the daylight behind him shifted, he noticed something more, just beyond the bars and dingy panes of glass.

The dark and distorted silhouette of something watching him through the window...

CHAPTER NINE

Startled, Joel hesitated at the front door. As far as he knew, Lonnie's apartment should've been empty. It was possible the landlord or perhaps the police were inside, but whoever was in that window didn't look like an adult. The silhouette was small in stature, more like a child or a dwarf, and appeared disfigured, as it stood at a strange angle, noticeably bent to one side, indicating an odd curvature of the spine and a rather unsettling, twisted posture, its arms drawn in close to its chest.

Whatever he was looking at was still registering in his mind when it slid away from the window and out of sight. He gave the street another quick scan. Nothing parked along either side that looked like a police car or official vehicle, nothing out of place, and nothing that looked like it didn't belong there. He pushed open the front door, stepped inside the building and found himself in a small foyer. Straight ahead stood a row of mailboxes built directly into the wall. To his left, stairs that presumably led to the second and third floor units; to his right, Lonnie's apartment door. He located the gold key on the ring, leaned in close to the door and listened a moment. No sounds of movement or anything else. He knocked lightly. Nothing. He knocked again, harder this time, but there was still no response.

Joel pushed the key into the lock, turned it and opened the door. "Hello?"

"Nobody's in there," said a raspy female voice from somewhere behind him.

He looked over his shoulder to the stairs and found a middle-aged woman standing on the landing, looking down at him with a quizzical gaze. Her face was pockmarked with scars from what were likely bouts of acne in her youth; her hair was shoulder-length, parted in the middle and dyed blonde, with black roots running the length of the part; she was clad in jeans, sneakers and a sweatshirt featuring three cats and the phrase *Crazy Cat Lady* emblazoned across it.

"Hi," he said. "I just saw someone through the window, actually."

"You sure?" she asked with a heavy regional accent. Her eyes were dark and rather attractive—the sole survivors, it seemed, on a face that had been much prettier many years before. Since then, life had taken its toll on her, and it showed. "There shouldn't be nobody in there."

"Are there any children in the building?"

"Nope, just me and a bunch of whiteheads."

"Whiteheads?"

"Oldsters. You know, senior citizens. I'm just bustin' balls, I like old people."

"Maybe the landlord's in there."

"Nah, he's never here unless he's collectin' the rent. He still comes to the door every month like it's a hundred years ago. You can't mail it. He has to pick it up. Real piece of work, this guy, nose hair for miles, you could bead these things, I shit you not—and far as I can tell he never got the memo about the whole deodorant thing. Smells like an Italian sub."

"Is he a little person, by any chance?"

"Huh?"

"A dwarf."

She squinted as if she were losing sight of him. "Dude, why the hell would he be a frickin' dwarf?"

"Never mind." Joel pushed the door, letting it swing open, and looked inside. He couldn't see the entire apartment, but from his position in the hallway, the areas he could see appeared to be empty. "Strange," he said, "I could've sworn…"

"I heard the knockin', but obviously you got a key so…can I help you, or…"

"I'm a friend of Lonnie's," he told her. "I have permission to be here. His daughter gave me keys to his place."

"Oh yeah? What's his daughter's name?"

"Katelyn Burrows."

"Okay, I guess you're legit." The woman frowned and nervously combed a renegade strand of bright blonde hair out of her eyes. "You know what happened to Lonnie then, huh?"

"Yeah," Joel said, his patience already waning. "I know what happened to Lonnie. Katelyn asked me to look into things for her."

The woman arched a penciled-on eyebrow. "What are you, like a private detective or somethin'?"

"I'm a reporter."

"Oh."

"Sorry to disappoint you. I'm off the clock anyway, just here as a friend."

"You and Lonnie were bros, huh?"

"Since high school."

"Was awful, what happened to him. He was a wicked good guy."

"Were you two close?"

She nodded, looking sincerely pained. "I only knew him for like a year, but we got pretty tight. He was a sweetheart. I miss him." The woman offered a quick, self-conscious wave. "I'm Bea."

"Joel Walker."

She moved down the stairs and offered her hand. "Good to meet you."

"You too." Her hand was warm, her wrist adorned with numerous bracelets. She continued shaking his hand long after it seemed appropriate, so Joel subtly pulled free. "I'm going to go look around now, if you don't mind."

"I don't mind," she said with a shrug, absently scratching the corner of her mouth with a hot-pink acrylic fingernail. "I work for the post office, but I took a vacation day, so if you need to ask me any questions or whatever, let me know, I'll be right upstairs."

"I'll do that," he said, slipping into the apartment. "Thank you."

"Top of the stairs, bang a left, first door on the right." Bea smiled, revealing teeth stained from years of cigarette smoking. "Number three."

"Got it." Joel smiled back, then closed the door behind him.

He stood there a moment, listening. Once he heard Bea going back up the stairs, he turned and saw that he was standing in a living room. Just off the main room were a bathroom and small bedroom, and a kitchenette filled the rear wall of the apartment. He remembered the shadowy figure in the window and, realizing he was alone in the apartment, felt his apprehension grow. "Is anyone in here?" he asked. "Hello? Look, I know someone's in here, I saw you in the window."

Joel quickly checked the bathroom and bedroom but found no one. Back in the living room, he crossed into the kitchenette area and checked the back door to the apartment, which led out onto a paved walkway surrounded by chain-link fence and a gate that opened onto the street. Other than climbing out a window, the back door was the only other exit, but it was locked. That meant if the person he'd seen had left that way, they had a key and used it to lock the door from the outside while making their escape.

He was obviously alone in the apartment now, but still felt uneasy. Could he have been mistaken? Could what he'd seen in the window have been a trick of light and shadow? It had to be. *No*, he thought, *I know what I saw. Whoever it was must've had a key and slipped out the back door while I was talking with Bea.*

He made a quick mental note to find out exactly how many keys to Lonnie's apartment there were and who had them. He knew all too well the dangers of both doubting what your eyes and ears told you, and in making more of things than they actually were. That uncertainty was what kept you off-balance and vulnerable to the darkness, and like all predators, it understood only strength and resistance administered with extreme prejudice.

He sighed and looked around. Feeling like the intruder he was, he began checking the place out while doing his best to ignore the voice in his head insisting he was invading his old friend's privacy.

Joel decided to return to Lonnie's bedroom first. It was a small, cramped room that was mostly taken up by the bed, which still had sheets and blankets on it, though they were mussed and thrown to the side. It looked as if the bed hadn't been touched since the last time Lonnie rolled out of it. On the nightstand next to it were an inexpensive lamp, and an ashtray with a half-smoked cigar and two beer bottle tops in it. On the floor between the bed and a small closet, a pair of ratty slippers lay side by side, looking as if Lonnie just recently kicked them off. In the closet he found some shoes and boots on the floor, two uniforms hanging along with some shirts, dress slacks and a few belts. The lone shelf housed folded blankets, another set of sheets and an empty sneaker box.

A printer, an extra inkjet cartridge and a ream of paper sat on a small desk against one wall. There was an empty space in the middle of the desk where Lonnie's laptop had once been.

After going through the bathroom and finding a leaky faucet in the sink but nothing of any import, Joel drifted back out into the living room. Everything looked just as Lonnie had left it, like he'd gone out for a few minutes and planned to be back any moment. There was no preparation here, no locked-down apartment he knew he'd never return to. Much as he might have believed people were after him and something bad was going to happen, he hadn't expected to die the day he did.

"Where were you going that morning?" Joel asked the apartment. "Who were you meeting? What the hell was going on, Lonnie?"

His eyes slowly panned across the room. A recliner…a remote for the television in the corner…a small couch and a coffee table…two end tables…a small bookcase housing knickknacks, magazines and mostly paperback books. On the coffee table, an empty glass, half a bottle of cheap whiskey, a disposable lighter and a plastic ashtray with another cigar stub in it.

"Tell me," he whispered. "Talk to me, Lonnie. Show me what I need to see."

His eyes fell upon a small storage unit located directly below the windows facing the street. Joel crouched down and opened the double doors. The first thing he noticed was a gun case, as it was the only thing on the lone shelf. That seemed strange. Why purchase a unit like this, then put only one thing in the top half of it that didn't utilize even half the space? Carefully, he pulled the case free and opened it. An extra clip and a box of ammunition were in place, but the foam cutout where a pistol should have been was empty. The weapon wasn't anywhere in the unit either, so he closed the case and returned it to the shelf. The bottom section was filled with DVDs and a few old VHS tapes. He pulled out a stack of them. Mostly comedies. Joel smiled. Lonnie always did love comedies. One DVD in particular stood out: *Animal House*. Joel remembered when it had first come out, his freshman year of high school. Along with Sal, Dorsey, and Trent, they'd skipped school and snuck into the theater at the Dartmouth Mall to see it. They'd never witnessed anything like it before, loved it, and every chance they got they'd sneak in or convince Sal's older brother to go too, as he could get them into the R-rated film as the "adult guardian." He pictured the whole group of them palling around and laughing, so alive and full of mischief, so…unaware.

My God, were we ever really those people? Were we ever really that lucky?

As the memories faded, taking his smile and any answers he'd hoped for with them, he returned the DVDs to the unit, closed the doors and stood up. Watching the street through the windows a while, he wondered how many times Lonnie had done the exact same thing.

Did you do it on the day you died? What did you see out there?

He turned away, focused on the apartment again and strode into the kitchenette area. Nothing out of the ordinary, but a few boxes partially packed with utensils and assorted items lay scattered across the small kitchen table and along the floor. Katelyn had said she and Adam had begun packing the place up but hadn't gotten far. This was apparently the fruit of their limited labor.

Something drew his focus back to the bookcase in the living room. He moved toward it, this time noticing numerous gaps in the rows, indicating several books had been removed from the shelves. What remained were mostly novels, predominantly crime and suspense thrillers, along with a couple horror and science fiction tomes. Some celebrity biographies, sports-related books and nonfiction pieces having to do with local history rounded out the collection.

Lonnie was everywhere here…and nowhere at all.

In the eerie silence of that empty apartment, with nothing but shadows and the residue of what had once been his friend moving all around him like the ghosts they likely were, more than anything, Joel felt a tremendous sense of grief. Sadness was tangible here, as strong and dominant as Lonnie had once been.

But there was something more here as well. Evil. Evil was here, in this place. Joel knew it well, recognized it for what it was when it slithered into his brain and curled up in the warmth of his blood, nesting in his mind before beginning its work. It hung in the air like the pungent and rotting *thing* it was, hidden in those same shadows, watching and whispering its lies from the world no one could see.

And it was pleased.

He remembered the forest all those years before, the makeshift stone altars his investigation had led him to, the blood and animal bones and carcasses he found there, the satanic symbols painted and carved everywhere, the evil dripping from the trees, oozing from the muddy ground, filling his lungs with each breath drawn. He'd never witnessed what actually happened in that awful clearing in the woods, but he didn't have to. Those responsible for it were gone, but the evil they had conjured remained. Waiting…

Waiting for you, Joel.

Rubbing his eyes and drawing a deep breath, Joel paced about for a moment, doing his best to clear his head and push away the darkness, the demonic growls and whispers that for so very long now had lived at the outskirts, the very edges of his sanity, so easily awakened even after all this time, ready to pounce like seedy scaremongers from some carnival funhouse, leering at him and bringing forth the same unbridled terror that had crippled him in the past, broken him and left him a shell of what he'd once been, curled up in a ball in the bowels of a hospital for the mentally ill.

"Stop," he said aloud, his voice cracking. He cleared his throat, ran shaking hands through his hair. "Stop. Now. *Stop* it."

The Devil closed his bloody eyes, returned to sleep amid the flames.

There had been a time when he would've needed pills to rescue him, but he'd learned breathing techniques and ways of distracting his thoughts and focusing them elsewhere when this sort of thing happened. He stayed with them, going through them again and again until he felt his heart rate return to normal and the laughter of demons in the back of his mind go quiet.

In that moment, Joel wanted nothing more than to go home and feel Taylor's arms around him, the warmth of her body against his, those eyes searching his with love and understanding, patience and kindness unlike any he'd ever known.

Instead, he moved quickly across the room to the bookcase and began scanning the book spines, going from title to title in search of…what? What was he looking for? He wasn't sure, but he'd been drawn to the books. Perhaps Lonnie had answered him after all. He pulled several, flipping through them, but came up empty until he selected an old, dogeared copy of the Philip K. Dick novel *The Man in the High Castle*. As he flipped through it, he noticed that a little over halfway through the book, a business card was nestled between the pages. He plucked it free, then tossed the novel back on the shelf.

The card read: *Jerry Simpson, Director of Human Resources,* TUSER INDUSTRIES. It listed a phone number and address in New Bedford.

Joel turned the card over. Hastily written in pen was the word *Tuser*, followed by the word *Resut*. He studied them a moment. It was the same word. Lonnie had written it normally, then backward.

Grabbing his phone, he opened his Internet browser and did a search for *Tuser Industries*. It returned a website verifying it was a real place, evidently still in business. A search for the word *Tuser* only offered a listing in an urban dictionary that read: *A user of a product who commonly raises ridiculous or otherwise hilariously daft questions relating to usability.* That certainly didn't seem to fit or relate to anything, so Joel wondered if Tuser was simply a person's name or perhaps a combination of names.

Next he did a search for *Resut*.

RESUT is an ancient Egyptian word for dream. The literal translation is "to come awake" or "awakening", and it is depicted in hieroglyphs as an open eye, symbolizing that when one dreams, one's eyes are open to the truth.

A search for Jerry Simpson turned up nothing related to the company.

Joel put the card in his pocket and left the apartment. Once in the hallway, he locked the door, then looked up at the stairs. Somewhere in the building a game show was blaring from someone's television.

He texted Katelyn and asked if Lonnie had ever mentioned Tuser Industries or anyone named Jerry Simpson. A moment later she texted back, explaining he had not. It didn't sound familiar to her at all. Joel let her know he'd be in touch soon, then put his phone away and slowly climbed the stairs toward Bea's apartment.

Following her directions, he followed a dim, dusty, windowless hallway to apartment 3.

Bea answered the door almost immediately. "Hey," she said with a smile.

"Hey. Quick question. Ever heard of Tuser Industries?"

"Yeah, it's in New Bedford," she told him. "Lonnie worked there."

CHAPTER TEN

A black cat jumped up on the kitchen table and began slinking toward him like a little panther. On the floor, three others—two calicos and one with white and black coloring like a cow—gathered around Joel's feet, rubbing their bodies against his legs and his chair and purring nosily.

"You like cats?" Bea asked from her position at the counter.

"Yeah," he said, petting the black one. "I love animals."

Bea's apartment had essentially the same layout as Lonnie's, although the living room was smaller and hers featured a full kitchen. Predictably, the décor was haphazard and inexpensive, and while the apartment was clean, it was cluttered and messy. Obviously she didn't spend a great deal of time tidying up, but she'd managed to turn an otherwise dull space into something attractive and homey.

"Good thing, 'cause they love you, huh?" She pulled two mugs from a cupboard and placed them on the counter next to a coffeemaker. "I never trust nobody my babies don't like, you know what I mean? They're always right when it comes to that kind of thing. You got any?"

"Used to have a dog and a cat," he said. "Not in a while, though."

"Yeah? How come?"

"It's so hard when you lose them."

"Everythin' dies." She poured the coffee, then added sugar and milk to hers. "No reason not to love. If you think about it, maybe it's more reason to."

Joel smiled. He hadn't expected Bea to wax poetic about much of anything. "You're right," he said as she set a steaming mug down in front of him. "Thanks."

"The landlord says I'm only allowed to have one, but fuck him, right? What he don't know, he don't know, you know?" She scooped up the black cat, kissed him on the head, then dropped him to the floor with the others. "So I called Katelyn, wanted to make sure you checked out."

"Did I pass?"

"Flyin' colors. I don't know Katelyn that good, to be honest. Between you and me she's kind of a snoot, you know? But she loved her father, and he loved her somethin' fierce. She said you and Lonnie were buds back in the day."

"We hadn't talked in a long while, but yeah, like I said, since high school."

"Just wanted to make sure I could trust you, that's all. Nothin' personal."

"Totally understandable. I'm not here to hurt you or Lonnie's memory in any way. I'm here to help if I can. Know that anything you tell me will be held in the strictest confidence. Everything will stay between us, okay?"

Bea nodded. "Okay."

Joel sipped his coffee as Bea retrieved her mug and joined him at the table, which was littered with celebrity and fashion magazines, and an ashtray brimming with spent cigarette butts. "What can you tell me about Tuser Industries?"

"I don't know what they do or nothin', but Lonnie worked there part-time for like seven or eight months. Couple nights a week kinda thing at first, then he did mostly weekends there. He even stayed overnight when he did weekend shifts. He spent his last vacation from his regular job working there too, a whole week, stayed there the whole time. Guess they had a place for employees to sleep or whatever. It's why he was always so frickin' tired. Lonnie worked a lot. He didn't make a lot at his regular job, though. Tuser was a way to make extra bucks. Coffee good, hon?"

"It's great." He held his mug up as if in evidence. "Thanks."

"Ain't Dunkin but it's not bad, right?" She had some of hers, then grabbed a pack of Camels from the table and stabbed a cigarette into the corner of her mouth.

"What did Lonnie do at Tuser, do you know?"

"Night security or some shit." She lit the cigarette, drew on it, then threw her head back and exhaled at the ceiling.

"When I asked Katelyn about it, she'd never heard of the company."

"He didn't want nobody to know. He said they had all these rules and he wasn't supposed to tell nobody he worked there. He told me, but he told me lots of stuff. Like how he was still dealin' with Katelyn gettin' married and all that. They were super close. He raised her by himself in an apartment not far from the bridge. When Katelyn got married, she moved out, of course, and since he was by himself, he didn't see no reason to keep a place that size, so he moved in here. That's when I met him. He was kinda lost, you know? He had some friends but he didn't hang out with them a lot. I felt bad for him. Maybe 'cause I get it, you know? I'm alone, and I got a son I raised on my own too. His dad—my ex—died when he was a kid."

"I'm sorry to hear that."

"Yeah, got up one mornin', said he wasn't feelin' good. Walked across the room, coughed and fell over dead. Hand to God, just like that. Heart attack. Thirty frickin' years old, Joel." Bea looked away, took another hard pull on her cigarette, then forced a smile. "Now I'm a grandmother, if you can believe that shit. Two grandkids. Twin girls. I don't see them much as I want 'cause my son and his wife live in Connecticut, so… Anyways, my point is, when it's just the two of youse, it's such a close relationship that it's really hard when they leave, you know?"

"Makes sense," Joel said. "Do the police know he worked at Tuser?"

"I told them."

"Was he still working there at the time of his death?"

"He quit a couple months before he died."

"Do you know why?

"He was havin' problems."

"What kind of problems?"

She hesitated, drank some coffee.

"It's okay to tell me, Bea. I know Lonnie was struggling with some issues."

"Me and Lonnie," she said, her eyes filling with tears, "we tried the whole boyfriend-girlfriend thing for like two weeks, okay? It wasn't bad. Sometimes it was even good. But we were better at bein' friends, you know? He was a sweet guy, always lookin' out for me, makin' sure I was all right and askin' if I had a good day. Nobody ever gives two shits what kinda day I had. Hardly anybody outside work even fuckin' talks to me. I live in this buildin' where nobody but me is under a hundred years old, not one of them can fuckin' hear anythin'—they're all deaf as shit—and then this guy my age moves in, you know?" She wiped her eyes, pawing away the tears with the back of her free hand. "He was by himself, didn't have a girlfriend or nothin', and far as I could tell he wasn't a fag. No disrespect, I love queers. My brother's a queer. I'm totally for gay rights and all that shit. I even tried it a couple times. I'm fifty years old, dude. I was a party girl in the eighties and nineties. Gimme a break, right? I know how to have a good time, and lemme tellya, I can still get it wet, okay? No bullshit! But end of the day, I love guys, what can I do?" She barked out a burst of baritone laughter, but it quickly turned into a hacking cough.

There seemed nothing else to do but laugh along with her, so that's exactly what Joel did, until her cough subsided. "You all right?"

"Yeah, I'm good. Don't mean to be a pig, but it feels frickin' good to laugh sometimes, you know? Especially lately." She plucked a paper napkin from a ceramic holder on the table and wiped her mouth. "Anyways, we just hit it off, me and Lonnie, you know? When he first moved in, he was different. Kinda sad, but wicked nice. Everythin' was good for months. Then things started changin'."

"Do you remember what was going on in his life when the changes began?"

"It wasn't too long after he started workin' that night gig."

87

"Do you think that had anything to do with it?"

Bea shrugged. "Dunno."

"Did he ever mention anything more about the job or the company?"

"I don't think so. He didn't really talk about work a lot." She smoked a while without offering more. "He just started gettin' weird one day. Paranoid, you know? He thought people were after him and that somebody was messin' with his head. Like fuckin' his mind over or whatever."

"Did he say who these people were?"

"He wouldn't tell me."

"Lonnie had a gun."

"Yeah, I know, a 9mm."

"It's missing from the case downstairs. Do you know what happened to it?"

She shook her head no. "Cops asked about it too."

"Okay, so they didn't confiscate it then."

"Fuckin' cops, please." Bea rolled her eyes. "Like they give a shit. They were all gung ho about catchin' Lonnie's killer at first 'cause the press was all over it like flies on a bag of shit. Good news story, right? Guy shot down in the street and all that. Sells papers, gets ratings. But then after a couple days nobody gives a fuck. Just some mall cop, who cares? Ain't like some senator got whacked or nothin'. Anyways, the cops took all kinds of shit out of his apartment. Actin' all high and mighty, like big shots. Oooo, they're gonna solve a murder! Look out! Yeah. Sure. Then everythin' just stopped. Douches couldn't catch a hand job in a whorehouse."

Biting his lip, Joel asked, "Do you have any idea where Lonnie was going the morning he was killed?"

"No." She crushed her cigarette in the ashtray. "But…"

"But what?"

Bea was suddenly having a difficult time making eye contact. "Did you really see somebody in there before, in his apartment?"

"I'm not sure. Why?"

"I never told nobody else this," she said, squirming a bit in her chair, "but ever since Lonnie died, sometimes I hear noises comin' from his apartment."

"Like what?"

"Sounds like somebody walkin' around in there. But it's not like a regular walk. Sounds like it's a cripple walkin', you know?"

Joel felt a twinge of fear brush his spine as he remembered the figure he'd seen in the window, and how it had appeared disfigured.

"It's like somebody that's…what's the word…"

"Hobbled?"

"Yeah, *hobbled*," she said, pointing at him. "That's a good one!"

"Go on."

"I've heard it a few times since Lonnie died. One time I was leavin' for work and it sounded like somebody was in his place, so I knocked and asked if someone was there, right? The sound stopped but nobody ever answered." Bea sipped her coffee. "It happens mostly at night. I don't know, I—I started thinkin' maybe it's Lonnie. Maybe it's like his ghost or somethin', and maybe he's walkin' funny 'cause he got shot in the head, right, and like maybe it fucked up his walkin' in the afterlife or whatever." She looked at him, her eyes still wet. "Is that retarded? It is. It's totally frickin' retarded. Almost as bad as that dwarf shit you were talkin' about. That was fuckin' mental, dude. I'm all like, why the fuck would he be a midget?"

"Yeah, sorry about that," Joel said through a sigh. "Bea, do you know anything about any notebooks Lonnie kept?"

She lit another cigarette and took several drags before answering. "You mean the one with the numbers and the scary pictures in it?"

His heart dropping into his lap, Joel sat forward. "Yes."

"I wasn't supposed to tell nobody about it." Bea stood up, walked her mug over to the sink, took one more sip, then dumped the rest. "Figured the cops took it."

"No, I have it. But I don't know what it means. Do you?"

She turned and faced him, but stayed near the sink. "He only showed it to me one time, couple weeks before he died. He was wicked drunk, said the numbers had somethin' to do with that shortwave shit."

"Shortwave? Like shortwave radios?"

"Yeah, some guy he knew was into that stuff. Talkin' on it or whatever. They talk to people all over the world, I guess."

"What guy, Bea? Do you have a name?"

"Jerry somethin'."

"Simpson?"

"Maybe, I don't remember. I'm not even sure he ever told me the guy's last name, to be honest. Anyways, he lives somewhere down near the cape. I forget the town, but Lonnie worked with him at Tuser. He told me he went to his house a couple times 'cause the guy has one of them radios."

"Did you tell the police any of this?"

"I didn't tell nobody, except for you, just now."

"Why were the same series of numbers written over and over again, page after page?"

"I don't know nothin' about it, but that night Lonnie kept talkin' about some signal that was dangerous 'cause it was fuckin' with his head and other people's heads and all this kinda shit. He was scared, Joel. He said they were gonna kill him. They were comin', and they were gonna kill him. He was drunk off his ass, and he sounded fuckin' insane, but that's what he said. I couldn't figure out what the hell he was talkin' about, but Lonnie was scared, I can tell you that. Real scared. So I'm like, *Who, Lonnie? Who's gonna kill you?* But he wouldn't tell me. He just kept sayin' they were gonna kill him." Bea puffed her cigarette. "And then they did."

Joel stood up and carried his mug over to the counter. "Thank you, Bea, you've been a big help."

She took the mug from him and placed it in the sink. "Are you gonna find out who did this?"

"I'm going to try." He offered his hand. "If I have any more questions, is it all right if I call on you again?"

"Any time," she said, taking his hand. "Like I got anythin' to do."

"Anyone else comes around asking questions—including the police—don't tell them anything about any of this, all right?"

"About any of what?" She smiled. "I don't know what you're talkin' about."

They shook.

"That a weddin' ring?" Bea asked.

"Yes."

"Married man, huh?"

"For a long time now."

"Happily?"

"Afraid so."

"Figures." She sighed. "Fuck me sideways. Or not, apparently."

Once they'd crossed the kitchen and living room, at the front door, Joel handed her his business card. "In case you remember anything else you think might be important, or need to call me."

She read the card over, then looked at him. "You like pork chops?"

Joel laughed lightly. "I do, yeah."

"Just so you know, I make delicious pork chops. If I ever invite you to come over and eat some with me, you should say yes, because they're frickin' awesome and I promise not to jump your bones."

"I'll be sure to keep that in mind."

She bowed her head. "Can I tell you somethin'?"

"Sure."

"Promise not to laugh at me?"

"I do."

Nearly whispering, she said, "Sometimes at night, when it's dark and I'm all alone, I...I get scared."

"Me too."

She gave a playful smirk, and then, realizing he wasn't joking, said, "Really?"

You have no idea.

"We all get scared sometimes. Just have to keep it from getting too tight a hold on us, is all. Most of the time there's nothing to be afraid of."

"But sometimes there is."

"Yes. Sometimes there is."

"When I hear those noises down in Lonnie's apartment, do you think it's him walkin' around in there?"

"Lonnie's dead, Bea."

"Yeah, he is," she said sadly. "But that's not what I asked you."

CHAPTER ELEVEN

The sky had turned an odd shade of gray, threatening snow, and the cold snap continued into the afternoon. Although traffic was heavy in the city, Joel didn't see the mystery car again, and had to assume that whoever had been following him earlier had called it off, at least for the time being.

Following the directions Katelyn had given him, Joel drove a few blocks until he reached the intersection and corner where Lonnie had been killed. He found a spot near the convenience store and pulled over. People and traffic moved through the streets, oblivious to the feelings surging through him in that moment as his eyes came to rest on the nearby corner.

Right there, he thought. *Lonnie died right there.*

Despite his best attempts to stop it, visions of Lonnie being shot and falling to the pavement fired across his mind's eye, his body writhing and head bleeding as he died in the street. Alive, then dead, just like that. He wondered if Lonnie ever knew what hit him, if he'd had time to react or be afraid or even feel pain. Joel hoped not.

He shut the car off, forced the thoughts and pictures from his head and called the number for Tuser Industries listed on Jerry Simpson's business card.

An automated program answered his call on the second ring. A vaguely pleasant female voice that might or might not have been human informed him he had reached Tuser Industries, and then offered an array of options. Joel selected the extension for human resources.

"Good afternoon, human resources. This is Peggy."

"Good afternoon, Peggy," Joel said. "Jerry Simpson, please."

"I'm sorry, Mr. Simpson's in a meeting right now. Who may I ask is calling?"

"My name's Joel Walker. Can you tell me when Jerry might be available?"

"Hard to say, really," Peggy assured him in a tone so cheerful it bordered on cartoonish. "May I ask what this is regarding, Mr. Walker?"

"It's rather personal in nature," Joel said as smoothly as he could.

"I see. Well, if you'd like to leave me a number where you can reached, I'll be sure Mr. Simpson gets it the moment he's free."

Joel left his cell number with the happiest secretary he'd ever encountered, then disconnected and thought a moment, allowing the conversation with Bea and the things he'd found in Lonnie's apartment to replay in his mind.

He didn't really have much to go on when it came to Tuser Industries, and couldn't be sure it wasn't a dead end, but Bea had said Lonnie's difficulties coincided with his employment there. Added to the fact that the strange notebook was connected to this Jerry Simpson character, at a minimum it warranted looking into.

Stepping from the car, Joel watched the corner a while, reenacting in his mind the morning Lonnie walked across the street toward the convenience store. Whether the shooter had arrived at the scene and/or fled in a vehicle of some kind, when the murder was committed the shooter had been on foot, because the wound to Lonnie's temple had been administered at point-blank range.

But where had the killer come from? If one applied the theory that Lonnie hadn't seen him coming, then the shooter had either approached him from behind or from his right. From the information Joel knew of the case, Lonnie had been shot in the right temple, meaning if the shooter had come from behind, he would've had to sidle up next to him, on Lonnie's right-hand side—the street side—press the gun against his head and fire. Certainly possible as well as plausible, but had the shooter come from the right to begin with, he could've walked directly up to Lonnie from across the street, following a straight line to his target. Either option worked, but the second seemed more efficient and therefore more likely. The third choice was that the killer had come from the front. If this was true, he passed on the right side and shot him as they passed each other. If the third scenario was correct, Lonnie either didn't know the shooter (because he would've seen him coming) or the shooter was the person he had come to meet, and he'd simply shot him so quickly Lonnie didn't have time to react. Regardless of scenario, the killing had to have happened quickly and without error, because it was a Sunday morning and there weren't a lot of people on the street. In one way that helped the killer escape without detection, but from another perspective, it also made the hit more dangerous because the fewer the people on the street, the more one stood out and the harder it was to approach someone without him realizing it.

Joel searched the streets, looking for cameras. In today's day and age there were always cameras. Always.

A gas station about a block away had surveillance cameras on the roof, facing the pumps. Depending on the angle, they might have picked up something, though it was unlikely that at that distance they'd yield anything useful. Beyond that, from what Joel could tell, the area was void of cameras. Coincidence or convenience?

Next, Joel thought about escape. Unless it had been a totally random and senseless execution, Lonnie's murder was premeditated and planned. There seemed no question about that. So, following that logic, it stood to reason that there also must have been an escape plan. Regardless of the day or how busy or not the area was at the time of the killing, no assassin shot someone on the street in broad daylight without having a pre-established escape route.

Joel turned and looked toward the gas station. At the far end of the drag, perhaps four or five blocks in the distance, there were signs for a highway. *If there was a vehicle involved*, he thought, *the shooter went that way*. Any other direction would've taken him deeper into the city and into more congested areas with a higher risk of encountering witnesses. It also would've made it far harder and longer to get out of the area, much less the city. Had he been on foot, he'd have done the opposite, walking in one of the other three directions, because on foot the congestion could provide cover and make it easier to get lost in the crowd or hustle and bustle of busier areas that morning, and had he opted for the quieter side streets, they could provide cover as well, as the shooter could simply walk away through numerous neighborhoods like someone going for a Sunday stroll.

Although he couldn't be sure, instinct told him a car had been involved. It just seemed more likely. This was murder, after all, and a damn efficient one that had worked and hadn't resulted in capture or detection, at least not yet. That meant it was likely perpetrated by a professional or, at a minimum, someone who'd thought this through and planned it in detail. And the odds that either would walk to and from any scene, much less this one, were difficult to conceive.

Joel imagined a car already parked somewhere in this area, with at least two people inside. They would've known which direction Lonnie would be coming from and would have positioned themselves in a spot where they could easily see him coming, but where they might blend in and not be seen by him. To Lonnie's right, Joel decided. This way, as Lonnie approached, the shooter could get out of the car undetected, approach Lonnie by crossing the street in a straight line—the shortest and most efficient distance between two points—and shoot him in the right temple before he probably ever saw him coming. The car could then pull out, and because the drag was wide enough, make a U-turn and stop at the corner where the killing took place. The killer got in and the car took off in the direction of the highway, where it disappeared and could either head toward New Bedford and Cape Cod or Rhode Island and New York in a matter of seconds.

A moment later, Joel found himself standing on the corner where Lonnie had died. He wanted to feel a strong sense of dread or horror, a residue of darkness where his friend had drawn his last breath and left this earth. But he didn't. He didn't feel anything. It was just a street corner like any other. There was no longer any sign or indication that, just weeks before, a man had been murdered here, on this very spot. All evidence was gone. Just like Lonnie. Gone.

His phone rang. Still distracted, he answered without checking the ID. "Yes?"

"Mr. Walker, Detective Rossi."

"Detective, hello."

"Are you in town?"

"I am, yes."

"I've got a brief amount of time, if you're still interested in talking."

"Absolutely," Joel said, heading for his car. "Where and when?"

The detective gave him the name of a Chinese restaurant on Rhode Island Avenue and told him he'd meet him there in ten minutes.

He made it in about five, and quickly found The Dancing Panda, a family-style joint located in a dark, rectangular building set back from the road at the rear of a small parking lot. A giant neon panda holding a wok danced on the roof.

Joel parked and went in through the bar entrance.

The bar and restaurant beyond were dimly lit and mostly empty. Hesitating just inside the door, he saw a female Chinese bartender with spiked blonde hair and heavy eyeliner flash him a bright smile. Joel smiled back and drifted deeper into the bar. He was about to take a seat when a Chinese waiter appeared in the doorway to the restaurant portion of the establishment and asked, "Are you Mr. Walker?"

"Yes."

"This way."

Joel followed the man across the restaurant, through a sea of tables with lighted candles under glass in the center of each, past some booths, and eventually into the darkest corner in the place.

A lone man sat sipping a drink at a small table off by itself.

"Detective?"

The man looked up with a noncommittal expression and waved Joel in. "Mr. Walker," he said, standing and extending his hand, "I'm Mike Rossi."

"Good to meet you." Joel shook his hand. It was a firm handshake, almost aggressive, but not quite. Once they'd finished, Rossi motioned to the chair across from him, then sat down. Joel joined him.

"Did you want anything?" Rossi asked. "You hungry? Maybe a drink?"

"No thanks, I'm fine."

Rossi nodded to the waiter and he moved away. The detective was a bit younger than Joel had expected, probably early thirties, with dark, wavy hair, an intentional five o'clock shadow and a modest suit. "I come here a lot," he said. "It's quiet, you know? Food's decent, drinks are strong and the help's top-notch."

"Well, I appreciate you seeing me," Joel told him. He already sensed a slight difference in the detective's tone. He'd seemed friendlier on the phone.

Rossi sat back and stirred what appeared to be a Coke with a plastic red stirrer. "I need you to understand that the Scott case is an open and ongoing investigation, so I'm not at liberty to discuss the case or any particulars associated with it."

"Of course. I was just hoping—"

"Here's the thing," Rossi said, leaning forward onto the table, the dark intensity of his eyes eerie in the limited light. "I know who you are, okay?"

And there it was. "Okay," Joel sighed.

"I know all about you and what went on here years ago."

"In all fairness—"

"I'm going to give you a little piece of advice," Rossi interrupted. "You know, just between us. It's not twenty years ago. That was then. This is now. If you think you're going to come here and start your carnival sideshow bullshit like you did back then, you're in for one hell of a surprise, Walker, because I won't have it, you hear me? I won't have it. I got a partner I didn't even bring with me because he was a rookie back in the day, and I wasn't sure I could stop him from putting his foot in your ass. You see where I'm going with this?"

Joel leaned forward as well. The candle on the table between them burned, the flame flickering and licking their faces with iridescent light. "I'm not here as a reporter. I'm here as Lonnie's friend, and because his daughter asked me to look into things."

"Did she now?" Rossi seemed genuinely surprised.

"Yes, she did. I'm here at her request, all right? I'm not looking to give you or the department or anyone else a hard time. I'm not here to cause trouble or to write a story or anything along those lines. I'm here as a favor and because Lonnie Scott was a friend of mine."

Rossi stared at him a while. "You hurt a lot of good people."

"I wrote a book."

"That was full of lies and fairy tales."

"I see. And when all that was going on, you were, what, in elementary school?"

His expression remained even. "I was fourteen, a freshman in high school. So what? I had family in the department back then, including a couple uncles. You hurt the reputations of a lot of people. Decent cops who were doing their best during a very difficult time and trying to do their jobs and find out who slaughtered that girl."

"That girl had a name. It was Cindy—"

"I know what the fuck her name was."

"That investigation still ongoing too? Was still unsolved last time I checked."

Rossi smoldered a moment or two more before responding. "You know as well as I do we have a very good idea of who the perp was, we just couldn't prove it. What it never was, though, was the big devil-shit conspiracy you made it out to be on every talk show from here to the moon."

"She was slaughtered in a church, on an altar, and—"

"Yeah, I know all about it, thanks."

"I never blamed the police."

"Not directly. You didn't have to. You implied. You made people think the departments in Fall River and New Bedford and a few other places were a bunch of bumbling Keystone Cops. You even implied some officers could've been involved in the cult activity, or were being paid off to look the other way. Do you have any idea the damage that caused those departments? Do you even give a shit?"

Joel sat back, breaking the showdown. "Look, Rossi, that—"

"*Detective* Rossi."

"That was a long time ago, *Detective* Rossi."

"Cops don't forget."

"Well, good for them. And yes, I give a shit. I never wanted to hurt anyone, least of all the police. I made some mistakes, I admit it, and I'm sorry for that. It's easy to pile on me too, don't forget that. I paid for my sins, Detective, trust me. And I wasn't entirely wrong, but—"

"But nothing. You're not a cop. You're not an investigator. You're not even a reporter. You're a joke, a sensationalistic, half-baked, almost-was has-been, and a piece of shit."

"Jesus, don't hold back."

"If you think I'm here to debate the merits of your character, Walker, you're out of your mind."

"Fine. Then why are you here?"

"To let you know we've got this situation well in hand, thanks."

Joel laughed lightly. "Is this where you tell me to get out of town before sundown?"

Rossi's expression made it abundantly clear that he was not amused. "Do yourself a favor, Walker. Go on back up to yahoo land and do whatever the hell it is you do up there these days. You know, like get those local Little League scores out to the masses and whatnot. And let us do our job."

"Are you aware of the fact that Lonnie worked part-time for a company called Tuser Industries in New Bedford?" Joel asked.

"Yes, we are aware of that."

"That's interesting, because his family had no knowledge of it."

Rossi shrugged. "As I mentioned, ongoing investigation."

"Do you know anything about the company?"

"They do research and development."

"What kind of research and development?"

"What am I, your personal assistant?"

"Gimme a break."

Rossi sipped his Coke. "And why would I do that?"

"How about professional courtesy?"

"The only professional at this table is me."

"Okay, how about just two guys talking?"

Several seconds lived and died before Rossi answered. "They're a privately owned company. They handle some government contracts, several with military applications, but they don't discuss them due to national security, which is standard operating procedure when it comes to such things."

"Thank you."

"You're welcome. Why are you so concerned with the company?"

"I was told that many of the difficulties Lonnie was experiencing started right around the time he began employment there."

"He was the night watchman, for Christ's sake." Rossi smiled, but there could not have been less humor in it. "Wait, let me guess, it's all a big cover, isn't it? It's a secret satanic cult company, part of a huge network of secret satanic cult companies that span the entire country, maybe the whole *world*. And almost everybody's in on it. Plus they eat babies, you know, whenever they can get hold of one, am I right?"

"I'm glad you can find such humor in the murder of Lonnie Scott, Detective."

"Don't get self-righteous with me, you fucking turd," Rossi snapped, sitting forward and stabbing a finger at him. Then just as quickly, he seemed to recall that he was in a public place. Relaxing his posture, he lowered his hand and his voice. "There's no connection to Tuser Industries and the murder of Lonnie Scott."

"You're certain?"

"Yes. Why the hell would there be? Only in your twisted mind would some place he worked part-time in the most menial of positions be connected to this."

"Are you aware that he often slept there? At one point, during a vacation from his regular job, he worked a week straight and slept there the entire time."

"So?"

"You don't find that odd?"

"Unusual maybe, but not unheard of. They must have employee barracks."

"For a night watchman in the most menial of positions?"

"There is no connection between Lonnie Scott's death and Tuser Industries, understood?"

Joel knew Rossi might very well be correct, but he wasn't ready to dismiss there being any connection just yet. "And how do you know that?"

"It's called investigation, Walker."

"Investigation or assumption?"

"They're not under any suspicion or investigation in these matters, is that clear? I suggest you stay away from them."

"Why's that?"

"Because, as I just explained, they have nothing to do with this."

It was a gamble, but Joel rolled the dice anyway. "Have you been told to leave them alone, Detective?"

Something shifted in Rossi's dark eyes, something telling. "I never said that."

"You didn't say no, either."

Rossi finished his Coke and put it aside. "I didn't say anything. Know why? Because I was never here and this little get-together never happened."

"In that case, do you have any leads?"

"I can't discuss the case."

"Now there's a solid no. Is it already on the back burner?"

"But Jesus *Christ*, you got some fucking balls on you." Rossi shook his head in apparent disbelief. "You're lucky you're technically old enough to be my father. Otherwise I'd drag you outside and teach you some fucking manners."

"Ever considered anger management? They have classes for that, you know."

"You here to do comedy, jackass? Huh? You a stand-up, a clown?"

"I just want to know what happened to my friend."

"You sure? You sure you're not here to get yourself back in the game by trashing decent, honest, hardworking people?"

"I'm sure."

"Your friend was likely involved in illegal narcotics."

"Come on, the guy smoked a little weed now and then, he was hardly a—"

"It very well may have been a drug deal gone bad. Choirboys don't get executed in the street, Walker."

"He was a mall cop."

"Go home. You came, you snooped around a little and you

came up with nothing. No shame in it; you gave it a shot, right? Now go home, cuddle with your wife, give her the baloney pony and forget all about this. Lonnie Scott's dead. You let us handle the investigation."

Joel continued as if he hadn't heard a word Rossi said. "You know Lonnie claimed he had no idea how he got the brand on the back of his shoulder, right? Not a tattoo, a *brand*. He told his daughter 'they' had marked him."

The detective stared straight ahead, offering nothing.

"He was also convinced that whoever 'they' were had plans to kill him," Joel pressed. "You don't find that troubling?"

"I find it troubling when people drink too much or do too many drugs, do stupid shit, then blame it on other people or some paranoid delusion those things cause in the first place. Is that what you mean?"

"You're saying you believe Lonnie was—"

"Did I mention Mr. Scott? I already explained I'm not at liberty to discuss an open and ongoing investigation, didn't I? You got wax buildup or you just deaf?"

"I'll be sure to pick up some Q-tips." Joel flashed his best contemptuous smile. "Meanwhile, Katelyn told me there was an unidentified bottle of pills that were taken from Lonnie's medicine cabinet. They were to be analyzed, but they were supposedly lost."

"Misplaced."

"Misplaced. Of course, misplaced. Any luck un-misplacing them yet?"

Rossi remained stone-faced. "Afraid not."

"She also told me you guys have Lonnie's laptop and cell phone. Are you planning to hang on to those indefinitely?"

"They'll be returned to Mrs. Burrows the moment we're done with them."

"Find anything interesting on either one?"

"We're done here." Rossi stood up, purposely positioning himself next to Joel's chair so he'd be towering over him. "Stay out of my way and let me do my job, Walker. I'm warning you."

"Sounds like a threat."

"It is. I'd take it seriously if I were you."

"One last question, if you don't mind." Joel remained seated but looked up at him. "Are you having me followed?"

"Oh, of course. It's not us though." Rossi looked around dramatically, as if to be sure no one else was listening. "I'm not saying it's aliens but…it's aliens. Satanic cult aliens, actually. Mean little fuckers."

"You really have trouble with the whole yes or no thing, don't you?"

"I hate to disappoint you, *Agent Mulder*, but you're not important enough to warrant a tail. You're not even important enough to warrant this meeting. I'm just trying to help you out, save us both some trouble and do my best to be nice."

"This is you nice?"

"Positively cheery, motherfucker."

"Your charm does appear to be effortless."

Rossi slapped him on the shoulder far harder than necessary. "Have a drink, something with an umbrella in it, maybe some lunch—the moo goo gai pan is out of this world—and then when you're done, go back to Maine like a good boy." He leaned closer, his mouth less than an inch from Joel's ear. "And fucking stay there."

CHAPTER TWELVE

Joel hadn't even driven a block from the restaurant when he noticed the Crown Vic was back in play. He drove directly to his motel, watching as the tail followed his every move, staying several car lengths back just as it had before.

When he turned in to his motel lot, the car continued on past. Joel parked but kept it in sight, watching as it took an exit and slid onto the highway. Within seconds it was gone, swallowed by heavy traffic.

As he stepped from the car, he noticed his room door was ajar. Assuming it was only housecleaning, he grabbed his case and approached the room with caution, as he couldn't be sure. He pushed the door open but remained outside. "Hello?"

The room was empty.

Nothing seemed disturbed or out of place, until he checked for his suitcase, which he'd left on the far side of the bed, sandwiched between it and the wall. It was no longer there, but had been left instead on the bathroom floor. It was open, and his clothes and toiletries, which were all he had in it, were scattered about the room. A quick inspection of the suitcase revealed nothing was damaged and nothing had been stolen. Still, the fact that whoever had done this hadn't even attempted to hide what they'd done was troubling. Their obviousness wasn't an accident. It was designed to send a message. They'd come into his motel room and done whatever they wanted because they could get to him whenever they felt like it. And they wanted to make damn sure he knew it. Heart racing, Joel packed everything back into his suitcase, then headed for the motel office.

The same disheveled college-age kid who had been there when Joel checked in was propped behind the counter on a stool. Slumped forward and reading a comic book, he looked up with disinterest when Joel came through he door. "Help you?" he said, as if mustering a complete sentence required far more effort than he could possibly expend at that moment.

"I'm in number 7," Joel told him. "I went out this morning and just got back. Someone was in my room while I was gone."

His bleary eyes narrowed into a squint. "No way."

"Whoever it was went through my suitcase. Nothing's missing, but—"

"Cool."

"Cool? Who the hell was in my room?"

"I don't know, dude. Only ones it might be is housekeeping, but they aren't here until tomorrow. Is the door jacked up?"

"No. It's fine. So is the lock."

He laughed for some reason, even doing that in slow motion. "So they didn't break in then. They had a key."

"Apparently, or they were able to pick the lock."

"You give your key to anybody?"

"No. I've had it with me the whole time."

"Maybe you forgot to lock the door when you left."

Joel glared at him.

"Okay, whatever," he said, the apparent humor he'd previously found in the situation no longer quite so amusing. "You want to file a complaint? I can give you a form. Or I can call the cops if you want, but they're not gonna do anything if nothing's missing."

"I don't suppose you saw anybody coming in or out of my room?"

He shrugged.

Rather than strangle him, Joel checked out, paid his bill and five minutes later was back on the road. It was later in the day now, but he still had a couple hours of daylight left and planned to have a new base of operations before dark. Although the events were unsettling, whatever he was into was important. He knew that now. Cops didn't threaten you to back off, and people didn't follow you or ransack your motel room unless you were onto something. But if Rossi was telling the truth, and at least at that point he had no reason to think he wasn't, who the hell was following him? More importantly, how had they known he was in the area, and even if they had, how had they found him so quickly and easily?

As he followed Interstate 195 toward New Bedford, he made the Crown Vic in his rearview again. Either this guy was the best tail Joel had ever seen, or there was more than one car following him. The use of multiple vehicles was not unusual when it came to tailing someone—especially when it was a police operation—but far as he knew, using identical cars was.

His GPS led him out of Fall River and, skirting his hometown of Westport, into North Dartmouth, where he found an inexpensive chain hotel not far from one of the malls where Lonnie had worked. From this location, which was less than five minutes from New Bedford, Joel could easily check out Tuser Industries when the opportunity presented itself.

Once he got into his new room, he fired up his laptop, ordered a pizza from a local place, then checked his email. He found nothing of any importance there, so he organized his notes from his chat with Bea. After going through them again, Joel decided to look into the shortwave radio angle. Bea had told him Lonnie had said the notebook was directly related to that subject, and unless there was some other Jerry in Lonnie's life no one knew about, odds were he'd been involved with Jerry Simpson, which in turn—directly or indirectly— brought Tuser Industries into the mix.

But what possible connection could there be between a night watchman and the head of human resources? On the surface, at least, it seemed an odd pairing. Besides, Lonnie worked there nights and weekends while Simpson certainly worked the day shift, Monday through Friday. Perhaps they'd met when Lonnie was first hired, as it was standard in most companies for employees to go through the human resources department at the time of hire. Maybe they'd hit it off due to a shared interest in ham radios? Although Lonnie told Bea he'd been to Simpson's home and listened to his radio, there was no evidence to suggest Lonnie had any interest in shortwave radios whatsoever. Even if he had, there was no way to know for sure until he spoke with Jerry Simpson personally, so Joel rummaged through his bag, found the notebook Katelyn had given him and flipped through it again.

All those numbers written over and over again, page after page—it was more than a little creepy. Why would Lonnie have furiously jotted them down again and again? They had to be a code of some kind, but what could they possible mean when there was no variance? They were identical numbers, written in the same order.

Joel checked the notebook again, going over it far more carefully this time, and while inspecting the inside front and back covers, noticed something he hadn't previously. A single set of numbers had been written in black pen in the bottom left corner of the inside front cover. They were different from those written on the pages, and were followed by the letters kHz, which Joel knew stood for kilohertz. It had to represent a frequency of some kind to a specific station or program, but he knew virtually nothing about shortwave radios and how they worked, so he plugged the numbers into his search engine.

The only thing of value the search returned was a basic site that explained the number fell within the Amplitude Modulated (AM radio) carrier frequencies, which ranged from 535 to 1605 kHz, and that carrier frequencies of 540 to 1600kHz were assigned at 10kHz intervals, whatever the hell that meant.

Joel put his laptop aside, then went through his notes until he came across the names and numbers Katelyn had given him of the two men Lonnie was closest with through work: Brian Currant and Pete Fernandez.

He got through to Currant first, introduced himself, explained how he'd gotten his name and number, and why he was calling.

"Was hoping I could ask you a few questions," Joel said.

"Captain Scott was a good man," Currant said in a deep, very officious voice. "I hope they get the bastard that did it, pardon my French, but I don't want to get involved in anything that isn't related to the official investigation."

"This is completely off the record," Joel assured him. "Just one friend of Lonnie's talking to another. You have my word. None of this will end up in print or anywhere else. I'm just trying to find some answers, that's all."

"All I know is what I read in the paper or saw on the news, sir."

Standing and wandering over to the window, which overlooked the back parking lot, Joel said, "Katelyn said you and Lonnie were friends."

"He was my superior officer and my boss," Currant explained. "But we also socialized off-hours occasionally. We enjoyed shooting pool, or sometimes we'd have a beer or a bite to eat after work and talk shop. Law enforcement is highly stressful and it's important to decompress."

Referring to a security guard job at a mall as "law enforcement" seemed a stretch, but it fit perfectly with Currant's official tone and cop-speak phrasing.

"Unless you're part of the brotherhood, it's hard to understand," he added. "I'm forty-six, been doing this for decades, and there are still days it gets to me. But that's how it is. You put the uniform on, you accept what comes with it."

Was this guy serious? "Yes, I'm sure it must be difficult," Joel managed.

"At any rate, Officer Fernandez spent more time with Captain Scott than I did. At least in a social context."

"Pete Fernandez?"

"Affirmative. He may be able to tell you more than I can, if you can find him."

"What do you mean?"

"Officer Fernandez doesn't work for the company anymore," Currant told him. "Just up and quit one day, no notice, nothing. Word on the street was he left the area for a while and no one knew where he was. He was having issues before all this, some sort of personal problems, apparently. Not long before Captain Scott died, he was back in the area, from what I heard, but since then he's moved out of his house—he owns a cottage in New Bedford over by the airport—and dropped out of sight. Strange, but then Fernandez always was an oddball."

Pot, Joel thought, *meet kettle.* "Does he still have the same cell number?"

"I really don't know, sir."

"Any idea where he is these days, still in New Bedford or—"

"No idea. I haven't heard from him in months, and frankly, I'm fine with that. The last thing I need is more drama." A burst of background noise rumbled through the line, and it sounded as if Currant tried to cover the phone. "Hold on, Mom! I'm on the phone!" Once back, he cleared his throat. "Sorry. You were saying?"

Joel felt himself grin. "Did Lonnie ever talk about shortwave radios?"

"Not to me, sir, no."

"Do you have any theories regarding Lonnie's murder?"

"Negative. Since I'm not personally involved in the investigation, I feel it would be irresponsible of me to discuss or form any theories at this time, as they'd be pure conjecture." Currant breathed heavily into the phone for a few seconds before he continued. "Captain Scott was hardworking, honest, a stand-up guy. I know of no one who had anything against the man. All I can tell you is that he started having problems a few months before he was killed, and I could tell he wasn't sleeping and had a lot on his mind. He wasn't himself. We weren't that close outside of work. I'm sure there were things going on in his life I was unaware of and know nothing about. But as to why anyone would want to kill the man? I really don't know. Then again, in our line of work, once you put the badge on, you never know what might happen. There's a lot of scum out there who have no respect for law and order, and even less for those of us who dedicate our lives to upholding it. Take down one of us, you make a statement."

Okay, Dirty Harry.

"Sure, I see what you mean," Joel lied. "Did Lonnie ever mention a company called Tuser Industries?"

"Doesn't sound familiar."

Joel believed him. He asked a few more cursory questions, but got similar responses. For all his bravado, it was obvious Currant was uncomfortable sharing what little he knew. He also didn't sound terribly upset about Lonnie's death, but perhaps that was just his manner; Joel couldn't get an accurate handle on it over the phone. He thanked Currant for his time and asked if it would be all right to contact him again, should more questions arise.

"I'm sorry about what happened, and I'll always have very fond memories of Captain Scott, as I'm sure you will. I appreciate that you're a family friend and trying to help—it's admirable, sir, and you have my respect—but I'd appreciate it if you didn't contact me again. No disrespect intended. I just think these matters are better left to law enforcement professionals." More sudden background noise, followed by what sounded like an elderly woman calling for him. A muffled sound came next as Currant hastily put his hand over the phone again. "Mom, hold on! What the hell!" A moment later he came back on the line. "I have to go, my *girlfriend* has dinner on the table. I wish you the best, sir, and please give my best to Captain Scott's family. But please don't call again."

The line clicked.

Joel watched the parking lot a while. No sign of the Crown Vic. It had been a long day, but he'd learned more in his first two days here than he'd expected in total. He didn't yet know what this was all about, but it wasn't nothing, as he'd originally hoped and even suspected. Lonnie's murder hadn't been a random killing or some drug deal gone wrong, as the police were evidently planning to frame it, and none of this was going to be easily explained away. Of that much he was certain.

Maybe Taylor had been right. Maybe he should've stayed where he was and lived his life. But it was too late for all that now. He'd already jumped into the deep end. Nothing left to do but swim. He kicked his shoes off, stretched, and then returned to the table, sat down and called the number he had for Pete Fernandez.

It rang numerous times but never went to voice mail. Joel was about to hang up when it was finally answered. "Who is this?" a jittery male voice asked.

"Hi, it's Joel Walker, I'm a friend of Lonnie Scott's. Is this Pete Fernandez?"

He muttered Joel's full name again and again in rapid-fire succession, like some scatterbrained mantra, and then said, "Where are you from?"

"Westport originally, but I live in Maine now. I—"

"What's your wife's name?"

"I'm sorry?"

"Your wife! What's her fucking name?"

"Why do you need my wife's name?"

"Answer the question or we're done talking."

"Taylor."

"What do you do for a living?"

"I'm a reporter."

"Where?"

Joel told him.

"You doing a story?"

"No, nothing like that. Was hoping we could talk."

"You calling from a home or cell phone?"

"My cell."

"I'll call you back."

The call disconnected.

Stunned to silence, Joel sat there staring at his phone and trying to make sense of what had just happened. His concentration was interrupted seconds later by an insistent knock on the door. His dinner had arrived.

He'd paid the delivery kid, devoured two slices and downed half a can of Coke by the time Fernandez called back.

"It doesn't mean anything yet," he told Joel in the same harried voice, "but so far your basics check out. If it's really you, Lonnie mentioned you a few times. I knew the name sounded familiar. If it's not, then none of this will matter anyway."

"It's really me," Joel assured him. "As I said, was hoping we could talk."

"What do you want to talk about?"

"What do you think I want to talk about?" Joel said, pushing back a bit.

"I don't talk about anything that means anything on the phone. If you're smart, you don't either."

"Fine, we can face-to-face it then. Where are you?"

"Where are *you*?"

"A hotel in North Dartmouth. Do you want to meet here?"

"No." The line crackled. Then he gave Joel an address on Shawmut Avenue in New Bedford, the road that led to the airport. "Come alone."

"When?" Joel asked, stepping back into his shoes.

"I'm gone and I don't come back or answer any more calls if you're not there in ten minutes, you feel me?"

"I'll be there in five."

Throwing on his coat, Joel quickly packed everything of value into his case, slung it over his shoulder and headed straight for the coming night.

CHAPTER THIRTEEN

Fifty miles south of Boston, the city of New Bedford, famous for its vast whaling history (and of course its ties to Melville's classic *Moby Dick*), was still known as one of the great fishing ports in the United States. But New Bedford had its share of criminal infamy as well, including the 1983 Big Dan's gang rape case (which later became the basis for the Jodie Foster film *The Accused*), the brutal and unsolved highway serial killings of the late 1980s that claimed the lives of at least nine young women, a ritual killing and other atrocities in the nearby Freetown State Forest, and criminal satanic cult activity throughout the area in the 1980s and into the early 1990s. But in recent years much of New Bedford had seen a resurgence, and was a place where most residents had put those incidents and times behind them, tucked away in the dark past where they belonged, and instead embraced the progress the city had made since.

For Joel, it brought up a tremendous amount of emotions. He'd expected his return to elicit some strong feelings, but he hadn't been ready for what hit him.

Though he only had to cover a small section of the city to

reach Shawmut Avenue, he broke out in a cold sweat as visions of the church where Cindy Mello had been murdered flashed in his mind, along with a flood of memories he couldn't control. Hands shaking, he gripped the wheel tight, grateful the church was located on the opposite end of the city. Fighting nausea, he passed a park where he'd once interviewed a heroin-addicted informant, remembering the terror in his eyes and the things he'd told him about the cult activity in the area. A diner where a local prostitute with ties to the dark underworld of the city had talked to him just days before her alleged suicide was now a generic-looking convenience store. A home electronics store, where he'd interviewed the manager regarding the strange visitations he and his staff had experienced from alleged satanic cult members, was now a dentist's office.

Quite a bit had changed in the city in the years since Joel had left. But one thing remained the same. Although it too had morphed, evolved and reinvented itself, as evil often does, a whole other world still existed here, hiding just beneath the one he and everyone else could see. In this historic old city, all those old ghosts were still huddled in the shadows, waiting and watching, stronger and more frightening than ever.

Dusk had settled over the city. Night was on its way.

Joel took a left onto Shawmut Avenue. He checked the mirrors. No tail. In fact, the road abruptly turned rural, and there was no other traffic at all. He drove by a few businesses, then the tree-lined road turned desolate. There were very few residences here, only a handful of small cottages scattered along the final stretch of road before the airport that were old and looked like they'd been there for decades. Joel found one matching the address Pete had given him, located next to an empty field on a small, mostly dirt lot set back from the road.

He turned in, slowed the car to a crawl and followed the short road to the cottage. The residence appeared vacant and unkempt. There were no other vehicles parked on the property, and although it wasn't completely dark yet, there were no outside or interior lights on. There were dingy curtains in some of the windows, however, signaling someone had lived there recently. In near darkness, there was something creepy about the run-down old cottage all off by itself, but then he was sure it looked just as spooky on the sunniest day. It shared something with Lonnie's apartment. Something troubling. No phantoms in the windows, but there was a feeling of evil here. Joel sensed it immediately, deep in his gut. Fighting the natural flight instinct, he parked out front and waited, but left the car running. Brian Currant had said Fernandez moved out of the cottage a while back, so Joel assumed he was coming from somewhere else and he'd simply beaten him there.

Alternating between watching the cottage and checking his rearview, Joel waited several minutes. Except for a few cars that passed along the road behind him, there was no one else in sight. His eyes slowly scanned the field to his right. Light was becoming scarce. No one. Nothing. Turning, Joel looked over at the property line to his left.

A dark silhouette stood just beyond the trees.

Motionless at first, it started toward him almost as soon as he'd seen it. Joel shut the car off and stepped out just in time to see the silhouette transform into a young man in dark clothing and a black baseball cap worn backward.

"Pete?" he asked, offering his hand. "I'm Joel Walker."

It was then that Joel saw the gun.

"Don't move," the man said, leveling a revolver at him. "Don't you—don't you fucking move!"

"You got it." Joel raised his hands. "Just take it easy, buddy. Easy now."

"Put your hands down," he ordered, glancing around nervously. "You alone?"

"Yes."

"Give me your driver's license."

Moving slowly and carefully, Joel removed his wallet from his back pocket, opened it, pulled his license free and handed it to him.

The man held it close to his face in the dying light, then quickly returned it. "You know you're being followed?"

"Yes," Joel said, "but I don't think I was followed here."

"You need to pay better attention." He tilted his head toward the road. "They're out there. Not too close. Not too far."

"Do you know who they are?"

Fernandez looked as if he hadn't slept in days. Of average

height and build, he was dressed entirely in black. His hair was dark and styled in a military-like buzz cut, and his face sported several days of scruff. "More or less."

"Care to share it with me?"

"Not yet."

"Think maybe you could do me a favor and at least lower that gun?"

He did. "I'm not gonna be out here long. Whatever you want, better get to it."

Joel let out a sigh of relief. He hadn't had a gun pointed at him in a long time. "I talked to Brian Currant. He—"

"He's a pussy, a poser. Lives with his mother, thinks he's G.I.-fucking-Joe."

Now that Joel had a good look at Fernandez, he realized he was younger than he'd expected, late twenties at most, and what he'd mistaken for nervousness was much closer to fear. His emotions were raw, barely within his control, and his body trembled and jerked like a drug addict in need of a fix. Glassy, bloodshot eyes blinked manically.

"Be that as it may," Joel said, "he told me you left your job, moved out of this place and dropped out of sight not long after Lonnie was killed."

"You found me pretty easy, right? If I want to be found, I can be."

Joel stuffed his hands in his coat pockets. The darker it got, the colder it was becoming. "What kind of trouble are you in? Why are you so frightened?"

He grimaced and shook his head, the words there but difficult to voice. "If you knew the things I did, if you had the dreams I have, you'd be frightened too."

"Why don't you live here anymore?" Joel asked. When he got no response, he said, "Would you be more comfortable if we talked inside?"

His bottom lip trembled. "I don't go in there anymore."

"Why's that?"

Fernandez shuffled his feet, looked away. "There's something in there."

As a shiver knifed through him, Joel pretended the cold was to blame, even as he looked back over his shoulder at the dark cottage. "You mean someone?"

"I mean some*thing*." Fernandez's face contorted into an expression of sheer torture. If it was possible for a human being to come out his skin, he was about to. "I don't...I don't know what they are," he said softly. "But they're not friendly."

"I saw something odd in the window of Lonnie's apartment."

"Yeah, I bet you did." Fernandez whipped around and glared at the field as if he'd seen something from the corner of his eye. "Can't be out here long, we...we can't be out here...long."

"Where do these...some*things*...come from?"

Fernandez pointed to his temple.

"I don't understand," Joel said.

"Me either. They don't go away, they...they stay...in my dreams." A cold wind blew across the field, slicing through them before escaping into the trees on the far side of the lot. "Lonnie thought they were demons. Maybe he was right."

"What do you know about Lonnie's murder?" Joel asked.

His dark eyes narrowed. "It was an execution."

"Do you know who did it?"

He nodded.

"Have you spoken to the police?"

"Once. Right after it all went down."

"Did you tell them what you know?"

A burst of maniacal laughter escaped him but he quickly stifled it. "I told them what they wanted to hear, what I'm supposed to tell them. Then I disappeared for my own safety. This is bigger than the cops. They don't give a fuck anyway. They do what they're told just like everybody else. They—they don't have the *dreams*."

"What happened to you? What happened to Lonnie? Tell me about the dreams, Pete."

"They put them there," he whispered, eyes filling with tears. "In my head."

"Is Tuser Industries connected to this? I know Lonnie worked there doing security part-time."

"He wasn't doing security," Fernandez told him. "He was there because they wanted him there."

"How do you know?"

"Because I was too." Fernandez tapped the gun against the

outside of his thigh. "I found out about it through Lonnie. He told me there was this company that wanted people for these pharmaceutical studies they were doing, testing out new drugs they were getting ready to release to the public. Part-time thing, paid good. Nobody was supposed to know about it if you got picked, but Lonnie knew I needed some extra green, so he told me about it and I signed up too. Had to take all these written tests and go through a bunch of bullshit psych and personality tests to make sure we were healthy and had the right frame of mind. They said most didn't pass. But Lonnie made it, and so did I. Once we were in, all we had to do was take some pills or drink some liquids or powders, then tell the doctors how we felt. There was no real danger, they said. Might get some minor side effects, but nothing serious, nothing life threatening or anything that would hurt you or even make you sick. Not even anything long-term, they said. Maybe you'd get achy muscles or a nosebleed, a headache or a little rash, they said. They'd give you a cream for it and fix you right up, they said, no big deal. They were all doctors and scientists. They know what they're talking about, right? They made it out like it was easy money."

"And this took place at Tuser Industries here in the city?"

"Yeah." Nearby trees swayed in the mounting wind. Something cracked in the distance, perhaps a branch. Fernandez jumped, then continued, talking faster than he had before. "The company has all these military contracts there in other areas of the facility, so everything has to be kept quiet. You aren't allowed to talk about the company or what you do there or even that you work there at all. We had to sign these confidentiality forms and swear under oath we wouldn't talk about anything that happened there. Even though they said the stuff we were involved with wasn't secret, because of their contracts, everything that took place on the premises had to be closely guarded. There were really strict privacy rules and regulations, and all employees—even us guinea pigs—had to adhere to them. At the time it made sense. National security and all that, you know? I'm a good American." He began to pace frantically in a small space, like he could barely contain himself, eyes still welling with tears. "I love my country. I was a patriot. Did four years in the army, two tours in Iraq. I was a good American, a proud American and they...they..."

"It's okay," Joel said in the calmest voice he could muster. Fernandez was a powder keg in danger of exploding at any moment. He needed to keep him steady and focused or he'd lose him in the blink of an eye. "I get it, Pete, I do." *Far more than you realize.* "I'm not the enemy, I promise you."

"That's the problem, isn't it?" He smiled but it was reflexive, as if he had a sudden gas pain. "We always used to know who the enemy was. Not anymore. These fuckers, they—they lie. Maybe they always did. It's all a front, all of it."

The more this came together, the more apparent it became that Tuser Industries was the wild card here, and that the police had likely been told to stay away from them and to not involve or tie them in any way to Lonnie's murder. If that weren't the case, surely the company would've already become a focal point of the investigation. The only ones with the power to call off local and state police were the Feds, but why would they? Regardless of how sensitive some contracts at Tuser were, from the sounds Lonnie and Pete had been involved in a basic medical studies and testing program, not higher-level hush-hush projects cloaked in secrecy for the sake of national security.

"Who is Jerry Simpson?" Joel asked.

"Just another lie."

"He doesn't exist?"

"I didn't say that."

"His business card lists him as the head of human resources there."

"That's not what he does. He's involved in…other things."

"Help me understand, Pete. Explain to me what he or any of this has to do with Lonnie's murder."

"Everything they told us was a lie." Fernandez moved a bit closer to the car as a small plane flew overhead, slowly descending toward the nearby airport. He glanced up at it briefly. "The company? Lies. It's a front for a government testing ground, black ops, stuff buried so deep and so top secret they can hide in plain sight because nobody's looking for them. They're ghosts, and so are their programs. They're conspiracy theories, folklore and horror stories that don't exist. Ask anybody and they'll tell you. And if you try to tell someone this shit is all real, *you're* the crazy one."

"What were these drugs they gave you?"

"More lies. We took their pills, but they weren't harmless pharmaceuticals like they said. It was subtle at first…then it got worse, they…they made you feel crazy. Before I knew it I…I couldn't remember things. I knew I was there, I got paid, I did what they said, but…I couldn't remember anything. Then I started having these dreams, these…these horrible dreams. Sometimes we stayed overnight or for whole weekends, even longer if we had to, but…sometimes I wasn't sure how long I was there or what was going on, because I couldn't remember. It was like they took it all away, like they took it right out of my head." As he moved away from the car, out of deeper shadow, the tears he'd managed to hold back began to stream down his face. "They got inside our heads," he said, voice shaking. "Then they broke everything up in there. And they did it on purpose. They made us see things no living being should ever have to see. I know it was bad but I…I can't remember exactly what it was. My dreams are getting worse, though. I think I'm starting to remember more."

"Did Lonnie experience the same thing?"

He nodded, then opened his jacket and pulled down his sweatshirt with his free hand. Branded into his skin was the same symbol Lonnie had on the back of his shoulder. "They marked us. I don't remember it, but…they marked us."

Joel wanted to look away, but didn't. "For what?"

"Magic is real, did you know that?" Fernandez steeled himself, let go of his shirt and angrily wiped his tears. "Lonnie had the dreams too. Then he started to remember, they—the dreams helped him to remember. Because maybe they weren't just dreams, he said. Maybe they were memories they tried to kill in us, but we still had them somewhere deep inside. He started looking into things. He said he thought they'd been giving us hallucinogens, heavy-duty doses of LSD and shit like that, fucking with our heads and breaking our minds."

"But why?" Joel pressed. "Did he know why?"

"Ever heard of something called MKUltra?"

"Vaguely. They were secret mind control experiments the government conducted on human subjects back in the 1960s."

"Yeah. In the nineties, during the Clinton Administration, they finally admitted it, and information was released to the public for the first time."

"From what little I remember, it was very disturbing stuff," Joel said, "but the MKUltra programs were all discontinued and shut down decades ago."

"You sure?" A spasm of a smile twitched across his lips. "Lonnie wasn't."

Stunned, Joel leaned back against the car. "Christ, this—I mean—"

"Lonnie had this friend he knew from when he was younger. Real freak, but he knew all about this shit. Some underground type that lived out west someplace. He's the one told him that while MKUltra was shut down, a few of the studies morphed into other projects that are still going on. We were in one of them."

Joel was afraid of what the answer might be, but asked the question anyway. "This friend of Lonnie's. Was his name Trent?"

Fernandez nodded.

"Lonnie was in contact with Trent? Trent Pierce?"

"I don't know his last name, never knew the guy. I only heard about him through Lonnie."

"I was told Trent fell off the radar and no one had heard from him in years."

He scratched nervously at the stubble along his chin. "You asked, I told you."

"Do you know how to reach him?"

"No."

"Is that why they killed Lonnie? He knew too much?"

"We all knew too much. They don't care. It's horror stories in the dark. Don't you get it? What do I really know? What do you? What did Lonnie? You can talk all you want, no one's gonna believe you anyway." Another wave of tears spilled free. "I can't even remember what I do most days, never mind what they did to us there. All I got are the dreams. They led Lonnie to the truth, but I can't...I can't remember... I just dream, Walker. Crazy, terrible dreams moving around in my head like snakes that can't find a way out."

"Then why did they kill him?" Joel asked.

In the growing darkness, Pete Fernandez's swarthy face was becoming harder and harder to see. "They were finished with him."

The answer hit Joel like a punch to the gut.

"They were finished with all of us. We weren't even human to them, just lab rats, expendable, meaningless. Most of the others in our group are probably all dead by now too."

"Then why are you still alive?"

"I won't be much longer," he answered evenly. "If Lonnie was right—if my dreams are real—they sent us to places no one should ever go. But no matter how deep they went into our heads, they knew they could bring us back. Maybe not the same, maybe all fucked up, but they could bring us back." He looked to the cottage, his eyes gliding from window to window before settling back on Joel. "What they didn't count on was something coming back with us."

"Lonnie had a notebook with these numbers written in it again and again," Joel told him. "It had something to do with shortwave radios and—"

"Yeah," he said, nodding rapidly. "The numbers, they—they run through my head all the time, they…they never stop, I—I just try to ignore them like I do my dreams, but they're always there, Walker, always. Right now I can see them moving through my mind, falling in rows like rain. And the sounds too, I—I can hear them when it's quiet, when I try to sleep, but I…I…"

"Easy," Joel said. He wanted to comfort the man, but he was so shaky he couldn't be sure what kind of reaction he'd get if he tried. "Take a deep breath. The numbers in your head, the numbers in Lonnie's notebook, what do they mean?"

"I don't know, I—they're trying to tell me something but—I don't know what it is, I—I can't *remember* what it is, Walker. But I don't just see them in my head and in my dreams. I can hear them, the numbers and the sounds. They're talking to me."

"Who, Pete? Who's talking to you?"

"The numbers stations," he said, turning back toward the road. "I dreamed about them. I had those words in my head. *Numbers stations.* I didn't think they were real. But they are."

"What are they? I don't understand."

"Anonymous shortwave radio stations. Nobody knows exactly where they are or what their purpose is, but they broadcast from locations all over the world. Look into them and you'll see. I found examples of their broadcasts online, and the minute I heard it I knew that's what they were, because I'd heard them before. They were exactly what I'd heard in my dreams." He squinted into the darkness, watched the road. "They use them. They're using them right now, broadcasting from them. There's just nobody listening. Not you, not me, nobody." Fernandez spun around and faced him with a level of fear and panic in his dark eyes that signaled he might flee at any second. "But that doesn't mean you can't hear it; you just don't realize it."

"What are they broadcasting?"

"Voices, but I…I don't think they're human. They sound artificial."

"And what do they say," Joel asked, "these artificial voices?"

"They recite number sequences, sometimes nursery rhymes. Other times they play parts of songs or broadcast signals that sound like electronic bleeps or Morse code." He brought a trembling hand to his head, ran it across his hair and obsessively scratched at his scalp. "It's creepy as fuck."

"What's the point?"

"Some think it's spy shit. It's not." Fernandez gazed out into the field, as if he'd seen something again. "They're out there," he muttered. "In the dark."

"Pete, look at me," Joel said. "I believe you. I do, okay? But I have to ask this. Other than these numbers stations, which could have a perfectly reasonable explanation, and the brand on your body, which you could've gotten in any number of ways, can you prove anything you've told me here tonight?"

"All I've got are my nightmares," he answered. "But if they're not true, then I'm crazy and a liar. So was Lonnie. And so are you."

"Me?"

"You."

"Why are they doing this?"

"Don't you think I wish I could remember? I didn't ask for this, I—I didn't deserve this. They had no right to do these things to us, to fuck up our brains the way they did." He visibly shuddered. "I'm afraid all the time. *All* the fucking time, dog. Sometimes I wish they'd just get it over with and do me like they did Lonnie, just so my head will go quiet. Run away from all of this. And pray they don't follow you."

"I did that once years ago," Joel told him. "This time it's not happening."

"You'll lose. Lonnie told me about what happened to you back in the day. It's still the same Devil. Always has been, always will be. He's just wearing a different disguise, finding another way to come alive inside our heads." Fernandez tapped the revolver against his temple. "He doesn't need to find a way in. He's already there."

Once the Devil takes you, he doesn't give you back.

"You went up against him before. How'd that work out for you?" Fernandez laughed a sad and helpless little laugh, then slowly backed away, raised his gun and pointed over Joel's shoulder at the cottage. "They're coming."

Joel turned and looked.

He couldn't be certain in the dark, but for the briefest moment it appeared as if something separated from the shadows and slid past one of the front windows.

Something less than human...

When he turned back, Fernandez was gone. Joel was by himself.

But he wasn't alone.

CHAPTER FOURTEEN

The night crashed in on him like waves from an angry ocean. Joel still had no idea how Pete Fernandez had vanished as quickly and quietly as he had, or what it was he'd seen pass by the window of the cottage. The only thing he knew for sure was that two silhouettes had appeared in the field, standing there watching him, their forms barely visible but unmistakable in the darkness. The men following him, he assumed, but he didn't stick around to find out. Instead, with his terror rising, he jumped in his car and rocketed back out onto Shawmut Avenue, putting as much distance as quickly as he could between himself and those men, the cottage, and whatever was wandering around inside it.

Rather than return to the hotel, he drove deeper into the city. There were no signs that anyone was following him, but he hadn't realized they'd tailed him to the meeting with Fernandez either, so he could no longer be sure.

Like so much else in life, just because something couldn't be seen didn't necessarily mean it wasn't there.

Settling on the first bar he saw, a modest but busy place that advertised local bands, dancing, and cheap beer, he pulled in and parked beneath a large neon sign that not only caught one's eye from the road but illuminated most of the parking lot as well. At that moment, Joel wanted—*needed*—to be around as many people as possible, and with his nerves shot, a drink wasn't such a bad idea either.

He stepped out of the car and let the cold air snap him back, but he couldn't help reliving what he'd just heard and experienced at Pete Fernandez's place. Like all those years before, he'd looked into the darkness, and something deep within it had looked back.

It's still the same Devil. Always has been, always will be.

Moments later, Joel was sitting at a busy bar, throwing back a Jack on the rocks while an awful eighties tribute band struggled through an old Def Leppard tune and did their best to keep the largely middle-aged crowd out on the dance floor.

When he returned to his hotel roughly an hour later, he was pleased to find his suitcase undisturbed. As far as he could tell, no one had been in his room. The booze had leveled out his nerves somewhat, but he was still on edge, so he secured every lock on the door, then took the hottest shower he could stand.

Later, wrapped in a towel, he lay on the bed without bothering to turn down the covers. Staring at the ceiling and watching shadows and light from the television play along the walls, he called home.

Taylor answered in a soft and sleepy voice. "Hello?"

"Hey," Joel said, certain her voice was the most beautiful thing he'd ever heard. Like always, it made everything all right again, even if only for a little while.

"Joel, hey."

"Did I wake you?"

"I'm on the couch; I must've nodded off. Are you okay?"

He felt himself smile. "Yeah, I'm all right," he said, hoping he'd effectively masked the unrest that still had hold of him.

"How's it going down there? Find anything out?"

"I'm working on it."

"Is there anything *to* find out?"

He bought himself a few seconds by drawing a deep breath. "Hard to say."

"Well, that sounds evasive."

"Not trying to be."

"No?"

"I don't really know that much yet," he said hesitantly. "We'll see happens."

She remained quiet a moment. "Are you sure you're all right? You sound—"

"Baby, I'm fine."

"If you're feeling like you need one of your pills, go ahead and—"

"I will." He clenched shut his eyes until the visions of Fernandez's tortured face faded. "How'd your day go?"

"Usual stuff, I won't bore you with it."

"Please do."

"Really?"

"Every last detail. Just as long as I can hear your voice."

"Miss me?"

"Something awful."

"Then come home."

"Soon."

Neither spoke for a while. Just listening to each other breathing was comforting somehow.

"Taylor," Joel finally said, "you may not hear from me for a few days."

"Why?"

"I'll be working late hours and I may not be able to call every night, so if you don't hear from me, don't panic; it's fine. I'll be in touch soon as I can, okay?"

More silence, and then, "I don't like any of this, Joel, not one bit of it."

"I'm not that wild about it myself."

"I know you're trying to do what you think is right," Taylor said, "but you don't have to save the day. It's not your responsibility."

"If we don't save ourselves and each other, who will?"

"Is that a stab at late-night romantic poetry?"

He pictured her smiling. "Sure, why not? Feeble as it may be."

"Beats your usual Roses Are Red routines, I guess."

"There Once Was a Man from Nantucket?"

"I dated that guy. He tended to exaggerate, trust me."

Joel laughed lightly and nuzzled the phone, wishing it were Taylor instead. All the evil in the world felt far less powerful just then, revealed for the coward it was in the glow of their love. "Go to bed and get some sleep," he told her. "I'll call when I can."

"Be careful, Joel. Please, sweetheart. Promise me."

"I promise," he told her. "And I love you."

"I love you too."

After they'd hung up, Joel wanted nothing more than to drift off to sleep, but he was wide-awake and his mind had begun to race again.

Magic is real. Did you know that?

"Yeah," he said softly. "As a matter of fact, I did."

He lay there thinking, his mind laden with the events of that evening and everything Pete Fernandez had told him. Were these things really happening? Had Lonnie been killed because of them? And he'd been in contact with *Trent*? How had that happened, and what the hell would Trent know about these things? When he'd last known Trent, he was an angry punk rocker, a rebel and an antiestablishment guy for sure, but hardly an expert on mind control and secret government programs. Then again, things changed, people changed, and he hadn't spoken to or even laid eyes on Trent in a very long time, so it was certainly possible.

Years before, Joel had come across several occult groups that claimed to use brainwashing techniques in their rituals and practices to control their members and influence them in certain ways. It was never clear if any of it worked or was even real, but those people he'd talked to about it swore it was quite effective and implemented on a regular basis. Shady occult groups were hardly the only ones allegedly involved in such things, however. Although he hadn't researched it directly, had rather come across it in his investigation of hardcore satanic activity years before, the government, the military-industrial complex, and espionage and intelligence groups had a long history of loose ties to the occult and to various occultists and occult organizations. Even the most perfunctory amount of research could yield examples of this, if one bothered to look for it. There was also no question that in years past the government had conducted hideous experiments on unwitting human subjects, and sometimes even society at large. They'd admitted it, and extensive amounts of verifiable information were available online and elsewhere—again, if one bothered to look. The real questions were, did these ties still exist, and were these programs still happening today, as Fernandez suggested?

A few minutes later Joel was on his laptop Googling *MKUltra* and *mind control experiments*. The information that came back was astounding and encompassed a wide range of victims, including the mentally ill and even children.

Later, on absolute overload, Joel shut everything down and did his best to convince himself he might at some point in his life be able to sleep again. He felt like Nero, fiddling away while the world around him burned to the ground. It was all so overwhelming, and oddly familiar, just as things had been years ago. And just as they'd been when he was a kid and that strange black car—whether a dream or reality—changed his and his friends' lives forever.

But this time it was even broader, deeper and more frightening, because there literally seemed no end to it. The more he looked, the more these things were thoroughly entrenched not only in his past and in his dreams, but in the flesh and blood, real-world power elite establishment. If the numerous conspiracy theories around government mind control programs were even partially true, there was likely nothing anyone could ever do to reverse or stop what had been done and what might still be happening. They'd attempted to create everything from super soldiers to sex slaves to spies to *Manchurian Candidate* assassins. Yet, if one was to believe the reports, these programs had gone by the wayside years ago, not because of moral awakening but because most failed to produce the results they'd hoped for.

Apparently wiping a human being's mind clean by bombarding it with nearly lethal doses of LSD didn't create a blank slate of a brain that could be rebuilt into anything the programmers wanted. Instead, it destroyed the test subjects' minds, left them horribly damaged and broken beyond repair, vegetables.

When Joel finally went to bed, he kept the television on with the sound muted so there'd still be light in the room. But every peripheral sound in the hotel hallways became amplified, every noise a potential threat, and he began to wonder if all these things could be connected somehow.

Do you believe the Devil is talking to you, Mr. Walker?

The terrible whispers and sounds that had once stalked the corridors of his mind returned, testing the periphery of his sanity and attempting to drag him back to the same hell he'd clawed his way out of all those years before. Wasn't that part of the trap he'd fallen into before, making connections where there weren't any?

Do you believe he's inside you right now?

But had he been wrong? Was he wrong now? Or right on both counts?

He slept fitfully, like a frightened child hiding beneath blankets and waiting for the monsters under his bed to strike, hoping his parents might arrive first, save him from his fears and assure him that there were no such things as monsters.

The luxury of fearing things that didn't exist eluded him, however; it had for several years now, and likely always would.

Because Joel knew those monsters were real.

CHAPTER
FIFTEEN

As the sun sets over Horseneck Beach, a two-mile stretch of sand and dunes in Westport, just part of the hundreds of acres of barrier beach and salt marsh that constitute one of the busiest and more popular locations in the Massachusetts State Forests and Parks System, the four boys sit in the sand, watching the water and sharing a case of beer. Crowded with tourists, out-of-towners, and locals alike during the summer months, in early spring it's far more quiet and less traveled. To locals like Joel and his friends, it's the best time—their time—to hang out here and enjoy the sand and sun and ocean.

On this early evening in 1982, the sun low in the sky but not yet down, they have come in Sal's '71 Mustang to a spot they've frequented their entire lives. They're all nineteen and nearly a year out of high school, but since the drinking age is twenty, none are old enough to buy. Luckily, Dorsey's older sister works part-time at a local liquor store and has managed to score them a case of Schlitz and a fifth of Southern Comfort. Trent has weed, Quaaludes, and mescaline, like Trent always does. Joel, assigned with "tune duty", has shown up with his new JVC boom box and a handful of cassettes. Lonnie, given the responsibility to snag food, has a bag of sandwiches.

They all met at Sal's house, then piled into his Mustang and hit the beach. The plan is to enjoy a few hours of relaxation and laughs before hitting a party another friend has scheduled for later that Saturday evening. Summer will be here soon. What they don't yet realize is that it will be their last together. After taking a year off between graduation and continuing his education, Joel will begin college the coming fall to pursue a degree in journalism. In the interim he's working at a local restaurant, waiting tables and saving as much money as he can. Between his own limited funds, student loans, financial aid, a small scholarship and the help of his parents, college is a possibility for him. The others are either not as fortunate or not interested in college. Sal, a former Golden Gloves boxing champion, is good enough to turn pro but has no desire to, and opts instead to pursue his love of cars and work as a mechanic at a local garage owned by his cousin. It's all he's ever really wanted to do. Dorsey, who had planned to enter the military, has changed his mind and instead taken a job at a hip clothing store at the nearby Swansea Mall. Lonnie is working security for a company in New Bedford, and Trent has already had a handful of jobs since graduation. None have worked out, so he has returned to what he did through most of high school: selling drugs.

By the following summer, Joel will have moved on with his college career and stopped spending a lot of time with the old crew. Trent will get into more trouble, including a few stints in jail, then move away and not be heard from again. Lonnie, Sal, and Dorsey will remain in touch and relatively close friends, but even Lonnie will go his own way once he becomes a father. In the years that follow, only Sal and Dorsey will remain tight, although they won't be able to maintain the level of friendship they enjoyed in high school. Life seems to conspire against them all in that regard. This close-knit group of five friends is doomed, but they have no idea, because in those waning days and nights of spring, it still feels as if they'll be friends forever, always this close and connected as they've been for years now. How could it ever be any other way? Sure, things will change along the way, and they'll all change a bit along with them, but they'll still be them, they'll still be buds and they'll always hang out and be there for each other. Won't they?

Few things lost can never be saved. This is one. They are one.

"You look ridiculous," Sal says to Trent as he flops down onto the sand, a beer in hand. "When you gonna quit this bullshit?"

Trent chuckles, shakes his head. His Mohawk is purple today. It changes color frequently. His outfit is punk all the way, from his jack-boots to his torn Dead Kennedys Holiday in Cambodia *T-shirt, to the large clothespins he sports as earrings, to the wide, spiked leather bracelet. It's a transformation he made at the beginning of their senior year of high school, and it's gotten continually hardcore since. But to them, he's just Trent, the skinny, soft-spoken kid with sad blue eyes, the weakest and most vulnerable of their group, reborn as a tough and rebellious punk.* "What do you care?" *he asks.*

"Because we hang out, and you look like a fucking asshole."

Dorsey waves at him, as if to swat his words from the air. "Leave him alone."

"I'm trying to help him out." *Sal opens his can of beer with a loud pop, then takes a quick gulp.* "Fucking peacock on acid over here."

"Christ, not this again." *Lonnie takes a pull of Southern Comfort.* "Every time now with this bullshit. It's his thing, okay? Let it go, it's got nothing to do with you."

"Joel," *Sal says, spreading his hands wide in an appeal.* "Help me out here."

"You're on your own," *Joel tells him, laughing.* "Only one it bothers is you."

"Here, this is for all of youse. Drink it in, ya fucks." *Sal flips everyone off and takes another swig of beer.* "You clowns cover for him all you want. I'm the only one with the guts to tell him how fucking retarded he looks."

"What, you look so good?" *Trent smiles, rolls a cigarette into the corner of his mouth and lights it up with a Zippo.* "Give me a break, big man."

"What's the matter with the way I look? I'm dressed normal, like a regular person, not some goddamn carnival freak."

Trent winks at Joel, knowing he's goading Sal but unable to stop himself. "So a KISS T-shirt with the sleeves cut off, jeans, sneakers, and your hair slicked back like some greaseball, that's normal?"

"Greaseball?" *Sal laughs, slaps Dorsey's shoulder hard but playfully.* "You hear what he just called me? You gonna sit there and let this Sex Pistol motherfucker insult my proud Italian heritage?"

Dorsey, who's busy rolling a joint, shrugs. "Hey, you're Sal 'The Volcano' Valano; knock his ass out."

"Least I'm the real deal," *he scoffs, motioning to Trent.* "You're *just pretending. You're not some punk rock dipshit from London or whatever. You're a regular white kid from the workingclass burbs like the rest of us."*

Dorsey looks up from the rolling paper in his hands. "I'm black, you idiot."

"Come on, don't start that racist shit with me. You know what I mean."

"Oh, I's sorry, Mistah Sal, I sho enough ams!"

Everyone laughs but Sal. "Don't fucking encourage him with that shit."

Dorsey begins singing "Nobody Knows the Trouble I've Seen".

"Yeah, okay, whatever. The point is Trent's just playacting. It's a bunch of bullshit. It's all for show, hair done up like that and looking like he hasn't had a bath in a year. Jesus, man, you need attention that bad?"

"Yeah, I do, but only from you." Trent blows him a kiss. "I'm dying for it, baby."

"In your fucking dreams, Mary."

"He's expressing himself," Lonnie says, passing the bottle to Trent. "Not the way I'd do it, but—fuck it—who gives a shit?"

"Exactly," Sal says, "it's not the way you'd do it because it's fucking gay and he looks like a jackass."

"What the hell difference would that make?" Dorsey asks. "Lonnie looks like a jackass anyway."

Everyone laughs, and Lonnie throws a handful of sand at Dorsey, which results in the group collectively scolding him for potentially ruining the joint-in-progress.

"You guys are asleep," Trent says. "All of you. Open your eyes; the world's in flames all around you."

"That's just your hair," Sal says.

"Keep laughing. It's all a lie, man. Anarchy, that's the only answer."

"Yeah," Sal says, "because I'm definitely gonna take you seriously in that getup. I wouldn't let you walk my fucking dog looking like that."

Trent raises a finger. "First of all, you shouldn't talk about Barbie like that."

Everyone bursts into laughter as Joel falls over and rolls in the sand.

"Ouch," Lonnie finally manages. "Come on, man, that's the love of his life."

"Yeah," Dorsey adds, "this week."

"Fuck you, Trent," Sal says, drinking more beer. "You wish you could get anywhere near something that fine. Fucking guy looks like he gets his dates at the zoo and he's busting my balls. And don't even get me started on that sorry excuse for music."

"Sorry I don't dig that radio-friendly, corporate sell-out shit you like. Packaged and sanitized for your protection."

"Yeah, yeah, heard it all before. Nonconformity and antiestablishment pukes think you're our only hope."

"There is no hope." Trent smokes his cigarette, and though still in a jovial mood, seems a bit more serious. "And since when did you become so conformist and establishment anyway?"

"Maybe I'm not," Sal says, "but I do it cool, you know, like a man. Not some whacked-out lunatic the way you're trying to do it."

"Wait, wait, wait," Dorsey says, sparking up the joint. "What do you mean there's no hope?"

"There's always hope," Joel says.

Trent flashes him a look. "Dude, seriously?"

"What?"

"You sound like a fucking child, man."

"Why?" Joel asks. "Because I don't think everything sucks and the whole world is one big hopeless cesspool?"

"Open your eyes."

"To what, your way of thinking? No thanks."

"So you believe everything's right with the world? Go along to get along, huh?"

"Can we lighten the fuck up, please?" Lonnie says. "Jesus Christ."

"We all deal with shit in our own ways," Joel says evenly. "Right?"

They all know exactly what he means, but don't intend to discuss it. Trent shrugs, and instead says, "Dorsey, what you do believe?"

"I believe we should smoke this doobie." He smiles mischievously. "And get very...very...small."

One by one, they faded away, taking their carefree attitudes and dated, politically incorrect humor with them, until Joel stood alone on the beach, watching the waves crash shore. For all their faults and foolishness, they were a family in their own way. Joel remembered how, later that night, someone at the party called Trent a freak and Sal beat the guy to a pulp. They could say anything to each other, but no one outside their circle had that privilege. He'd forgotten how close they'd all once been, how comfortable and safe they'd been with each other. He'd forgotten how badly he missed that, how badly he missed them.

Joel walked the sand a while longer, but the wind and the cold were too much, and he soon found his way back to his car. He drove across town to their old neighborhood. He, Dorsey, and Lonnie all had lived on the same street. Sal and Trent had lived on the next street over. Their neighborhood consisted of rows of modest homes lined up on mostly quiet streets.

Not much had changed in all these years.

Joel cruised the neighborhood, his car crawling along the streets where they'd all grown up. There was Freaky Harold's house, a middle-aged guy everyone was told to stay away from and never talk to. The town pervert, complete with a windowless van, a creepy stare, and a perpetually itchy groin, he often followed kids home from school and scared his share of little boys and girls, but no one ever heard of him actually doing anything. Joel's freshmen year of high school, Harold killed himself, slit his wrists. It was the talk of the town for weeks. The house was now a different color, but Joel recognized it as Harold's right away. Then there was the Silva's house, where Mr. Silva had a bicycle repair shop in his garage. Everyone took their bicycles to Mr. Silva, a kindly older man who often made minor fixes for free. The garage was still there, but no longer a repair shop.

Joel turned at the corner onto the street where he'd grown up.

Ray-Ray Jennings had lived right there, he remembered, in that Cape with the extra wide driveway. A few years older than Joel, he was a bully who constantly chased him from the bus stop at the corner all the way to his house. This continued through most of seventh grade, until he became friends with Sal, who, with one memorable beating, put an end to Ray-Ray's reign of terror.

Dorsey's old house was updated, now sporting lots of shrubbery along the front of the property and a paved driveway that had once been gravel. Joel wasn't sure who lived there now, or if the house was even still in Dorsey's family.

Everything looked so cold and still, locked down, as if no one lived in any of these old houses anymore. Despite the years since he'd last been here, and there'd been plenty, the memories kept coming.

There was Lonnie's house. The screened-in side porch looked pretty much the same as it had when they were kids, as did the rest of the place. The property had not been particularly well maintained and was in need of some major repairs.

Joel slowed the car to a creep, then pulled over onto the side of the road.

A few doors down from Lonnie's, there it was: the house he'd grown up in.

He could almost see a younger version of himself running around and playing in the yard…his mother gardening in the summer heat…his father mowing the lawn. It all seemed so clear in that moment, so alive and tangible, as if it were still going on just like it had all those years before. None of those people were gone, it seemed, just out of sight, hiding perhaps, until he was on his way and no longer looking.

But Joel knew the truth all too well. His mother, a secretary at the local elementary school, had been diagnosed with lung cancer just weeks after he graduated college. Five months later she was dead. Although his father, an electrician, lived in the house a couple more years, he eventually sold it and moved to Florida, where he remarried and still lived to this day. Joel's mother missed so much. She never saw him marry Taylor, never really got to know her. She never even got to know him as an accomplished adult. She also avoided his collapse and fall from grace, and for that he was grateful, as it would have devastated her to see her only child ushered into a mental institution. His father, on the other hand, acted as if nothing ever happened. He was already in Florida at the time, and that's where he stayed. They had literally never discussed it. Even these days, they only saw each other every few years, and when they did, both pretended all was right with the world and always had been.

My God, he thought. *This life—my life—really existed. Here, in this place.*

Yet it seemed so impossibly far away, a dream he'd had years before and was just now remembering, like the memories of the black car haunting his nightmares.

Before his emotions got the better of him, Joel pulled back out onto the street and continued on until he'd found Trent's old house on the next street. While Sal, Dorsey, and Trent all had siblings, Joel and Lonnie were only children. Of their group, Trent was the only one raised in a single-parent home. His mother, a former hippie, worked as an art teacher at a private Catholic high school in nearby Dartmouth, and although she had a series of boyfriends over the years, never lived with any of them and raised Trent and his sister Delilah alone. Joel had no idea who lived there now.

A few doors down, he found Sal's house.

It looked the same, only older and with relatively new vinyl siding, a dull beige. Same big bay window facing the street, same overgrown, weed-infested front yard, same rusty auto parts and crap littering the side yard and small section of woods beyond. The paved driveway, which led to a two-stall garage, housed a pair of cars, including one up on blocks. An American flag mounted just outside the front door flapped in the cold wind.

Joel parked out front.

Even before he'd gotten out of the car, Sal appeared, all six feet and four inches of him framed in the doorway to the garage, a can of beer in one hand held down by his hip, a soiled rag clutched in the other. He squinted, stepped out onto the driveway, apparently oblivious to the cold in a sleeveless sweatshirt, a pair of old jeans and work boots. Filthy as any respectable grease monkey, he adjusted the brim of an equally dirty New England Patriots hat, then turned his head and spat on the ground.

Joel walked around the side of the car, heart pounding. He stopped halfway up the

driveway and smiled.

"Son of a bitch," Sal said. His face remained expressionless and weathered, his nose flattened and wide from years of boxing, his complexion red, leathery and loose from years of hard drinking, eyes tired and encircled with black rings from the rest of his vices and stresses and everything else life had dished out. "Joel Walker."

"Hey, Sal," Joel said, still smiling.

A smile finally broke, slowly spreading across Sal's otherwise menacing face. "Had a feeling you might be around sooner or later."

"It's good to see you, man."

As they closed the gap between them, Joel offered his hand. Sal engulfed it with his big, meaty paw and gave it a firm shake. His body still looked powerful, but he'd acquired a sizable gut that hung over his belt. Once-chiseled arms, while still thick, covered with bulging veins and likely solid, were wrinkled and no longer sculpted as they'd been in his youth. He took a long pull on his beer, killing it, then crushed the can and fired it over into the side yard. "That tasted rather *moreish*. You want a brewski?"

"Little early in the morning for me, but thanks."

"Don't worry about it. Light beer, pussy shit. You'll be fine." He belched, gave Joel's shoulder a playful slap that nearly knocked him over, then motioned to the garage. "Come on, let's get out of the cold and talk."

Inside, the house looked a lot different than it had years before. It hadn't been updated and was cluttered, messy and old. When they were kids, Sal's parents had always kept the house immaculate. Now it looked like it needed a thorough cleaning and straightening.

Feeling as if he were following his old friend back into the past, they entered the house through the side door and walked directly into the kitchen. Sal grabbed a couple beers from the refrigerator, tossed one across the table to Joel, then headed into the living room.

"Need to get somebody in here to clean," Sal said, pushing some magazines from the couch to the floor before sitting down in a recliner across from it. "Had a chick that used to come in and do it, but she went back to school or some shit."

"No worries." Joel sat on the couch, which looked almost as old as he was, and noticed a dusty hutch against the far wall showcasing all of Sal's old amateur boxing trophies and belts, including his Golden Glove trophies, now faded and in serious need of polishing. Much like Sal, they'd lost a good deal of luster with time and age.

"Me and Barbie divorced a few years back," he announced.

"Sorry to hear that."

"Yeah, I was banging this cocktail waitress worked over at the dog track in Raynham." Sal shrugged, and popped open his beer. "Got bagged. Wasn't the first time she caught me with my pants down, if you get my drift, so I knew I was fucked."

Unsure of what to say, Joel just nodded.

"How about you, still married?"

"Yup. Taylor and I are doing well."

Sal took a gulp of beer. "Good," he finally responded. "That's good."

The eight-hundred-pound gorilla in the room watched from the corner as silence fell over the house.

"Kids?" Sal asked a moment later.

"Nope, didn't do the kids thing."

Sal's right leg bounced nervously, like it had when he was a kid. "I got three," he said. "Two girls and a boy."

"No kidding? That's great."

"Ready for this shit? I'm a fucking grandfather, dude."

"No way."

"What are you gonna do?" Sal waved at him the way one might at a flying bug. "My boy—Sal Jr.—he's just like his old man. Little bastard can't keep it in his pants for five minutes. Lives with his girlfriend in Warwick, she dances over in Providence. You should see the tits on this kid. *Madone.* Anyway, they had a little girl few months ago. So it's official, I'm old as fuck. The other two, the girls, they're still living at home with Barbie and the dick she married over in Acushnet. They're all living happily ever after in my house, got to love it. Lost it in the divorce."

"That's rough, but congratulations on the granddaughter."

"Yeah." Sal sighed. "My father died in 2000, and we lost Ma a few years ago."

Joel remembered Sal's father as a gruff and unpleasant man who rarely spoke, and his mother as a sweet, heavyset woman who loved to cook and feed Sal's friends whenever they were at the house. "Jesus, man, sorry to hear that."

"Thanks. So I'm a fucking orphan now too." He laughed and powered down more beer. "Ma left us the house and I needed a place to live, so I bought out my brother and sister. Got to live someplace, right? Why not the old neighborhood?"

"Doesn't look like it's changed that much," Joel said.

"Not much does." Sal killed his beer, dropped it on a cluttered coffee table between them, then sat back. "Except for you, maybe."

"I'm still me, Sal."

"I don't know, with them khakis and that nice button-up shirt, you look like a fucking yuppie over here. One of them little prissy boys from Maine now, huh?"

Joel knew he wasn't serious, it was just Sal's way, and as he'd said, not much had changed. "Listen, I know I lost touch with all you guys and…"

"That's how the cookie crumbles, *paisan*. You got out of college and moved on, had new friends, a different life. We all understood that. But you cut us loose and never came back. People got married, had kids, lived, died, and you were never there for any of it, man. For Christ's sake, you even had a private wedding and didn't invite any of us."

Now he was serious, and he'd left no room for misunderstanding that. "Sal, it was a small ceremony with just immediate family."

"Hey, all I'm saying is that we were a band of brothers growing up, right? Figured that meant something."

"Come on, man, of course it did."

"Seemed like you washed your hands of us, you know? Like we didn't matter. Same way Trent did. But Trent was a mess. We expected it from him, not from you."

Joel opened his beer but didn't drink any. "I'm sorry, Sal, for everything. I had a lot of what I thought was success very quickly, and it went to my head. Then when it all came crashing down, it took me with it. I had to run if I wanted to survive it, had to start over somewhere else. I needed to let the past go. *All* of it."

"That don't forgive everything, but I understand. We all got our problems. You did good, better than any of us. You got your chance and you got your education and you got the hell out of here. Used to piss me off, 'cause I thought you got too good for us, too fancy, and kinda left us in the dust, you know? But when I got a little older, I understood."

"You could've gotten out if you wanted to. You were a great boxer, could've gone pro. Might've been heavyweight champ one day."

"Nah," he laughed, his emotions turning on a dime just as they had when he was younger. "Remember when I got that chance to go to New York City and train at Gleason's with the big boys? That pro trainer and manager were looking at me, seeing if the hype was justified. Turned out it wasn't. I was just a big fish in a little pond, dude. I might've been a badass around here, but out there, I was one more punk barely good enough to spar with those guys. Got my ass kicked from pillar to post, and then I knew: boxing wasn't supposed to be my life. Cars, that's my life. That's what always made me happy, working on cars. I boxed 'cause that's what my old man wanted me to do. All it ever got me was headaches, a bunch of scars, a busted nose and a cabinet full of trophies from a hundred years ago nobody gives a shit about. But being a mechanic? That got me my own place, my own business. I supported my family and put food on the table, toys under the tree at Christmas. I'm my own man. I don't answer to nobody and I do what I love all day. So, fucked up as my life is sometimes, I done okay, you know?" He sat forward. "But you hit the big time."

"Not really. It just looked that way for a while."

"I read your book when it came out, saw you on all them shows."

"You learned how to read?"

"Little bit." He grinned. "You fuck."

Joel laughed lightly, hoping it might defuse the awkwardness of the situation.

"Word was it all fell apart though, and you had to go away for a while." After seeing Joel's discomfort, he added, "Westport's a small town, man, then and now. People talk."

"I had to get some help," Joel explained, "but that was years ago. I'm fine now. Been fine for a long time."

"Glad to hear it, bro." He cracked his knuckles with a loud pop. "But good as it is to see you and catch up, we both know you're here about Lonnie."

Joel nodded.

"Me and Dorsey, we figured we'd see you at the funeral."

"I didn't know, Sal."

He raised a skeptical eyebrow.

"I had no idea Lonnie was dead until his daughter came to see me," Joel told him. "Lonnie knew about what I'd gone through, and he told Katelyn to leave me alone if anything ever happened to him. She did, until she had nowhere else to turn and asked me to look into his death."

Sal nodded. Apparently the response was acceptable. "You still a reporter?"

"More or less."

"You on the clock, then?" With another sigh, Sal removed his hat, tossed it on the coffee table and ran a hand through what was left of his hair.

Joel hadn't expected that. Sal's thick locks were all but gone. He still combed what little remained straight back, but there wasn't even enough hair left to slick it back like he had in his youth. "No, I'm here as a friend."

"Hard to believe Lonnie's really gone. We were still friends, still hung out every once in a while. Now I wish we spent more time, you know?" He caught Joel looking. "Yeah, lost my lettuce. Nice, huh? I'm fat now too, in case you were wondering. The chicks still dig me, though, who knows why?"

"I'm thinking it's your charm."

"Could be my giant cock."

"See? What could be more charming than that?"

Sal smiled but it faded quickly. "So you find anything out, or what?"

"Few things. I think Lonnie was into something heavy, Sal."

"Like what?"

"Not sure yet."

"Or maybe you just don't want to tell me yet."

Sal was many things, but stupid wasn't one of them. "You mentioned Trent before," Joel said, then took a sip of beer. "Katelyn said he's out west somewhere."

"Last I heard, yeah. I haven't seen or talked to Trent in years, dude."

"Any of his family still around?"

"His sister lives in the Midwest someplace. His mother got Alzheimer's and they put her in a nursing home few years back."

"Any idea where?"

"New Bedford. Whaling City Shores, it's in the south end."

"How do you know all this?"

"Like I said, man, small town."

"And what about Trent?"

"What about him? He lost his fucking mind. You know how he got all weird right after high school with all that punk rock bullshit and all that paranoid crap about the world going to hell? He got heavier into drugs and drinking, had a lot of problems. Married this real cunt from Swansea, bitch acted like her pussy dripped diamonds. You know the type. He was crazy in love with her, though. It didn't last a year, and when she divorced him, he really went off the fucking rails. I mean, you remember Trent, he was always weird, and I used to bust his balls about his look and all that, but I never let anybody else hassle him or any of youse. Shit, like you used to say, we all deal with things different, right? That was Trent's way."

Joel nodded. He knew what Sal was referencing without actually saying it.

"But he got worse, started talking all this crazy shit, conspiracies and how the government was coming to get us all, crap like that. He came by, said he was going to the desert to live by himself until the end of the world, 'cause it was coming soon. Poor bastard did too many drugs. You ask me, it rotted his brain, scrambled it all up, you know? Last time I seen him, to be honest, I didn't really want him around me. He was bad, Joel. Real bad. I'm talking full-throttle, motherfucking crazy."

"And that was it, he was gone just like that?"

"Never saw him again." Sal stood up. "Why, what's Trent got to do with all this?"

"I was told Lonnie was in touch with Trent not long before he was killed."

Sal flashed a questioning look. "Told by who?"

"Somebody that worked with him. The information's solid, and I believe it."

"Lonnie never said shit to me about Trent being back in the picture." Sal thought a moment. "You tell the cops this?"

"No. Far as I can tell, they're going to pin Lonnie's murder on a drug deal gone bad or something along those lines."

"Dickheads. Wasn't no drug deal, I'd bet my life on that."

"You got any theories, Sal?"

He seemed surprised at being asked, but rather than answer, disappeared into the kitchen and returned a moment later with a fresh beer. "Like you, I was born and raised here. It's my home.

I love it. There's no place like it. We got our share of assholes, but mostly there's good people here." Like a black cloud passing over the moon, something dark and deadly crossed Sal's face. "There's darkness here too, though. Who knows that better than us? It was here long before we were here, and it'll be here long after we're gone. We all know it. We all feel it. We all live with it. And we all look the other way. We pretend it's not there. But deep down we know better, don't we? We knew about it from the time we were kids. Back in the day, you found out what goes on in that darkness. Maybe somewhere along the line, Lonnie found out too."

A heavy burst of wind rocked the house.

"Did Lonnie tell you something before he was killed?"

Sal remained standing, but was having trouble staying still. "He was seeing shit, did you know that? Said there were things after him. *Demons*. It was crazy."

"Crazy like Trent?"

"No, not like Trent."

"I don't understand."

"See, Trent thought he was fine and it was everybody else that was crazy." Sal looked down at the floor. "But Lonnie…Lonnie was going nuts…and he knew it, Joel. The poor bastard knew it."

Joel had another swallow of beer. "Did he ever mention a Tuser Industries?"

Sal shook his head. "No, don't ring a bell."

"What about a man named Jerry Simpson?"

"Never heard of him."

"Does the term *numbers station* mean anything to you?"

"What's that?"

Joel put his beer can down on the coffee table. "Still working on it."

"I know Lonnie was into something, like you said. I just don't know what." Sal squared his stance. "But if you do, you need to tell me, man."

"I'm still trying to figure out what's real and what isn't."

"Good luck with that."

"It's like years ago, when I was investigating the cult thing. Some of what I ran across was so insane, so impossible, and yet there were these kernels of truth that couldn't be denied. It

145

makes you start to second-guess everything, but sooner or later, you come to realize that not everybody can be crazy."

"You sure?" Sal asked.

"No. I wish I was, but I'm not."

"Seems that way sometimes, don't it? Look at us. Trent. Lonnie. Even you."

"I'm not insane, Sal."

"Maybe not now."

"Maybe not ever."

"They put you away for it."

"Afraid you'll be next?"

Sal flexed his arms, then shook them loose like he had years ago, before he'd pound on his heavy bag. But he wasn't intimidating anyone. Even after all these years, they knew each other too well for that. He was afraid, just like the rest of them, because he'd been hanging on by his fingernails for years, and it was only a matter of time before he lost his grip. It was who they were, what they knew.

And what they didn't.

"What do you want from me, Joel?"

It took everything he had to get the words out. "Do you ever think about it?"

Sal stared at him with dark, angry eyes.

"The black car," Joel pressed, "do you ever think about it?"

For what seemed an eternity, only the wind answered.

The big black Cadillac at the top of the street...

"I still dream about it sometimes," Joel admitted.

Sal walked over to the bay window, looked out at the street. "Me too," he finally said, his voice uncharacteristically soft. "But we always said we'd never talk about that again."

Just...there...motionless...the windshield and windows tinted dark and impenetrable...

"Maybe it's time."

"There's nothing to talk about. We don't even know what happened."

Four boys on their bicycles...watching...wondering why it's stopped there and looks as if the car itself is staring them down...

"Don't we?"

"Don't go getting all cutesy clever with me, bro." Sal remained at the window, his back to Joel, his arms hanging at his sides and his hands clenching into fists, then releasing, again and again. "This is me you're talking to. All I know is, nothing was ever the same after that day. That's what I got."

And then the tires screech and it's barreling toward them, rocketing down the street straight for them, the summer sun reflecting off the shiny hood, blinding them...

"Something happened, Sal. To all of us."

"We were just kids," he said suddenly, turning away from the window and stuffing his hands in his pants pockets. "It was just a game."

"We told ourselves that, but it's bullshit. Something got in our heads and—"

"Why the fuck you bringing this up? I don't see you for twenty years and you come into *my* house talking *this* shit, are you ribbing me? I thought you were here to find out what happened to Lonnie."

"Sal, listen to me. I think everything might be connected, what happened when we were kids, what I went through as an adult, Trent going off the deep end, Lonnie's murder—all of it. Lonnie was mixed up in some bad shit. At the end, he may have even involved or recruited others. But people were fucking with his head. I think he was involved in mind control experiments."

"Mind control."

"Yes."

Sal licked his lips, a nervous habit he'd had for as long as Joel had known him. "What in the *fuck* are you talking about?"

"Look, I know how it sounds, but—"

"You been to see Dorsey yet?"

"No, wanted to talk to you first."

"Then leave him out of it. He's got enough problems. Let him be."

As broken-down as he'd become, Sal was still doing his best to protect them all. Time had stolen a lot, but it hadn't taken that from him yet.

"I can't do that," Joel told him.

Sal angrily snatched a battered leather jacket from a chair in the corner and threw it on. "You know who killed Lonnie, don't you."

It wasn't a question, and they both knew it, but Joel answered anyway.

"Not exactly. Not yet."

"What are you gonna do when you do know?"

"I'm not sure."

"Awesome. Great plan, dipshit."

"There's a chance all of our lives could be in danger," Joel said.

"Yeah? Well, life's a dangerous game, chief. It don't scare me."

"Yes, it does."

"Okay, whatever you say, slick." Sal pulled a ring of keys from his jacket pocket. "I know my life's shit, but it's what I got left, okay? My business, my kids, my grandkid, it's all I got, *cabeesh*? And nobody's taking it away from me. Not old memories, not bad dreams, not some bullshit mind control maybes, and not you or anybody else. Lonnie's dead, man, and it breaks my heart. It does. Tears me up inside, and if I find out who pulled the trigger, I will *personally* put the fuck down. So when you got something real, you come see me and we'll end this once and for all and make it right, yeah? Until then, no offense, Joel, but fuck off. I don't need this shit. I got enough demons." He headed back into the kitchen. "I'm going to work. Lock the door behind you on your way out."

"Sal, wait."

Joel followed him, but before he could get another word in, Sal had already jumped behind the wheel of one of the cars in the driveway. He backed out, burned rubber, and sped off down the street.

The cold air hit Joel like a slap to the face. He hurried across the yard to his car, and was about to get in when he saw a vehicle parked on the side of the road at the top of the street.

The Crown Vic was back.

CHAPTER SIXTEEN

Joel stood his ground, watching the car without subtlety. It remained where it was, parked on the side of the road. This time he had an unobstructed and stationary view of the vehicle, and was clearly able to make out two men sitting in the front seat. Both wore dark suits and ties and looked straight ahead as if in a trance, their eyes shielded by dark sunglasses. Had they been at all concerned with being seen, they would've driven off or at least attempted to remain undetected, but it was obvious they wanted Joel to see them this time. So he gave them what they wanted, staring them down for nearly a minute before getting into his car.

Once behind the wheel, he cranked the heater. He was freezing, but knew that wasn't the only reason he was shivering. He watched the Crown Vic a while longer in his side mirror. *Okay you bastards,* he thought, *come on then.*

Joel pulled out and turned at the top of the block. By the time he'd made it halfway up the next street, the Crown Vic appeared in his rearview. He crossed through the old neighborhood, less concerned with his tail and focused more on the discomfort and fear rising in him as he approached the crossroads where every-thing had gone down that day when they were kids.

It took him several seconds to realize where he was, as unlike the other part of town, this area had changed drastically since his youth. He slowed the car and, due to the heavier traffic, pulled over and parked. Across from him there had once been a huge open field. When the carnival came to town each summer, that's where they'd set up, but where the field once resided there now stood a large supermarket and considerable parking lot. And the crossroads, rural and desolate years ago, was now home to numer-ous businesses and residential properties.

But Joel knew where he was. The sweat breaking across his body despite the cold told him so. *Hold it together*, he told himself. *Hold it together.*

The Crown Vic drove right by him and continued on until it was out of sight.

Joel looked to the supermarket. All he saw was the old field on that strange and frightening summer afternoon all those years ago…

He clenched his hands into fists and tried to will them to stop shaking.

They see the big black Cadillac at the top of the street. On their bi-cycles, and saddled with camping gear and sleeping bags, they wait, watching to see what it might do next. Surely there has to be a reason it's sitting there in the middle of the road, its black windows and dark windshield mesmerizing…like a dream…

And then the screech of tires, and it's hurtling toward them, the glinting sunshine reflecting off the body and shiny chrome…

"Look out!" Sal screams, hopping off his bike and leaving it there as he runs for the side of the road.

Dorsey and Lonnie follow, abandoning their bikes and scrambling out of the way in a frenzied rush, as Trent and Joel do the same.

The Cadillac swerves, avoiding their bikes and gear, then rushes by in a blur of black and silver, shooting off down the straightaway and out of sight.

Baffled and relieved all at once, the boys slowly return to the middle of the street to stand up their bikes and gather their things.

"Everybody all right?" Sal asks as he walks back over to his bike.

"Yeah," Joel says. "What an asshole."

"The fuck is that guy's problem?" Dorsey snaps. "Prick almost hit us!"

"That was fucked up." Trent throws his sleeping bag over his shoulder and walks his bike to the side of the road. "We need to get the hell out of here, you guys."

"Bullshit," Sal says. "We came to camp in the field and that's what we're doing."

"Yeah, it's cool." Lonnie reaches for his bike. "Come on. We all got an overnight pass; let's not blow it just because some jackoff tried to scare us. Besides, he's long gone now anyway."

But the big black Cadillac isn't long gone. It's already turned around and coming back for them.

Joel sees it first. The car moves slowly this time, creeping toward them. He looks around frantically, but there's no one else on the road, no one else in sight. They're alone with this car and whoever's inside.

He's frightened, more frightened than he's ever been in his life.

And his fear is justified.

As his surroundings blurred, Joel realized his eyes had filled with tears. He angrily wiped them away, but they were quickly replaced. The more he tried to calm himself, to stop the shaking and tears, the worse both became.

"What the hell is wrong with me?"

He slammed shut his eyes and let his forehead rest on the steering wheel as he drew a series of slow, deep breaths and practiced the focusing and breathing techniques the doctors had taught him when anxiety attacks took hold of him.

After a few minutes, he felt himself slowing down, his emotion coming back under his control and his fear lessening. Now all he wanted was to get as far away from this place as possible, and that's exactly what he did.

With his fear giving way to steely determination, he headed for New Bedford. It was time to up the ante and go directly for the belly of the beast.

Before he'd reached the town line, the Crown Vic returned. It followed him all the way to New Bedford, but once he crossed into the south end of the city, it vanished into heavy traffic and was gone.

Following his GPS, Joel eventually found himself on a lonely dead-end road not far from the water. Deserted, the side street was littered with old mills closed and abandoned long ago. Left to rot, many were barely standing, the parking lots weed-infested, cracked and neglected. There were no residences here, just a ghost town of dead and decaying factories. A little more than a mile in, at the end of the road and housed in a converted but still-dreary old mill building, stood Tuser Industries. Except for one small sign attached to the chainlink gate out front, there was no other signage or markings indicating what the establishment was. A handful of small buildings were scattered about the property, with the main facility located in the center of the complex. The entire property was encircled with electrified and barbed wire fencing, and a uniformed guard sat in a hut just outside the front gate.

With a strong sense of dread hanging in the cold air, Joel rolled to a stop. The guard, a large, swarthy man in mirrored sunglasses who didn't exactly strike him as the accommodating type, stepped out of the hut and cautiously approached his car.

"Can I help you?"

"I'm here to see Jerry Simpson in human resources," Joel answered in as curt a tone as possible. He was done with formalities and niceties.

"Do you have an appointment?"

"Do I need one?"

The guard considered Joel a moment. "Your name?"

"Walker."

"First name?"

"Mister."

The guard turned on his heel and returned to the hut, where he grabbed a phone. After having apparently spoken on it for a few seconds, he emerged again from the station and approached Joel's car. "Mr. Simpson's gone for the day."

"It's not even noon yet."

The guard stood there, expressionless and silent.

Joel looked up at his own face reflected in the guard's mirrored sunglasses. "Is he expected back tomorrow?"

"I wouldn't know, sir."

"Yeah," Joel said, powering up his window, "of course you wouldn't."

The guard remained where he was, watching Joel as he turned the car around and headed back out the way he came.

He'd only driven a short way when he saw the Crown Vic. It

was parked diagonally in the middle of the street, blocking his way. Joel stopped several feet from the car, his heart racing. Tuser Industries and the guard were no longer visible in his rearview, and on either side of the road, abandoned rundown buildings with blown-out windows stood amid overgrown weeds and garbage.

"Okay," he muttered. "Here we go."

Joel watched as the passenger side door opened, and then the driver's side. Two tall, thin, tidy-looking men with short haircuts stepped out of the vehicle. In their dark suits and black shades, they looked like Secret Service agents straight out of central casting. The passenger was older, with vacuous good looks and dark hair graying at his temples. The driver, a bit taller and with broader shoulders, was a moonfaced blond with a flattop.

Keeping it hidden from view, Joel grabbed his phone, activated the video camera option and hit Record. Then he slid it back into his jacket pocket as the two men made a slow, casual approach toward his car.

Like cops, they separated and took different sides of the vehicle. The older one came over to Joel's side while the blond moved around to the passenger side. Doing his best to appear cool and collected, Joel pressed the button to lock all the doors, then dropped the window about an inch. He could feel Flattop's eyes on the back of his neck, but hoped his sunglasses helped hide his fear.

"Good morning, Joel," the older man said with a smooth, deep voice.

He wasn't surprised they knew his name, but hearing one of them speak it was still disturbing. "Who are you?"

"Do me a favor and step out of the vehicle, would you, Joel? So we can talk."

"How about you show me some ID first?"

"No need to be so formal." The man smiled, revealing teeth too white and straight to be real. "My name is Mr. Novak." He pointed to his partner. "And his name is Mr. Kavon."

Kavon. Strange name, Joel thought. "K-A-V-O-N?" he asked. "Sounds like his name is the same as yours, only spelled backward. That's quite a coincidence."

"How very perceptive. But I'm afraid I don't believe in coincidences, Joel."

"Not sure I do either, so you know what? Let's go ahead and be formal. Show me some ID."

"Why don't you step out of the car, Joel? We'll get this all worked out."

"All what worked out? Who are you?"

Mr. Novak's smile faded. His voice remained smooth, friendly, completely non-threatening but condescending. "Step out, Joel."

"What do you want? Why have you been following me?"

"Step out, Joel."

"No, I don't think so."

"Why make this more difficult than it needs to be? We just want to talk, Joel."

"Isn't that what we're doing?"

"Step out, Joel."

"Show me ID or we're done here."

Novak produced a small device from his pocket and pressed it against the door. The moment it made contact, all the locks disengaged. Before Joel realized what had happened, the man had opened the door and was motioning for him to get out. "Go ahead and step out, Joel."

This time he did, as Kavon slowly made his way around the rear of the car so that he and Novak had Joel bookended.

The cold air was jarring, and Joel immediately began calculating which avenue of escape would give him the best chance. Could he outrun these men if he bolted for one of the abandoned factories?

"There we go," Novak said. "Wasn't that easy?"

Hands in his jacket pockets, Joel tried to position his phone as casually as possible so that it would better pick up the audio. "What do you want?"

From behind, Joel felt a strange pinch on the side of his neck. His brain told him to spin around toward Kavon and to reach for the source of pain, but his body refused to cooperate. His feet felt as if they'd been cemented to the road, and his arms dangled at his sides, dead and immobile.

It was then Joel realized Kavon had stuck him with a needle.

He tried to call out but couldn't, and as a tingling sensation flooded through his entire body, the world blurred. Strange rushing sounds surged in his ears, and he felt himself falling.

The last thing Joel saw before darkness claimed him was Novak's creepy, smiling face.

CHAPTER SEVENTEEN

What do you remember, Joel?

The field. I remember coming awake in the field.

Why were you in the field, Joel?

We all passed out...or...maybe we fell asleep in the grass...but I remember coming awake and seeing the sky. It was so beautiful... so...blue. And the clouds...there were these giant clouds, they...they looked so peaceful.

Had you and the others been sleeping in the field, Joel?

I don't know. I think so. But maybe...maybe it was just a game.

Were you pretending?

Maybe.

Did you all lie down in the grass, Joel, and pretend to be asleep?

I don't know. I...I only remember the car...the big black car...and then...

What do you remember about the big black car, Joel?

It tried to run us down. We thought it was someone trying to scare us.

And did it scare you, Joel?

Yes. It scared all of us.

Then it was gone?

Yes, but it came back.

The big black car came back?

Yes. I remember seeing it coming. Slowly, it…it was coming slowly toward us.

And then what happened, Joel?

I don't know.

What's the next thing you remember?

Waking up in the field.

And how did you feel when you woke up in the field, Joel?

Tired…confused…afraid. We all did.

What happened with the big black car, Joel?

I don't know.

You don't know? Or is that you don't want to remember?

I don't…I don't want to remember.

Why don't you want to remember?

Because I…

Why don't you want to remember, Joel?

I'm not supposed to. None of us are.

A slight headache tingled behind his eyes even as the first moments of consciousness returned. Light from a row of filthy little windows high above him illuminated an intricate pattern not far from where he was lying. It took him several seconds to realize it was a large, very intricate web. Slowly, like a swimmer rising toward the surface of the ocean, Joel ascended toward consciousness, his mind firing and linking thoughts with sight and sound. The web belonged to a plump black spider hanging in its corner, slowly devouring the remains of a butterfly.

Joel hated spiders, was afraid of them, and with this memory came horror. In his mind he scrambled away, putting as much distance between himself and the spider as possible. But in reality he was still sluggish and barely moved at all, only managing to roll over slightly from his left side to his back.

The floor was cold and hard. The ceiling above consisted of old rafters and rotting beams. And then the smell…body odor, urine, fecal matter and…something else…something that actually smelled quite good. Soup? Beef of some kind?

Joel tried to move his arms. His hands flopped against his

face, and he rubbed his eyes with fingers that tingled and felt like they were asleep. Still groggy, he raised his head, pressed his palms flat against the cold floor, bent his legs at the knee and pushed himself up into a sitting position. Everything tilted and spun for a few seconds before coming to a blurry stop.

He felt nauseated and cold. Shivering, he drew his knees in closer to his chest, then wrapped his arms around his shins. It was all coming back now, gradually, and he wanted to run. Unfortunately Joel wasn't even in a position to stand up yet, much less flee, so he remained where he was and worked on focusing his vision and clearing his head.

"Relax," someone said. "Breathe. Give it a minute and you'll be good as new. It's normal to be groggy for a few minutes. Need to clear the cobwebs, is all."

The word web reminded him of the spider. He looked for it, but the spider, the web and the butterfly were gone. Had he dreamed them?

Joel kept dragging himself away from where it had been until he felt a wall against his back. With a wider and clearer view of the area, he guessed they'd taken him to one of the abandoned factories. The building was enormous but gutted and falling apart. His head lolled to the side, following the smell of soup, and he found an older man huddled in the corner, eagerly slurping at a steaming can of beef stew. The man looked to be in his sixties or early seventies, was horribly unkempt, and had a long gray beard that hung nearly to the middle of his chest. Dressed in filthy clothes that more closely resembled rags, and shoes that were literally falling apart, the homeless man was obviously unconcerned with anything but his stew as he noisily scooped plastic spoonful after plastic spoonful into his toothless mouth like he hadn't eaten in days, which he probably hadn't.

Sunglasses still in place, Novak and Kavon stepped from the shadows. Kavon had replaced the needle with a handgun, which he held down by his thigh.

Novak smiled and motioned to the homeless man. "This is our new friend Barney," he said. "Say hi, Barney."

Barney looked up long enough to nod at Joel, then continued shoveling.

"There's a lot of homeless people in the city," Novak explained.

"Lots of them take refuge in these old buildings. Hey, beats the streets, right, Barney? Anyway, he looked awful hungry, so we got him some nice discount beef stew in a can. Looks yummy, doesn't it, Joel? Eating good today, huh, Barney ole boy?"

Barney nodded and gave a toothless grin.

Joel attempted to ask Novak what they'd done to him, but his words came out slurred and unfamiliar. A string of spittle drooled from his mouth and dangled from his bottom lip.

"It's okay," Novak assured him. "Sounds and looks like you've had a stroke, but it's nowhere near that serious. The effects wear off fairly quickly. First minute or two can be a bear, though."

"Why are you doing this?" Joel asked, the words still slurred but discernible.

"It's awfully cold out today, even in here." Novak's breath tumbled forth like smoke, as if for emphasis. "So I've got an idea. How about we do our best to get along and have our little talk as quickly as we can? Then you can get back in your car, turn the heat way up, get nice and cozy and warm, and be on your way. How does that sound? Does that sound good to you, Joel?"

Spitting the drool free, he swallowed, coughed and wiped his chin. "I want to know who you are, why you've been following me and what you want."

Novak responded in a tone still eerily pleasant but unmistakably threatening. "Joel, it's been my experience that things tend to work out best when one person does the speaking and one person does the listening. So I'd like you to listen while I speak. Think you could do that for me, Joel? Think you could listen while I speak?"

Joel nodded, hopeful his feigned annoyance masked his anxiety.

"Super." Novak removed his sunglasses to reveal dull hazel eyes. "That's a good decision, Joel, and good decisions are the way things ought to be, because if you think about it, life is really all about decisions. To a large degree, the decisions we make determine the kind of lives we ultimately have, wouldn't you agree, Joel?"

An icy wind whipped against the building, infiltrating the numerous fissures and openings and blowing debris and trash about. Joel was sure he'd never be warm again. Novak continued grinning at him like a psychotic catalogue model, awaiting his response. "Yes," Joel answered. "I agree."

"Great, because as it turns out, you have a very important decision to make right now, Joel." Very subtly, Novak moved closer. "You can go on back to Maine and your nice, quiet life with your beautiful, loving wife, your fat little bald friend and your nifty job. Or you can stay here and continue to do things that are detrimental to your health and well-being, and maybe even theirs. Now I want you to think about that a minute, Joel. I want you to think about it very carefully. Can you do that for me? Can you think about it very carefully, Joel?"

"Threaten me all you want," Joel told him. "But don't you ever threaten my wife. I don't give a shit who you are."

Novak exchanged glances with Kavon. "Oh, this is so disappointing, Joel. I asked you to listen just now, didn't I? Didn't I ask you to listen and then to think very carefully? Jeez Louise, was I not clear on that?"

Before Joel could answer, Kavon stepped forward and kicked him in the stomach. The blow was so violent it took Joel's breath away and sent sharp, slashing pains from his gut all the way up into his chest.

As he gasped and slid to the side, Kavon grabbed him by the shoulders, then slammed him against the wall, releasing him to sit up on his own. Joel wobbled but remained upright.

Barney let out a cackling laugh, then continued eating.

"Decisions," Novak told him. "It's all about good decisions, Joel."

Joel's breath slowly returned, and the sharp pain eventually turned to a dull ache in his lower abdomen. "Is this what you did to Lonnie? Did you threaten him too? Did you kill him when he wouldn't leave things alone?"

Kavon stepped toward him, but Novak stopped him with a quick shake of his head. "Joel," Novak said, "I want you to take a good look around. Can you do that?"

Joel stared daggers at him instead.

"Do you see where you are, Joel?" Novak asked. "Here we are in the middle of a city, and yet, we're kind of in the middle of nowhere, aren't we? Gosh, I'd imagine a grown man could scream his head off for help out here at the top of his lungs and no one would ever hear him. I'd venture to say someone could even disappear on a road like this, with all those lost little spaces in all these big old buildings, and no one would ever find them. Except for maybe the rats, right, Barney?"

The homeless man was so engrossed with his stew he didn't answer.

"It's kind of scary if you think about it," Novak said. "Are you thinking about it yet, Joel? Give it a try. Think about it for me, and let's see what you come up with. How's that sound?"

The pain finally subsiding, Joel straightened his posture but remained sitting. "You're not going to kill me. Too many people know I'm here looking into things. If I turn up murdered too, it's going to be impossible to explain."

"*Murdered?* I don't recall saying anything along those lines." Novak looked to his partner. "Mr. Kavon, do you recall me saying anything along those lines?"

Kavon shook his head.

"Who are you?" Joel pressed. "Who do you work for, Tuser Industries? The government? Who?"

Using his free hand, Kavon fired a vicious uppercut to Joel's jaw.

As his teeth clacked and his head snapped back, slapping the wall, he let out a grunt, doubled over and fell forward into Kavon's waiting arms. He propped Joel up, leaning him against the wall again. Joel coughed, then gagged, struggling to catch his breath as nausea and horrific pains raced along his jawline up into his temples.

"Anyhoo," Novak said, "I'm going to need to see your phone now, okay, Joel?"

"I don't have it," he said, his jaw sore and crackling and the back of his skull throbbing. "I left it at the hotel."

Kavon thrust a beefy hand into Joel's jacket pocket, yanked the cell out and handed it to Novak.

"Well, aren't you a Sneaky Pete? I had a feeling, you rascal." Novak ran his finger over the screen. "Let's see. Stop…and…Delete. Now, I'm going to give this back to you, Joel, because I know how expensive these darn things can be and just how attached we get to our cell phones these days. But if you try that again, Mr. Kavon is going to break it up into teeny-weeny little pieces, okay?"

Finally able to sit erect again, Joel took his phone back when it was offered and returned it to his pocket, keeping a wary eye on Kavon throughout. He'd been in his share of fights in his youth, but no one had ever hit him that hard.

"Here's what it boils down to, Joel." Novak crouched down in front of him, took Joel by the chin and gently lifted his head until he was looking at him. "Like I said, it's all about making good decisions."

Kavon sidled up next to Barney, but the old man didn't seem to notice.

"Take ole Barnabas for example," Novak continued, eyes locked on Joel's. "Nobody's born a filthy homeless loser. I'd be willing to guess this old man has made numerous decisions over the course of his miserable and useless life, wouldn't you, Joel? Wouldn't you say he's probably made a lot of decisions in his miserable, useless lifetime?"

In his peripheral vision, Joel saw Kavon straighten his arm and aim the gun just inches from the side of the homeless man's head. Still slurping and focused on the stew, Barney had no idea a weapon was pointed directly at his temple.

"Yes," Joel said. "I would."

"He *decided* to sleep in this building last night. He *decided* to stay when we came in. He decided to have some stew on us and hang around. Barney didn't have to do any of those things. He chose to. Decisions, Joel, decisions."

As Joel looked into Novak's dull eyes, he had no doubt that the man before him was a vicious sadist who had killed many human beings. Kavon was the brute and muscle of the two, but Novak was the truly frightening one. "Stop it," Joel said softly. "Please. He's done nothing to you. He has nothing to do with any of this."

Novak stood up. "That's the thing about our decisions, Joel. They can reward us or they can punish us." He motioned to Barney. "On one hand, Barney's decisions rewarded him with that no doubt delicious gourmet beef stew he's so delicately scarfing down as we speak."

"You've made your point, please—"

"But on the other hand—"

"Novak, don't!"

"—Barney's decisions have also led to him to being in the

wrong place at the wrong time. You see what I mean, Joel? You see how Barney's in the wrong place at the wrong time?"

A deafening blast exploded through the building, echoing along with Joel's cry as the homeless man's head exploded, spraying him with a mist of blood, brains, and bodily fluids.

As the body fell over, the can of stew dropped into the growing puddle of blood around Barney's mangled head, and Joel scrambled away as best he could, vomiting onto the floor as he went.

The ringing in his ears eventually subsided, and Joel worked himself up onto his hands and knees and vomited again. With a shaking hand, he wiped his face clean with the back of his sleeve.

"You with us, Joel?" Novak asked. "Need your attention on this. You think you could give me just a few more seconds of your undivided, Joel?"

With blood and gore dripping from his face and chin, and his body violently trembling, Joel forced himself to look Novak in the eye again.

"It's all up to you, Joel. We're not playing games here. I'm going to go ahead and assume you've got that through your head now. What do you say, Joel? Is that a safe assumption for me to have? Have you got it through your head now?"

"Yes," he answered softly.

"Speak up for me so I can be sure I heard you properly. Think you could do that for me, Joel? Think you could speak up for me so I can hear you properly?"

"*Yes.*"

"There you go. I knew you could do it." Novak smiled. "It's all up to you from here, Joel. Do the right thing and you won't ever see us again. Do the wrong thing and you'll see us one more time. The choice...the decision...is yours."

Joel hung his head, drooling blood now, still in shock and unable to process or fully comprehend what he'd just witnessed. A few feet away, Barney's body continued to twitch and convulse after death.

"Don't worry about ole Barney and the rest of this mess," Novak told him. His voice seemed farther away now, and Joel could hear his and Kavon's shoes clicking against the cement floor as they walked off. "We've got people that'll come in and clean this all up nice. Be like it never even happened. Who knows? Maybe it didn't. Maybe it was all a dream. You have a nice day, Joel. Bye now."

Joel had no idea how long he lay there with the corpse in that blown-out old factory, praying for his strength and sanity to return, but it seemed like forever.

Eventually he got to his feet and stumbled around the building until he found an exit. Without looking back, he made his way through several yards of tall grass until he reached the side of the road. His car was parked nearby, as if he'd left it there himself.

His stomach, back, and jaw throbbed with pain, his mouth tasted like blood, his head was pounding and his arms and legs felt shaky and weak. His emotions were raw and all over the place, switching second to second from tears to rage to fear to disbelief, then back again. Head spinning, Joel dropped behind the wheel and hit the ignition, savoring the warm embrace of the car heater.

When he closed his eyes, all he saw was Taylor staring back at him. There could be no life, no happiness until this was over. To solve the mysteries tormenting him, to stop whoever these people were and the horrible things they were up to, Joel knew what he had to do, and running home with his tail between his legs was not it. He'd come for answers—not just about Lonnie but himself, the others, all of it—he understood that now. People had died for those answers, and he was closer than he'd ever been or ever would be again to getting them.

Novak was right. The decision was his.

Slumped in his car, alone in a dead zone long forgotten, at the edges of a haunted old city, a city of ghosts and shadow, Joel made his choice.

There was no turning back. He'd find the truth or join the dead trying.

CHAPTER EIGHTEEN

Joel steadied himself against the wall, negotiated the stair-well, then the long hallway to his room. Legs still shaky, he fell against the room door, stuffed a hand in his jacket pocket and retrieved his room key. He inhaled slowly, did his best to ignore the sharp pains that fired along his side and up into his chest with each breath, and exhaled through his mouth. He unlocked the door, pushed it open with his shoulder and staggered in. The door closed on its own and he leaned back against it, eyes slowly adjusting to the low light. The ticking of a clock on the night-stand transcended the constant din in his head, and he focused on it a moment, counting along with the clock, concentrating on something—anything—but the pain. His mouth still tasted like blood. He'd been spitting out globs of it all the way back. He slid a hand along the wall until he found the switch, then flipped the overhead light on.

The fixture came to life, casting the room in a dull yellow haze. It was only midafternoon, and the light wasn't necessary, but it made him feel better. He waited a while, and once his heart rate slowed, he pushed himself away from the door, struggled out of his jacket and tossed it onto the bed.

Swaying a bit, he made his way to the bathroom.

Joel turned the light on so he could see his reflection in the large mirror over the sink. Although he'd wiped his face and neck clean as best he could, they were still speckled and stained with blood. He looked down and studied the dark crimson soaked into the front of his shirt, which was pasted against him like a second skin. He pulled his shirt off and let it fall to the floor. It hit the tile with a splat. He leaned forward, hands on the counter in front of him, and slowly raised his head. There was a tiny hole in the flesh near the base of his neck, a reminder of the needle Kavon had stuck him with, and the lower part of his throat was slick with the homeless man's blood. He touched his jaw, worked it up and down and back and forth. It wasn't broken, but it was stiff and sore and still grinding a bit. He bit down and felt pain up into his ear. Running the water, he spit blood into the sink, then began checking his teeth. One bottom tooth on the right and near the back was loose and bleeding, courtesy of Kavon's uppercut.

"Son of a bitch," he sighed, spit more blood, then cupped water in his hand and drank, swishing it around the tooth before spitting again. A quick inspection of his remaining teeth revealed the rest were intact and undamaged.

Once the water had warmed, Joel washed himself gently around the right side of his rib cage, which was already sporting a bright purple bruise. His stomach was red and hurt to the touch. He cleaned himself for several minutes, then toweled off and pressed a wet cloth against the back of his head. When it slammed against the wall, it hadn't broken the skin, but a lump roughly the size of a marble had already formed, and there was a pulsing pain all the way down into his neck.

He left the bathroom, grabbed his bag and dug out a white tank-top tee, a pair of jeans, and a black sweatshirt. As he dressed, he groaned occasionally, reminded of the pain even such basic physical maneuvers caused. Gathering his old clothes, right down to the jacket, which was also stained, he threw them into a plastic bag and then into the closet. Once night fell, he'd ditch the bag in the Dumpster down in the parking lot.

An urgent knock on the door froze him in his tracks. Had he

locked it behind him? No. The knob turned and the door swung open, the sound echoing through the room like a warning.

Joel was about to snatch the lamp from the nightstand and swing it like a baseball bat when he realized the person tentatively coming through the door was Billy Gill.

"Joel?"

"Billy," he said. "Jesus Christ, what are you doing here?"

"Yeah, nice to see you too, my man." Billy finished his entrance, let the door close behind him and then looked around. "Wow, this place is…um…adequate."

"The Ritz was booked. What are you doing here?"

"I talked to Taylor this morning and decided to come check on you. She's worried."

He walked deeper into the room. "Haven't made that drive in a while, forgot how mindnumbingly boring it was."

Joel lowered himself onto the edge of the bed and slipped his shoes on.

"What's the matter?" Billy asked. "You're moving and groaning like you got hit by a train."

"Close. The guy hit like one."

"What? Somebody tuned you up?"

Joel nodded. "Yeah, kind of."

"You all right? Did you go to the hospital and get checked out?"

"I'm fine."

"You don't look fine. You look like shit."

"You shouldn't have come here. You need to go home."

"Hey, I came all this way," he said, wandering over to the window. "If you think I'm getting back in that car anytime soon, it's not happening. Unless I've got you with me, in which case you can drive and I'll take a nap because—"

"*Billy*," Joel snapped.

"What?"

"You've got to go."

He stood there in his cheap and wrinkled trench coat and his cheaper polyester suit, looking uncomfortable and overweight, his comb-over mussed and his chubby cheeks bright red from the cold. "Why?"

"I've got this."

"Taylor's worried about you. Hell, I am too."

"She shouldn't have asked you to come here."

"She didn't; this is on me. She's worried to death, Joel. I heard it in her voice, so I told her I wanted to give you a call and needed to know where you were staying. Once I had the info, I decided to get in the car and come find out for myself what you'd gotten yourself into. From what I'm seeing so far, kemosabe, it's not good."

Joel got to his feet with a muffled grunt, then grabbed his coat from the closet and laid it on the bed. What was he supposed to say? That an hour or so before, he'd seen a man executed in cold blood right before his eyes? That the man had been so close to him that his blood and brains and God knew what else were all over his clothes and soaked into his skin? That this whole thing was tied to government mind control programs, secret radio stations and evil entities running around in the dark? That the same men he'd seen kill the homeless man could very well be the same duo who murdered Lonnie and left him dead in the street? That at any given moment those men could come looking for him again, and that this time he might not walk away at all? Or maybe he could tell him about how the big black car that terrorized him and his friends in their youth was somehow connected to this mess as well? Whatever was real, whatever wasn't, and whatever existed in between, Joel knew one thing for sure. What he was into was deadly, and no place for anyone he cared about.

"Who kicked your ass?" Billy asked. "Did it have something to do with that license plate you had me run?"

"Billy, listen to me. I appreciate you coming all this way to check on me. But you need to go home, and you need to do it now. Should Taylor ask, you were never here, okay?"

"What are you talking about? What's happening?"

"Go home, Billy."

"Joel, I—"

"Go home." Joel walked to the door and held it open. "Now. Go."

"Close the door and sit down," Billy said, using his best authoritative voice. "You heard me. Close the goddamn door and sit down."

Joel let the door go.

"Sit down." Billy pointed to the bed.

"I'm too fucking sore to sit down."

"Fine, then stand up, you miserable prick." He put his hands on his hips. "Now what is going on?"

"I can't tell you everything, I—"

"Everything? You haven't told me anything."

"It's not safe here. I need you to get back in the car and go home. You need to keep an eye on things for the next few days, and you need to make sure Taylor's safe. I might still be able to defuse this; I don't know. If I can, I'll be back and everything will be okay. But if in the interim anything unusual or strange happens, or if anyone suspicious shows up or calls or emails or texts or sends smoke signals or fucking carrier pigeons, you need to let me know. In the meantime, you two get out of there and go to your cabin up north. You tell no one what you're doing or where you're going, and I mean no one. Hit an ATM on the way out of town and use cash only from that point forward. No credit cards or checks. Don't use your cell phones. Once you land, stay there until you hear from me, got it? You still have the shotgun?"

"The shotgun?"

"Yes, do you still have it at the cabin?"

"Yeah, I—"

"Load it. Anyone shows up you don't know, use it. Ask questions later."

Billy frowned. "Christ, what in the hell are we dealing with here?"

"*We're* not dealing with anything."

"Oh, we're not?" Billy held his hands out to his side, then let them slap against his thighs. "You've got some granite fucking balls, my man. You're really going to stand there and tell me my life and your wife's life are in danger, to the point where I have to round her up and hide her away at my cabin in the woods, and that—oh, by the way—I might have to fucking *shoot* someone, but you're not going to give me any indication as to why or what's going on? Really? What the hell is the matter with you?"

Joel ran his hands through his hair, crossed the room and began to pace near the table. "In investigating Lonnie's murder, I've unintentionally rattled some cages, all right? And there are some very dangerous types who aren't happy about it."

"There are these people called the police, maybe you've heard of them?"

"The police can't help me."

"Why not?"

"Because they can't."

Billy thought a moment. "Are you saying the police are a part of this, or somehow in on whatever it is that's going on here?"

"Doesn't matter. They can't help me either way. It's bigger than the cops."

"Bigger."

"Yes."

"Than the cops."

"Yes."

Billy shook his head and sighed. "Okay, then why not take the hint from these people, quit while you're still alive and come home?"

"Because I can't."

"Correct me if I'm wrong," Billy said, stabbing a finger at the air between them, "but wasn't this supposed to be some basic, half-assed snooping around that wasn't going to amount to a piss hole in a snow bank? Isn't that what you told me?"

"That's what I thought."

"Well, obviously you were wrong, so cut your losses and jettison your ass out of here."

"I can't do that."

"Am I missing something?"

"I can't, Billy."

"Joel—"

"I *can't!*" He slammed a fist onto the table. "Goddamn it, you're just going to have to trust me on this one."

"Okay." Billy took a step back as what little color was left in his face drained away. "Take it easy."

"This goes deeper than you can understand. For Christ's sake, it goes deeper than I can understand." Joel turned to the window and looked out at the cold afternoon and parking lot below. Every car seemed suspect now, every person walking the street a potential threat.

"I'm concerned, man, okay? Taylor is too." Billy forced an awkward smile. "With the things you went through before and all, we just—"

"I'm not crazy."

"Never said you were."

"I wasn't then and I'm not now."

"Okay." Billy held his hands up like the victim of a robbery. "But in the past you had problems that made you ill. I need to know you haven't run into those problems again. Try to see it from my side, okay? I'm not here to hurt you, Joel. I'm trying to help. You look terrible, someone's physically assaulted you, and you're talking about this whole thing—whatever it is—being bigger than the cops and going deeper than either of us can know and being dangerous to the point where people could die, and—don't get pissed, but—a lot of this sounds kind of familiar, okay? I'm seeing similarities here, is what I'm saying."

"What do you want from me?"

"I need to know you're all right. You're not exactly coming off rational."

Maybe because I just washed another human being's brains off my face.

"I wish I could tell you more," Joel said. "But I can't."

"Taylor said you have pills that calm you when you need to—"

"I don't need pills."

"Look me in the eye."

Joel did. "I don't need my pills. I'm not coming apart like before. I'm *not.*"

"Okay," Billy said softly.

"Do you really want to help?"

"Of course I do."

"Then you need to listen to me and trust what I'm saying."

"All right."

"Please—*please*, Billy—go home and do as I asked. This is serious shit, and I need you to have my back. I need to know I can count on you."

"You know you can."

Flashes of the homeless man's head exploding blinked in Joel's mind. He squeezed shut his eyes but it only made the images more vivid. "I don't want you to get hurt. I don't want anyone to get hurt."

Billy stood there staring at him, disheveled and confused.

Joel reached out, took his friend by the shoulders, pulled him in close and hugged him tight. "You're my best friend," he whispered in his ear, "and I love you like a brother. I know you're worried about me, but you need to do like I say. *Exactly* like I say, Billy. There's no other way. Now go home."

Moments later, from the hotel room window, he watched Billy cross the parking lot to his car. As he pulled away and out of sight, Joel could only wonder if he'd ever see him again.

There were no guarantees now. There never had been.

Evil wasn't in the guarantee business.

CHAPTER NINETEEN

Dorsey stands in the field, smoking a cigarette and trying to look cool. He can usually pull it off without a problem, but not today. They've all tried cigarettes by now, but only he and Trent have taken to them, and Trent rarely even inhales. At thirteen it's difficult to get hold of cigarettes, but Dorsey managed to score an entire pack of Winston Lights for their overnight camping trip. He taps the pack until another butt comes free, then holds it out for Trent, who plucks the cigarette out and stabs it into the corner of his mouth. He doesn't light it. Instead, he stands next to Dorsey with a perplexed look on his face. Like the others, he attempts to make sense of what's happening, what has happened.

"It's just a game," Sal says. It's the third or fourth time he's said it.

The sun is high and bright in the sky. Joel looks up at it, as if for answers, while the others stand around in a daze.

How long have they been lying down in the grass? When did they decide to pretend to sleep in the field? Why did they pretend to do that? What game were they playing? Nothing makes any sense, and yet somehow their minds tell them it does. You came to the field and pretended to fall asleep for a few minutes. The game is over now.

"Stop saying that," Dorsey finally tells him.

"What?" Sal asks.

"It's just a game."

"But it is just a game."

Dorsey draws on his cigarette, exhales through his nose. "I don't feel right."

"Me neither," Lonnie says, nervously running his hands up and down his torso as if searching for wounds.

Trent, who has still not lit the cigarette, begins to tremble. Tears spill across his cheeks. He wipes them away fast as he can, takes a few steps away and turns his back so the others won't see. But it's too late. They have seen.

Dorsey and Lonnie begin to cry too. Silently, tears stream down their faces.

Joel nods as if he understands—even though he doesn't—and feels tears dripping from his eyes as well. What is the matter with them? What's going on?

Only Sal is dry-eyed. "It was just a game," he says dully.

"The car," Dorsey says, like he's just remembered it.

The others turn to him. Yes. The car. They'd all forgotten about the big black car. But wasn't that the last thing they all remembered?

"The big black car," Dorsey says, the cigarette smoke circling him.

"It tried to scare us," Sal says. "It's gone now."

Lonnie puts his hands to his head, holding his temples. "When was that?"

"Something happened," Trent says, pacing about awkwardly. He removes the unlit cigarette from his mouth, then brings it to his lips and takes it away over and over again. "Something happened. Something bad."

"When did the car try to scare us?" Lonnie asks.

Dorsey hangs his head. "I don't know."

"I remember the car," Joel says.

"We all remember the car, Einstein," Lonnie snaps. "When did it happen?"

"A few minutes ago." Joel looks to the others. "Right?"

Dorsey shakes his head. "I don't...I don't think so."

Trent stares at the trees on the far side of the field, like he expects to see something emerge from them at any moment. "Something happened," he says.

"Let's split." Sal marches away, over to their bikes, which have all been left in a pile in the grass along with their camping gear. He tosses the other bikes aside until he gets to his own, stands it up and brushes it off. "Stop being pussy squirts."

"What happened to the car?" Lonnie asks, barely containing himself.

"It left," Sal answers. "It drove off. What the fuck with you guys?"

"No," Joel says. "It came back. I saw it turn around and come back."

"Me too," Trent says.

"Okay." Lonnie moves closer to them. "Okay, then what?"

Dorsey stumbles through the grass. "I don't feel right."

"Somebody fucking answer me!" Lonnie screams. "What happened when the big black car turned around and came back?"

"I don't know," Joel tells him.

"Nothing happened," Sal says, straddling his bike. "You guys are acting like a bunch of wimps. Letting a car scare you this bad and all crying and shit? Come on, man, you got to be fucking shitting me."

Trent spins around and flicks his still-unlit cigarette at Sal. "Eat shit, man! You're as scared as the rest of us!"

The cigarette bounces off the side of Sal's head. He glares at Trent. "What am I supposed to be scared of, dipshit?"

"How the fuck did we get here?" Lonnie asks.

"We were lying down in the grass," Sal says. "What's wrong with you guys?"

Dorsey takes a slow drag on his cigarette. "Did we go to sleep?"

"We were pretending. It was just a game."

Trent moves toward him. "Say it was just a game one more fucking time."

"Blow it out your ass, Trent." Sal gets off his bike, lets it fall to the ground as he squares his stance. "Any time, faggot."

Lonnie cuts Trent off, blocks him from reaching Sal and probably the worst beating of his life. "Knock it off, both of you!"

"We're not supposed to do this," Dorsey says.

The others turn to him, unsure of what he means.

"We're not supposed to talk about it. We're not supposed to remember."

Joel wanders away from the group, trying to sort his thoughts. He looks at his watch. It's new. His parents got it for him for his birthday this year. It displays not only the time, but also the day and date.

"Wait," he says, turning back toward the others. "Wait, what—what day is it?"

"Saturday," Sal says.

"My watch says Sunday."

"So what? It's wrong."

"No," Joel tells him, "it isn't."

The cigarette falls from Dorsey's mouth into the grass at his feet. "It's Sunday morning, cuz?"

"It's Saturday," Sal insists. "We just got here."

Trent says, "But if it's Sunday morning, then..."

Joel sinks to his knees. "Where were we all day yesterday?"

"And last night?" Lonnie adds.

Trent begins to cough. It quickly escalates to choking.

The others look to him. Panic and confusion paint his face.

As his eyes roll back in his head, a mass of butterflies pours from his open mouth, swarming the air around him to form a cloud of fluttering wings both horrific and curiously beautiful.

Much like the chorus of screams ripping to shreds the blissful silence of an otherwise peaceful Sunday morning.

Joel watched the neighborhood as best he could, scanning the area again and again. Through the large front windows, he saw men in whites working in the bakery across the street. Delivery trucks from the soft drink bottling plant on the corner came and went with regularity. The windows and door of a convenience store a few doors down were plastered with advertisements for discount cigarettes, coffee, and breakfast burritos. A liquor store with bars across the windows occupied the next corner, the exterior of the building covered in graffiti.

Above it was the small apartment where Dorsey Hill lived with his girlfriend.

Dodging traffic, Joel crossed the street. He entered the building through a door to the side of the liquor store entrance and was met by a battered, graffiti-covered hallway and a staircase leading to the second-floor apartment.

He climbed the stairs and arrived at a door scarred and worn, its paint old and badly chipped. Joel knocked, and a harried-looking woman in a tan polyester dress with a white apron answered the door a moment later.

"Yes?" she asked, annoyed.

Joel tried to smile, probably failed. "Is Dorsey in?"

The woman looked him up and down. "Who's asking?"

"If you could tell him Joel Walker's here to see him, I'd appreciate it."

"What do you want with Dorsey? Leave the man alone."

"I need to talk to him. Is he here or not?"

"Nita, it's all right," a voice said from behind her.

The woman sighed, gave Joel one last dirty look, then moved away.

Before Joel could fully process her reaction to him, Dorsey stepped into view. He looked a lot older and very tired, his Afro gone, the hair now buzzed close to his scalp and peppered with gray. His body was still thin and well muscled, but his posture was hunched, and he moved as if it was difficult for him to do so without pain. Though his eyes were not as bright as they'd once been, like he always had, he smiled with them first. "Sally said you'd come." His voice was raspier than in his youth. "How you been, cuz?"

"Been better, man. What do you say?"

"I say it's been too long." Dorsey wrapped him up in an unexpected hug.

He smelled of cheap cologne and cigarettes, but it was such a pure and genuine gesture Joel couldn't help but be deeply moved. "Good to see you, Dorse."

His old friend let him go, and they both stood there awkwardly.

"I'd invite you in," Dorsey said, "but I don't like white people in the house."

Joel laughed lightly. If nothing else, Dorsey's sense of humor was still intact. "Can't blame you there."

"You're not missing anything, and besides," Dorsey said, lowering his voice, "Juanita's the protective type, dig? She's getting ready for work, doing the dinner shift tonight, so let me get a coat; we'll talk outside and stay out of her way."

Moments later, as they took the stairs and ventured out onto the street and into the cold air, Joel noticed that Dorsey, now wearing a gray knit hat and a pea coat, walked with a slight limp. Traffic was heavy, but otherwise there weren't many people on the street. Dorsey motioned to a nearby playground surrounded by chain-link fence, and they headed in that direction.

It smelled like the ocean here, as it wasn't far, but mixed with engine exhaust, grime, baked goods, and a mingling of other foods—largely a combination of fresh and fried fish—from local establishments. At the far end of the avenue, wind blew in off the Atlantic, bringing with it an icy chill. Joel stuffed his hands in his pockets, tucked chin to chest and walked on, ignoring the pain in his ribs and along his jaw.

"Sometimes I feel the need to get out on the street," Dorsey told him. "Walk the neighborhood and breathe the air, feel the city pulsing and moving all around me. Helps me remember I'm not so alone in the world, reminds me I'm connected to something bigger and alive. Makes me feel…normal. Close as I ever get, anyway."

Normal, Joel thought. He had no idea what that even meant anymore.

"Didn't think I'd ever see you again," Dorsey said.

"Didn't think I'd ever be back."

"Still doing the reporter thing?"

"So they tell me." Joel slowed his pace a bit so Dorsey could keep up.

"I haven't worked retail in years," Dorsey explained. "Had a couple babies with my ex and all that changed. Needed more money, so I started fishing. Worked the same crew for years. Good money, but hard work and away from home a lot. Stopped a while back, had to go on disability. My body can't take it anymore. Bad back, my knees are all fucked up, got to take a handful of pain pills just to get out of bed in the morning. Sucks to get old, man. And the babies, a boy and a girl, they're all grown up now. Don't have much time for their pops these days, got their own lives and families. Always been partial to their mother anyway. Can't blame them; she raised them and I was hardly ever home. Just paid the bills. Got lucky and met Nita a few years ago. She's a good woman. Tough as leather and mean as a snake, but a good woman." They passed through the gates to the playground, which consisted of a run-down swing set, jungle gym, and basketball court with rusted hoops sans nets, and settled over by a couple out-of-the-way picnic tables. "Sad sight, isn't it? Empty playground, I mean. Even in winter, doesn't look right."

Sad was a good word for it. The entire neighborhood was draped in an intrinsic melancholy and dreariness so thick it was palpable. "Dorsey—"

"Never got the chance to tell you," he interrupted, pulling a pack of smokes from his pocket. "But I was proud of you, cuz. You lit it up back in the day."

"I crashed and burned, that's all."

"What, all that devil shit? It got crazy toward the end, sure, every nut in the country got in on it, every bad psychologist and church-lady lunatic, but that doesn't mean it was all lies. The radical religious types took it too far, not you. Never seen a group of people go on and on about Jesus this and Jesus that, then do everything they can to drive folks as far away from Jesus as they can get." With a great deal of effort, he stepped up on the bench, sat atop the picnic table and lit a cigarette. "Smoke?"

"No thanks."

He put the pack back in his coat pocket. "I read your book. You got it right. People around here lived it. Few even died. Shit, look what it did to you."

Joel held his tongue and stood between the tables and the fence, alternating his gaze between Dorsey and the street.

Sounds of the city filled the silence until Dorsey said, "Never thought Lonnie would go first." He let the cigarette dangle from his mouth, then put his hands in his coat pockets. "Maybe me. Or Trent, that crazy bastard, but not Lonnie."

The day was overcast and bleak, and in a few hours it would be dark. Joel didn't want to be there once night fell. He didn't want to be anywhere once night fell.

"I used to bust balls, call him Deputy Dog. He'd get so pissed." Dorsey smiled, took a drag on his cigarette and exhaled through his nose. "Remember how he'd get so pissed he'd start laughing? Could always make Lonnie laugh."

Joel wanted to smile too, because he did remember that about Lonnie, but he couldn't seem to summon it. "Dorse," he said, "we need to talk."

He looked out at the playground and street beyond, his smile dead. "Yeah."

"Did you know Lonnie was in contact with Trent before his death?"

The sound of Trent's name caused him to turn back to Joel.

After a moment he looked away again, then shook his head no. "I didn't think anybody saw or heard from Trent in forever. You sure about that?"

"Relatively."

"Lonnie would've told me."

"If he felt he could've. He did talk to you about what was happening to him, didn't he?"

Dorsey puffed his cigarette. "Nita didn't like him coming around. He was having problems and it upset me. I...I started having nightmares."

"About what?"

"Hadn't had them in years. It was one of the things I loved about being out at sea. Never had them out there. One of the most dangerous jobs in the world, but I never felt safer in my life. Before or since."

"What were the nightmares about?"

"You know what they were about, Joel."

"Tell me anyway."

Dorsey finally plucked the cigarette from his mouth. "I thought it was over," he said, his voice beginning to shake. "Lonnie did too—shit, we all did—but then it started up again. Whatever got to Lonnie triggered it, I..."

"Triggered what, the nightmares?"

"He was seeing bad shit." Dorsey flicked the cigarette away. "*Demons.*"

"Were you seeing them too?"

Dorsey looked at him, his face a grimace of pain and terror.

"Are you seeing them right now?" Joel pressed.

As if in answer, the wind blew paper and refuse across the otherwise empty basketball court. A few blocks away, a siren blared, then faded.

"Everything was okay for a long time," Dorsey said, wincing. "Wasn't it?"

"I thought so."

"Why now? After all these years?"

"Ever heard of Tuser Industries?"

"No. What is it?"

"Company over in the south end."

"What's it got to do with us?"

"The name Pete Fernandez mean anything to you?"

Dorsey shook his head.

"Fernandez worked with Lonnie," Joel explained. "But he and Lonnie were both also involved with some sort of program over at Tuser Industries. I think Lonnie might've even been unknowingly recruiting for them and brought Fernandez into the fold. Either way, they're serious people, man. Dangerous people. They were experimenting on him and others there. Mind control experiments, Dorse."

Dorsey dug out another cigarette and lit it, this time with shaking hands. "What the hell's that even mean?"

"Something happened to us."

"Keep dazzlin' and I'm gonna start calling you the Amazing Kreskin."

"Hilarious."

"Beats crying."

"Dorse, whatever happened, it happened to all of us—when we were kids—and whatever it was, it's connected somehow to what was going on with Lonnie at Tuser and what's happening to all of us now."

Dorsey manically smoked his cigarette a while. "Have you seen them?" he finally asked, his voice nearly a whisper.

"No," Joel said. "But I…back when I had my problems, I thought…I thought things like that were inside me, inside my head and…talking to me."

"But not anymore?"

Growls and whispers at the very edges of his perception…

"No. Not anymore."

He opened his coat enough to reach his free hand inside and pull out a piece of paper. It was folded up to about the size of a business card. Dorsey put his smoke in his mouth and, using both trembling hands, unfolded the paper. "Sometimes if I draw them, they get out of my head for a while." Placing it across his knees, then smoothing it out, he held it up for Joel to see. "This is what they look like."

Done in pencil, a crudely drawn series of frightening humanoid figures filled the paper, their limbs long, distorted and extended, as if reaching out for him. They looked exactly like the ones Lonnie had drawn in his notebook.

But this drawing included something more.

In the upper right-hand corner was a much smaller but clearer depiction of a car and four stick figures lying down in what looked like grass or weeds.

A single snowflake appeared in the sky, slowly spiraling down toward the basketball court. Joel and Dorsey watched it ride the wind, dancing for them before making its final descent to the pavement. Just like the thoughts and visions in their heads, more would follow. This was only the beginning.

"I never told anyone," Dorsey said softly.

"Me either."

Dorsey smoked the rest of his cigarette, then flicked it away. Smoke swirled around him like rolling fog. "Nita knows something happened when I was a kid, but she doesn't know what. Never been able to tell her."

"Do you even know yourself?" Joel asked.

He folded up the paper and slid it back into his coat. "The car."

"To this day Sal still says it was all just a game."

"For years I had myself convinced that's what it was. Bunch of kids lying down in the grass, pretending we were…"

"We were what?"

Dorsey shrugged. "We were gone a day. A whole day, man, just…gone."

"We were in that car, weren't we?"

"I think so." Dorsey ran a hand across his mouth and sighed. "We weren't in the field the whole time, I know that much. We never even set up our gear."

"What did they do to us, Dorse?"

"I don't know, but whatever it was, it wasn't the first time."

The revelation slammed Joel like a punch to the chest. He'd never thought of it before, yet the moment the words registered, he knew Dorsey was right.

"Whoever they were, they already knew us," he continued. "It wasn't like they came across some random kids and made their move, dig? They knew we'd be there. They knew *us*. They'd taken us before, plenty of times, just not all at once."

A tremor shuddered through Joel's body. "Why do you say that?"

"I remember being in a place. It was all white, like a hospital maybe. I was on a gurney, and these people were wheeling me down a long hallway. I remember the lights overhead passing by real slow. I dreamed about that for years before the day with the big black car. But when I remember that weekend, I remember the same thing happening, like in the dream. I feel it, and I know it's something I felt before. Not once, but a lot of times."

"Do you remember anything else?"

"Being afraid." Dorsey seemed to come back from wherever he'd been in his head and quickly dug his cigarettes out again. "Now it's just the dreams. I don't know how much more I can take, cuz. I'm scared all the time."

Joel remembered Pete Fernandez telling him the same thing. He decided to test the waters and cast a line. "What about the numbers, Dorse, the sounds?"

"They're in my head too," he said. "Falling through my mind like..."

"Rain?"

Dorsey looked at him with equal parts terror and hope. "You too?"

"No, but I have the dreams. The numbers and sounds were things Lonnie suffered from, and so does the guy he worked with I told you about."

"There's a message in them, but I don't know what it is. It's just out of reach. Like whispers you know you heard but can't make out."

On the other side of the fence, three young guys in heavy jackets walked parallel to the playground. Joel watched them until they turned the corner and disappeared from sight.

"It's like sometimes the whole goddamn world's inside my head," Dorsey told him. "And it's all in flames."

Joel wanted to comfort him somehow, but it was beyond that. It had been for a very long time.

"Like the shit you ran into in your book." Dorsey took a hard pull on his cigarette. "You think all that went away? What, evil got cured? That cult disbanded and they're all living good lives now, baking cookies and shit? That what happened to those fucks? You *proved* connections existed between them and a nationwide group of sick-ass motherfuckers. That all went up in smoke, dissolved into nothing, huh? The psychos that slaughtered that poor Portuguese girl—what—they went straight? Shit, listen to people now and you'd think none of it ever happened. You'd think the Devil's the good guy in all this and the rest of us are crazy."

Joel nodded but refrained from answering, the fear he'd felt back then boiling to the surface, strangling him along with all the rest.

"That's the beauty of evil," Dorsey said. "It hides for a while, that's all. Waits. Changes. Comes back. Stronger. Meaner. Not a villain anymore, but the hero. And we all open wide and swallow it down."

"Like the dreams," Joel said.

"Like the dreams."

"I need to find Trent. I need to know what he knows. We all do."

"Sal says Trent's nuts."

"Maybe so. Maybe we all are. But this is no game, Dorse. Whoever these people are, they killed Lonnie, and there's a good chance they'll come after the rest of us too. I've already been threatened. I've seen firsthand what they're capable of, and it's hardcore, man. Serious hardcore."

"What are they going to do, kill us like they did Lonnie? We're already dead, cuz. Been dead for years, just didn't know it. We all died in that field back home. Didn't none of us get out of there alive."

"I'm going to end this," Joel told him. "One way or another."

Something shifted in Dorsey's face. He smoked his cigarette a while. "That's what Lonnie told me," he finally said. "Last time I saw him alive."

A few more renegade flakes fell from the sky, riding the wind.

"Trent's mother's in a nursing home here in the city," Joel said.

"He was never that close to his mother." Dorsey's cigarette was smoked down to the filter. He stared at it as if he'd only then realized it was in his hand. "Think about it. None of us were close to our parents. Before that day or after."

Joel nodded. Dorsey was right again. "Still, she might know where he is."

Dorsey flicked the butt away. "You think he's close?"

"I think he might be."

They were quiet a while. The snow picked up, but still wasn't accumulating.

"There isn't as much of me left as there used to be, but I can still rumble pretty good for an old man." Dorsey smiled sadly, as if he'd remembered something. "You need me, I'm here. Sal too."

"Sal didn't seem too receptive."

"You let me worry about that stubborn-ass guinea."

Just like old times, Joel thought. *He can call Sal that all day, but let someone else do it and it's time to throw.* It brought back so many happy memories, it made him want to smile. Almost.

Instead, screams whispered to him from the farthest reaches of his mind, dragging him back to the dark, and the madness that nested there.

"I'll be in touch." Joel offered his fist. "Be safe."

Dorsey bumped his fist against Joel's. "Ain't no such thing."

CHAPTER TWENTY

As night drifted over the city, Joel stood on a corner across the street from the Whaling City Shores Nursing Home and Rehabilitation Facility, a three-story rectangular building that looked like a hospital out of the 1930s. Drab and run-down and located in a less than prime neighborhood, this was not a place that housed the wealthy or privileged. Though a few renegade snowflakes still sputtered about, the temperature had gotten a bit warmer, and the air now felt more like rain.

Watching the facility, Joel dialed Katelyn Burrows' number. This was beyond her, and for her own safety, she needed to be removed from anything that might happen from this point forward. He owed Lonnie that, and the only way to assure his daughter was out of the equation was for Joel to sever his ties with her as quickly and with as much finality as possible.

"Katelyn," he said when she answered, "Joel Walker."

"Hello," she said tentatively. "How are you making out?"

"I was going to come by and see you so we could talk face-to-face," he lied, knowing this would be the first of many, "but I have some things back home I have to attend to."

"You're going home?"

"Katelyn, I've looked into things as best I can. I even spoke, off the record, with the police. I know you don't have a lot of faith in them right now, but within the next few days—if not sooner—they're going to be in touch with you regarding your father's murder."

"Have they discovered something new?"

"Odds are they're going to tell you that their investigation has led them to believe Lonnie was killed in a small-time drug deal gone wrong. They don't know who did it yet and they may never know, but Katelyn, you need to listen to them."

"And why would I do that? You and I both know that's nonsense."

Joel drew a deep breath and did his best to sound sincere. "A few days ago I would've agreed with you. Now, I think you need to listen to what the police have to say. You need to accept it, understand it for the horrible and senseless tragedy that it was, and then you and your husband need to move on with your lives. Start a family of your own, be happy. It's what Lonnie would want."

A long silence, and then, "What changed your mind?"

"The police weren't at liberty to go into much detail since it's still an open investigation, but after looking into things myself and speaking with one of the detectives directly, my advice is to listen to what they have to tell you." A cold blast of wind blew along the avenue and slammed into him. He turned his back to it and pressed the phone tighter against his ear. "It's over, Katelyn. It is what it is. I'm heading back to Maine tonight. I'll drop Lonnie's keys in the mail to you."

"Mr. Walker, can I—"

"Joel."

"*Mr. Walker*, may I ask you one more question?"

"Of course."

"Are you telling me the truth?"

Joel watched the cars pass along the avenue. None were the Crown Vic. "Yes." When she offered no reply, he said, "Lonnie was a casual marijuana user. I believe he may have been suffering from some serious depression and paranoia. That may have been what the pills the police took were for. I think he wound up on the wrong street with the wrong guy at the wrong time and paid the price for it. We may never have all the answers, Katelyn, or even any that make sense to us or in any way make us feel better. But that certainly appears to be what happened."

"When you agreed to do this, you told me—"

"I told you not to get your hopes up. I did my best. I'm sorry."

"If I get additional information, should I let you know, or would you rather I leave you alone?"

"I'd rather you remember and take comfort in how deeply your father loved and adored you. And I'd rather you get on with your life, Katelyn."

"All right. Then I'll let you do the same. Thank you for your help."

Before he could say anything else, Katelyn hung up.

With a sigh, Joel put his phone away. *You might hate me right now,* he thought, *but I may have just saved your life.*

Waiting for a break in traffic, he hurried across the street to the nursing home just as an icy rain began to fall.

Once he made his way across a large front parking lot, Joel entered through two sliding doors. A security guard greeted him in the foyer. Old and frail enough to be living there, the guard looked up at him from the plastic chair he was sitting in but said nothing. Behind comically thick glasses, the old man's gigantic eyes blinked at him.

"Evening," Joel said. "Reception?"

The guard returned his attention to a crossword puzzle book he was working on. "Straight ahead, son," he muttered.

Joel went through another doorway and down a short hallway to a reception desk, where a woman in a flowered top was chatting on a telephone. As she saw Joel approaching, she held a finger up, signaling him to wait. When she'd finished, she hung up and smiled at him pleasantly. "Yes?"

"I'm here to see a resident."

"Who is it you'd like to see?"

"Theresa Pierce."

"And you are?"

"Joel Walker."

"Your relation to Ms. Pierce?"

"Friend of the family."

"One moment." The woman consulted her computer, clicking at the keyboard before her with bright red fingernails. Frowning suddenly, she pointed to a nearby waiting area and said, "You can have a seat over there and someone will be with you shortly."

"Is everything all right?"

"If you'll just have a seat, someone will be out to talk with you shortly."

Joel nodded and wandered over to the waiting area, which consisted of dated, cheap furniture and a bevy of magazines older than he was. Rather than sit, he stood in the otherwise empty area and watched the television suspended in the corner. The sound was turned down but the local news was on. He looked over his shoulder at the double doors and lot beyond. It was getting dark and the rain had picked up.

"Mr. Walker?" a female voice asked from behind him.

Joel turned to find a nurse moving toward him. "Yes."

"Reception said you were here to see Theresa Pierce?"

"Yes. I'm a friend of the family."

"I'm Brittany Baptiste. I run the unit Ms. Pierce is on."

He plastered the warmest smile he could muster across his face. "Hi. I'm visiting from out of town, thought I'd stop in and see her. Haven't seen Theresa in ages—is everything okay?"

"I'm sorry," the nurse said, "but Ms. Pierce had an episode earlier and she's been taken to the hospital."

"An episode? Is she all right?"

"I'm afraid I can't go into any detail or disclose anything more regarding her medical condition," she said. "Sorry. HIPAA laws."

"Of course, I understand. Gosh, I hope she's okay. I'm only in town tonight and won't be back for quite some time." Joel sighed dramatically. "Are you allowed to tell me which hospital she's been taken to?"

"I'm really not supposed to."

"Saint Luke's?" he asked quietly.

The nurse pursed her lips, looked behind her at the reception desk, then moved closer and quietly said, "She was transferred over there a few hours ago."

"Thank you so much."

"She's a sweetheart. I hope she's going to be all right."

"Me too. Thanks again."

The nurse turned and walked off down the hallway from which she'd come. Joel looked up at the television in the corner. A breaking news story banner flashed across the screen beneath the talking head reading the news. Without volume he couldn't hear what was being said, but the graphic at the bottom of the screen read: SECURITY GUARD DEAD. Joel frantically looked around, found a remote control lying next to the stack of magazines and aimed it at the set until the volume rose enough for him to hear it.

"The man," the newscaster said in his best sorrowful voice, "identified as Peter Fernandez of New Bedford, was a former security guard at the mall in North Dartmouth. Police found the body in a car in the mall parking lot after it was reported by passersby earlier this afternoon that there was someone in the car, covered in blood and not moving or responding. Fernandez, in an apparent suicide, slashed his own throat and was pronounced dead on the scene. Police say he had been deceased for several hours when they found him in the driver's seat with the car doors locked. Family told *Action News 3* that Fernandez had been fired from his job recently and had become despondent due to his inability to find employment…"

"Not too loud, please," the receptionist said.

Joel muted the TV, dropped the remote back atop the stack of magazines and stood there in stunned silence. The terrified face of Pete Fernandez drifted through his mind. *God Almighty*, he thought. *They're going to kill us all.*

Magic is real, Pete whispered to him, as if from the grave. *Did you know that?*

He headed back out, passed by the old guard in the plastic chair and slipped away into the darkness and falling rain.

CHAPTER TWENTY-ONE

Tell me what you remember, Joel.

What I remember isn't possible.

What do you remember?

The car...the field...but...I can see it like when it was happening.

Did the car come back, Joel?

Yes. It circled back for us and then stopped. We couldn't see inside because the windows and windshield were tinted dark. Only the back window was clear, but the way the car was parked and facing us, we couldn't see that yet. Everyone was nervous and didn't know what to do. Sal was the one that approached the car first.

What did Sal do, Joel?

He walked to the edge of the field and started yelling at the car, asking the people inside what they wanted and why they'd tried to run us down. But no one answered or got out. The car just sat there.

Did you try to run, Joel?

I wanted to, but I couldn't move. I couldn't stop looking at the car.

Did they take you, Joel?

I only remember wanting to sleep...needing to sleep.

Do you remember The Wizard of Oz, Joel?

It used to be on TV once a year when I was a child. I never missed it.

Do you remember Dorothy and the others running toward Oz through a field of poppies?

Yes.

They fell asleep before they reached Oz, do you remember?

They fell asleep in the field.

Yes.

Just like us.

Yes, Joel.

But Dorothy and the others woke up in Oz. We didn't wake up in Oz.

Where did you wake up, Joel?

They took us, they...

Where did you wake up, Joel?

We were in the car, but I don't know how they got us inside. I re-member standing on the edge of the field and watching the car speed away. I wanted to do something. I wanted to stop them, but I couldn't because I was in the car too. I could see myself in the backseat, my face and hands pressed to the back window, my mouth open in a scream, I...I was standing at the edge of the field...watching myself being taken away with the others in that big black car.

Where did you wake up, Joel?

I can't breathe, I— I want to breathe, I—we didn't wake up in Oz.

Where then? Where did you wake up, Joel?

In Hell...

The rain fell in icy sheets, coming down hard and soaking the city. Joel hurried across the lot, visibility low in the darkness and downpour, feet splashing puddles as he went. He'd nearly made the curb when something separated from the darkness to his right, a blur that registered in his peripheral vision just seconds before it slammed into him with such violence that he left his feet and crashed to the wet pavement.

Landing on his shoulder and rolling through the fall, he scrambled to his feet, disoriented and trying to find his bearings as the form emerged from the dark rain. From behind it came a second figure.

A slash of headlights from a passing car glided past, briefly illuminating two faces otherwise cloaked in shadows and darkness: Novak and Kavon. Novak was smiling, but it was the knife in Kavon's hand that drew Joel's attention.

"You just couldn't leave it alone for me, could you, Joel?" Novak said, his voice barely audible above the rain. "So now it's dying time."

Drenched and still trying to catch his breath, Joel took a step back. He could run for the street or try to make it back across the lot to the nursing home entrance, but neither choice held much hope.

"Go ahead," Novak said. "Run."

Instead, he raised his fists and held his ground. "Fuck you."

Novak began to laugh.

Kavon rushed him, turning the knife back and forth and thrusting it at Joel as he circled away, trying to keep both men in his line of sight. I'm in the middle of a city, he thought. *How can this be happening? Where is everyone? Where are the police?* But the storm had forced nearly everyone indoors, and those on the streets were driving, their visibility limited and attention distracted by the rain.

He and the others were little more than shadows in the rain.

As Kavon closed on him, Joel threw a combination with everything he had. Both punches landed flush on Kavon's chin.

Unfazed, he walked right through them.

Stumbling away, Joel threw a wild backhand, but it was too late. The knife was already moving; he could see it coming for his chest as if in slow motion. At the last moment he spun away, and the blade struck his arm. What initially felt like a hard punch quickly turned to searing pain as Kavon yanked the knife free of Joel's shoulder. Ribbons of blood flew through the darkness, and Joel's arm went limp. Numbness exploded and spread all the way to his fingertips.

My God, I—I'm stabbed.

In shock, Joel froze, unable to believe what was happening even as Kavon slammed a granite forearm into his face, clipping him with the point of his elbow on the followthrough. Pain erupted across his brow, and Joel felt his knees buckle. Head spinning and stomach turning, he dropped and fell over onto his back, flopping onto the pavement in a splashing spray of blood, ice, and rain. Vision blurred, he tried to will himself back to his feet, but his body refused to comply with his mind's frantic demands. The rain, cold and wet, fell across his face and into his eyes.

Kavon straddled him, pulled him up into a sitting position, then yanked his head back by his hair and leveled the knife at Joel's throat. The tip of the blade pricked his skin as Kavon pressed it harder against the flesh, ready to slash Joel's throat from ear to ear.

I'm going to die, Joel thought. *Here, in the rain.*

Suddenly a shadow dressed in black emerged from the surrounding darkness behind Kavon and, utilizing uncanny speed and efficiency, wrapped arms around Kavon's head, sliding one beneath his chin and across his throat, the other over his forehead. A single violent twist snapped Kavon's neck with a loud, gut-wrenching crack. His body collapsed, falling next to Joel in a heap, the knife clanging against cement as it bounced away into the night.

Still on his back, Joel squirmed away as the shadowy figure was absorbed again into darkness. Another passing car briefly illuminated the area, revealing Novak with a gun in his hand, spinning like a top while frantically trying to locate the phantom.

But there was no one else there.

Joel rolled over. Spitting blood, he raised his head and peered through the darkness. With Novak still distracted, he struggled back to his feet and staggered away. Light-headed, legs rubbery, and his face and shoulder throbbing with pain, he somehow managed to make it back to his car without falling.

Fighting the pain, and with one arm rendered all but useless, he sped off, letting the night hide him behind its curtains of darkness and rain.

Weak and bleeding heavily from his shoulder, Joel fled the city.

Driving through the heavy downpour, he struggled to remain conscious. Hazy, his vision still slightly blurred, he dropped the window and let the cold air and icy rain spray against his face. He couldn't go back to his hotel room, and he couldn't risk going to Sal's house or Dorsey's apartment without putting them in more danger than they were already in, so those options were out too. He had to go somewhere no one would think to look for him.

What seemed like hours but was only minutes later, Joel crossed the Braga Bridge and slipped into Fall River. Eventually he reached Lonnie's neighborhood, parked a street away, then stumbled through the rain to the apartment building.

Once inside and out of the rain, Joel looked at Lonnie's front door and felt a twinge of fear. He didn't want to pass by that door, and he wasn't sure he could climb the stairs in his current condition, but he needed to do both or he'd collapse right where he was and be at the mercy of whatever was wandering around in the building.

Keeping his eye on the door, he dragged himself to the stairs and began to climb. He hadn't gotten far when he heard rustling behind him. Either something had scurried across the foyer below, or things were alive and moving inside that first-floor apartment.

Without looking back, Joel kept on, fighting to remain conscious until he'd reached Bea's door and managed two solid knocks.

Bea opened her door to find him slumped against the wall, battered and drenched, his face bruised and bloody, a gruesome gash more than an inch in length above his eyebrow, and his shoulder and coat covered in blood.

"Oh my God!" she said, reaching for him. "Joel, what happened?"

"I'm sorry," he muttered. "No police, no ambulance."

Then he fell into her as everything went dark.

Moving…motion…lights mounted in the ceiling overhead slide past. Lying atop a gurney that is being wheeled down a long hallway, he is not strapped down or restrained in any way, yet he is unable to move. He looks up and tries to see behind him, but all he can make out in the periphery is the shape of a man dressed in white, pushing the gurney, a surgical mask covering his face.

Sounds. Strange sounds echo throughout the corridor from hidden speakers. Music and voices, but in short, peculiar bursts interspersed with loud noises—clangs and screeches and trumpeting—they assault his mind and make him uneasy, edgy, afraid.

Where am I?

The lights blink and he is in a room, a dark room.

Colors and faces appear, drift, sliding along the walls and ceiling like ghosts. Odd tones sound, coming from all around him, as if alive and flying about the room in circles. A severe burst of blinding white light suddenly fills the room, and Joel tries again to raise his head. He fails, and in an attempt to look away from the bright light flooding down on him, looks to the floor.

It is covered in a black-and-white checkerboard pattern.

His eyes drift upward, just before the bright light goes out, and he realizes the walls are covered in the same pattern. "What's happening to me?" *he asks. Or did he only think it? He cannot be sure.*

Everything stops. Darkness and silence fill the room.

All Joel can hear is the thudding of his heart in his chest.

But he is not alone. There are others here with him, hidden in the dark. He can't see them.

He can feel them, their presence. Leering at him and coming closer and closer still, until he can smell and feel their hot, rancid breath against his face.

He wants to move, has to move; he needs to get out of here, but he can't move because they've done something to him and he doesn't know what it is or where he is or what's happening, but he's so afraid, so very afraid. He can't think straight and—

Please, dear God, help me!

Through the darkness, strange shapes converge on him.

They're touching me. No, I—I don't want them touching me—please make it stop, please stop touching me please—

Something is fitted to his head, affixed to his temples.

Please, what are you doing to me?

Fingers—smooth and tasting like chemicals—are forced into his mouth. He feels a liquid running across his tongue and down his throat. He chokes but it keeps coming, and just when he's sure he'll vomit, it stops and the hands leave his mouth.

And then, pain. The worst pain Joel has ever felt in his young life.

Were he able to speak, he would beg them for mercy, for death. But all he can manage are gurgling sounds and occasional wails of agony.

The torture stops, only to begin again seconds later.

In time, when Joel believes he will die—is dying from the daggers ripping through his temples and into his eyes—the pain gives way to something else.

Floating. He's floating. So peacefully floating. He's sure of it.

Like a butterfly, *he thinks.* I'm floating on air. How can that be?

195

It is then that Joel realizes he can see the air, the molecules and the atoms and the whole of the universe right there with him. His brain is burning and changing and becoming something else. Something more.

Spiraling down into the darkest pits of hell, he is reborn.

Through a fog and haze, a woman's pockmarked face and bleached-blonde hair came into slow focus before him, and Joel realized he was lying on a couch, covered in a blanket. "Bea," he said, throat raw and sore.

Seated next to him, she gently stroked his forehead and told him again and again that he was all right and not to be afraid. "I'm right here," she assured him. "It's okay. You're safe now."

Joel tried to sit up. "How long have I—"

She placed a hand on his chest. "Stay there. You need rest."

Exhausted and sore, Joel complied. His face hurt, and as he tried to move his arms, the pain in his shoulder reminded him of the knife wound he'd sustained. He winced. "Everything hurts. How long have I been out?"

"Couple hours."

As Joel crept farther from unconsciousness, his other senses began to sharpen, and he smelled something good. Soup. Chicken soup. "You didn't call—"

"I didn't call nobody," she said. "You got a bad wound on your shoulder. I cleaned it up and bandaged it best I could, but I don't know what the fuck I'm doin'. You need to go to the hospital. If that gets infected, you could—"

"No hospital, no cops." He pulled the blanket away far enough to see that he had no shirt on. She'd done a competent job dressing the wound with gauze and medical tape. Blood had seeped through the bandage, but the bleeding had stopped.

"A doctor needs to look at that," Bea said, standing. "And you got a huge gash over your eye this frickin' long." She demonstrated by pulling her thumb and index finger as far away from each other as she could. "I packed it with Neosporin and put a big-ass Band-Aid over it, but you need stitches. Lots of 'em."

"Thanks." Joel struggled up into a sitting position, his legs still stretched out before him on the couch and covered with the blanket. "Where are my clothes?"

"Your shirt was ripped and soaked with blood," she explained. "I threw it out. I tried washing your coat off by hand, but it's still stained. It's hanging on the back of one of the kitchen chairs. There's also another shirt out there on the table. Lonnie left a few things in the closet from when we were… Anyway… It should fit all right."

"I'm sorry for showing up like this, but I had nowhere else to go."

Bea folded her arms across her chest. "Do I want to know what happened?"

"No, you don't."

"Hon, you need to see a doctor. For real."

Joel swung his legs around to the floor. "I won't be here long, I—"

"Where the hell you think you're goin'? You're not in any condition to go anywhere tonight. Stay right there. Unless you gotta take a squirt. Do you? Do you gotta take a squirt?"

"No, Bea, I don't *gotta take a squirt.*"

"Don't you make fun of the way I talk, you fuckin' prick." She waved a reprimanding hot-pink fingernail at him. "I been playing nursemaid since your stupid ass got here, okay?"

"Sorry."

"You should be. Go showing up at my door lookin' like you got mauled by a goddamn lion, for Christ's sake. Scared the shit out of me. I'm still scared. Nobody else is gonna show up lookin' to finish the job, right?"

"There's no reason for anyone to look for me here," he said, head pounding.

"When's the last time you had somethin' to eat?"

"I can't remember."

"Well, I made chicken soup," she said softly. "Because I'm frickin' awesome."

"I don't know if I can hold anything down at this point, I—"

"You're gonna have some because it's good for you." Bea headed for the kitchen. "And because if you don't, I'm gonna stab you in your other arm."

Rain sprayed the windows, startling him. With a sigh, Joel tried to move his injured shoulder. The numbness was gone, replaced with a horrible ache, and while he couldn't move the arm before at all, he'd since regained limited mobility. But the pain in his shoulder was still nearly unbearable.

Bea appeared with a small folding table in one hand and a steaming, oversize mug of soup in the other. She put the table down and opened it before him, then set his soup atop it. She left again and returned with a paper napkin, a tablespoon, a bottle of water and three aspirin.

He downed the aspirin and drank nearly the entire bottle of water in one attempt. Then he tried the soup. It was delicious. "Thank you," he said.

"You're welcome. Can I get you anythin' else?"

"No, this is great." He sipped more broth.

Bea sat on the arm of the couch and lit a cigarette. "So you get run over by a truck or what?"

Rather than answer, Joel had more soup.

"Did the person who killed Lonnie do this to you?" she pressed.

"I don't know."

Bea reached down to the end table and scooped up a small, black plastic ashtray. "Yeah you do," she said. "After all this, you could at least tell me the truth. Think I deserve that much, no?"

Joel put the spoon down and wiped his mouth. "I don't want you to get hurt, all right? The less you know, the better. Once you have knowledge of certain things, you're responsible for it. Do you understand?"

"Yeah, I speak English and I'm not a moron."

He collected his thoughts. "I was almost killed tonight. Someone saved my life. If it weren't for that, I'd be rotting in a ditch somewhere right now. I don't want any of that darkness anywhere near you."

"Thanks, 'cause I'm not already scared out of my mind or anythin'." She took an angry draw on her Camel. "Like I need any of this shit."

"I know, and I'm sorry. I'll be gone in the morning."

"Story of my frickin' life. Am I ever gonna know what happened?"

Joel reached over and put a hand on hers. "It's better that you don't."

She nodded but wouldn't look at him.

"If anything happened to you because of me, I'd never forgive myself," he told her. "Once I'm gone, forget all this. Go on with your life. Be happy. If anyone comes around—and I mean *any-one*—you don't know me and we've never talked. You've never even met me, got it?"

She exhaled a stream of smoke and gave a quick nod. "What about you?"

"I don't know." He took up his spoon and had another mouthful of soup. "Maybe I'll make it, maybe I won't, but I have to end this. I don't have a choice."

"There's no other way?"

"Not anymore. I'm in too deep."

"You got somebody back home that cares about you."

"You think I don't know that? She's my whole world."

"And you're hers, right? You need to remember that. She's your wife. Somethin' happens to you, what's she supposed to do?"

It was a good question, but one Joel didn't have an answer for.

"You got to be there for her," Bea said. "Don't leave her alone, Joel. It's an awful thing to be alone. Makes you feel like you could disappear or die and wouldn't nobody notice or care."

"I'd care, Bea."

"Don't be a retard." She winked at him, then rolled her eyes. "You know what I mean."

"Yeah," he said, managing a slight smile. "I know what you mean."

"Eat your fuckin' soup, you pain in my ass."

"Yes, ma'am." He had another swallow of soup as Bea's two calico cats appeared as if from nowhere. One jumped up on the back of the couch while the other curled up in his lap. Across the room, in a window, the black-and-white cat sat watching the rainy night.

A thudding sound emanated up through the floor from the apartment below, then fell silent. Bea kept smoking and pretended not to hear it, but Joel could see the fear in her eyes. "You don't have any ties here, do you?" he asked her.

"Not anymore."

"You said you have a daughter in Connecticut."

"Yeah, and my grandbabies."

"You should leave the city, Bea. Go there and live. Leave all this behind."

She crushed her cigarette butt out in the ashtray. "Been thinking about it."

"You need to get away from this building."

"You mean Lonnie's apartment."

He nodded.

She clutched the ashtray with both hands. "What's down there?"

"I don't know."

"But there is somethin'."

"Yes."

She cleared her throat and tried to appear calm, but her terror was rising and it showed. "Is it Lonnie?" she asked in a loud whisper.

Joel didn't answer right away. "No. It's not anything even close to Lonnie."

"Somethin' else I don't want to know, right?"

This time he didn't answer at all.

"Is it gonna come out of there?" she asked.

He thought about the same things moving around in Pete Fernandez's cottage. They hadn't left the house, even though he and Pete were right outside. Maybe they couldn't. "I think they might be...confined."

"Does it want to hurt me?"

"Just stay out of there." He pushed the soup aside and sat back. "Get away from it. Get away from all this. Go be with your family. There's nothing good here, Bea."

She put the ashtray down and picked up one of the cats. Petting it gently, she held it close to her chest. "Makes you wonder if there's any good left anywhere."

"There's more than we know."

"Says the guy somebody almost killed tonight."

Kavon's face flashed before Joel's eyes, a face full of confusion as his neck popped and shattered and he fell away, swallowed in darkness and rain. *So much violence*, he thought. The cackling homeless man reappeared in his mind, alive and gulping down stew one minute and dead with his brains sprayed all over him the next.

Almost killed.

Even then, amid all the horror, Joel knew the likely identity of the phantom. He just couldn't bring himself to acknowledge it, then or now. It all felt like a blur, a nightmare where nothing made sense, yet everything fit together as if it did.

"That's why evil lives in the dark," he said quietly. "The rest belongs to us."

Without saying a word, Bea sat next to him on the couch. Still holding and petting the cat, she slowly let her head come to rest on Joel's good shoulder.

Together, they waited out the night.

CHAPTER TWENTY-TWO

By morning the rain had turned to snow. Joel left Bea asleep and snoring softly on the couch, her cats cuddled up all around her. A fresh shirt and his coat were in the kitchen, just as she'd said. It felt odd putting on something that had belonged to Lonnie, but he distracted himself by inspecting his coat. One shoulder had a tear and bloody hole in it, and though a good deal of blood had dried or been washed clean, quite a bit was still evident. He threw it on anyway, went back to the living room and, ignoring the pain throughout his body, bent down and gently kissed Bea on the forehead. She stirred and moaned but didn't come awake.

Downstairs, Lonnie's apartment was quiet. Joel stepped out into the cold morning air. Big, fluffy flakes fell slowly and steadily, draping the still and quiet city in a beautiful shroud of white, the morning light causing it to glisten like it had been sprinkled with tiny diamonds. He found his car where he'd left it, two blocks away. Nobody followed him, and the streets were empty, the snow still fresh and undisturbed, as if the entire neighborhood was still asleep. Perhaps it was.

He drove toward New Bedford, and the cemetery waiting for him there. He'd put it off long enough, but it was time. There would be no more chances.

Although it was located in the middle of the city, Saint Joseph's Cemetery covered more than fifty acres and sat atop a large hill surrounded by pine trees. Ornate wrought-iron gates opened onto a paved path that the led up the hill and to a sea of headstones, tombs, and mausoleums for as far as the eye could see.

Joel slowly followed the narrow avenues, doing his best to remember the exact spot he'd come looking for, and within a short time was able to find it. He sat there a moment with the engine running and watched snow fall across the graves.

So beautiful, he thought, *even amid all these monuments to death.*

His mother's body had been cremated, per her wishes, the ashes scattered in the Atlantic Ocean, but Joel often wished she'd been buried instead. Whenever he wanted to visit his mother's memory, he'd go to the ocean and watch the waves. There was something so vast and impersonal about it, though. He envied those who had a more specific spot to grieve. A spot like this, where one could stand before a headstone, something tangible and directly related to the person one missed.

Somewhere in this cemetery they'd buried Lonnie, but he hadn't come here for that.

One day perhaps he'd return and visit it, just not today. Not now. Not yet.

Joel got out of the car and walked toward a headstone bookended by a small pair of granite angels, winged cherubs kneeling on either side of the grave, stone faces forlorn and tortured, one's tiny hands folded in desperate prayer, the other's reaching skyward as if for mercy or aid.

He walked closer, through the flurries, until the name etched on the stone came into clearer focus: CYNTHIA MARIA MELLO, followed by the dates of her birth and death.

Heart sinking, he moved closer and realized that although a good portion of the headstone was obscured by snow, there was a second name etched into it as well. The large stone sat before three plots, one containing Cindy's remains and two more for her parents. A second grave had been filled since Joel had last been here.

He crouched a few feet from the family plot and read what he could of the stone. Cindy's father had died five years ago. Joel wrestled with his emotions, that poor man's tormented face forever burned into his memory, his soul possessed by crippling sorrow beyond comprehension. Somewhere in the back of Joel's mind, he'd convinced himself that one day he'd make things right and at least help bring Cindy's daughter's killers to justice. He'd believed his book would help facilitate just that. Instead it had become a joke, and now fate had beaten him to the punch. Joel could only hope the man's questions had been answered, and that, wherever he was, he'd been reunited with the daughter he so adored.

You have to see, you—you have to see who my little girl was.

Joel closed his eyes and was greeted by the VHS version of Cindy Mello as a little girl, tromping through wet beach sand and building sandcastles with her dad.

My…my baby…

"I'm sorry," he said, his voice quiet but carrying in the boundless silence, riding the breeze through the nearby trees. "To both of you, I'm sorry."

"You did your best."

Joel whirled around to find a woman dressed in black standing behind him. Her head was bowed and wrapped in a black scarf tied beneath her chin, and she'd aged a great deal, but he recognized her nonetheless. "Mrs. Mello…"

"I didn't mean to startle you," she said, still possessing a slight accent.

"It's all right, I—I didn't hear you coming, is all." He took a tentative step toward her. "I didn't expect to see you here."

"I come every day." Her dark bloodshot eyes, saddled with heavy black bags, looked beyond him to the graves containing her husband and daughter. "Even if just for a little while."

If they became widowed, many traditional Portuguese women wore black for seven years, or sometimes for the remainder of their lives. Particularly common among older women, it was a tradition Cindy's mother apparently adhered to, as her dress, stockings, shoes and even her pocketbook were black. Joel looked around for her car, but his was the only one in sight. Had she walked from the street below? Why would she do such a thing, particularly in this weather?

"They've brought you back," she said through a sigh.

"They?"

Rather than answer, she reached into her purse and removed a set of rosary beads. "That's why you're here."

"A friend of mine was killed."

She looked at him with sorrowful eyes, but had no response.

"I came back to see what I could do to help," he went on. "I wanted to visit your daughter's grave because I wanted to talk to Cindy. I wanted to tell her I was sorry."

"Cindy's not here." She gazed out at the rows of stones. "None of them are."

"I know, but…"

"It was a horrible time."

"No one involved was ever the same."

"You did your best," she said, her fingers nervously running across the beads from one to the next, then back again. "We always believed that. My husband, until the day he died, believed you were a good and decent man who truly cared about our daughter and what was done to her."

It took everything Joel had to hold back tears. "Thank you, Mrs. Mello."

"You told the truth, but people only want to hear truth for so long. Then, like all truth, it becomes…muddled…infected…and people no longer have any interest in it. They prefer lies."

The snow kept falling all around them, graceful and alive.

"It was a terrible thing they did to our little girl, and a terrible thing they did to the rest of us afterward. You told the truth, as you knew it, about who hurt our daughter and why they did it. And people laughed." Her bottom lip quivered. "They *laughed*. They laugh at God; why should we expect they wouldn't do the same to us? Lucifer's tail slowly wraps around them, his wings close over their eyes, and they don't even realize it's happening. They're too busy laughing."

"Yes, ma'am."

"A group of people took my daughter, tied her to an altar in a Catholic church, cut her open and played with what they found inside. Painted the walls and statues with satanic symbols and prayers and desecrated everything holy in that building with my baby's blood and bodily fluids. They took the eyes out of her head...my little girl's beautiful eyes...and had sex with her corpse." Her hands, shaking now, continued to work the beads, but she shed no tears. "They were doing the Devil's work when they murdered my Cynthia, Mr. Walker. The *Devil's* work, just like you wrote. And people laughed. They still laugh, even all these years later."

"Where was God that night, Mrs. Mello?" Joel said before he could stop the words from escaping him. "Where was God when they were slaughtering your precious child?"

Where was He when that black car took us?

"The Devil was in that church that night," she told him. "But God was there too, holding Cynthia in his arms and crying along with her. Crying for all of us, Mr. Walker, all of us. While we laugh, He cries."

"But He's *God*. Why didn't He *do* something?"

"He did," she said. "He comforted my baby, took away all her pain and fear even in the midst of pure evil, and loved her more than she ever thought possible. Not just that night, but forever. What's more powerful than that? God's not an action-movie hero, Mr. Walker. He's something much greater, so much so we can't even begin to understand it. There is no hate there, no violence, anger or judgment. Only love. Love beyond anything we can imagine. All the rest are the weaknesses, the sins and the excuses of man."

Joel wiped snow from his face with a shaking hand of his own. "I have those things inside me, Mrs. Mello...violence and anger...rage."

"Do you think I'm unfamiliar with those things?"

"No, ma'am. But there are people who have hurt me too, and those I love. Not the same people who hurt your family, but they're just as evil. That's why I came here. I wanted to tell Cindy I was sorry, and to ask for her permission to hurt these people. I don't have a choice anymore, it's about survival now, but I want—*need*—her to tell me it's all right...even if it's only in my head."

"Why do you need this from her?"

"Because she was good. She was special. That's why they chose her."

"And what makes you think this permission is hers to grant?"

"I know it's unfair of me to even ask, but I'm no action-movie hero either, Mrs. Mello. I'm just a flawed and damaged man, a husband, a small-town reporter."

"You're a frightened child trying to find your way in the dark." She continued running the beads through her fingers. "We all are."

"They're trying to kill me, Mrs. Mello."

"You wrote in your book that the coroner stated Cindy fought back against her attackers with everything she had, that she fought them tooth and nail before they finally killed her."

"That's right."

"Then fight, Mr. Walker. With everything you have."

It wasn't Cindy's blessing, but it was enough.

"They brought you back here," she told him, her eyes wandering across his bruised, battered and swollen face, and the remnants of bloodstains on his coat. "They brought you back here to die."

"Who?"

She looked to the trees along the ridge above the headstones.

Joel followed her stare.

Things moved between the trees, but he couldn't make out what they were, or if they were even there at all. Small, dark forms, he thought, moving slowly but just barely discernible—visible through the curtains of snow, then gone—or was it only a trick of the light? Like the entities before, and yet this time there was something more. They seemed oddly familiar this time. He'd seen them before, not only in Lonnie's apartment and Pete Fernandez's cottage.

Joel had seen them in his dreams.

He turned back to Mrs. Mello. She was gone. He was alone in the cemetery, the freshly fallen snow all around him undisturbed but for his own footprints.

Profound silence filled the cold air.

Stumbling forward, he took a second look at the Mello family headstone, this time dropping to his knees, then frantically wiping away the remainder of the snow blocking its face.

Cindy's mother's name and dates appeared before him.

She'd been dead more than two years.

CHAPTER TWENTY-THREE

The eye. It blinks. Slowly. Watches him. Stares at him through the strange keyhole shaped like a pyramid. Fading...blurring...the keyhole vanishes little by little until it has dissolved into nothing, revealing two dark eyes and a woman's face. She stands watching him, adorned in an unusual but striking piece of jewelry strewn across her face like a web, all of it black and connected, a single piece. As she moves closer, the thin chains and small stones, circles and triangles and complex butterfly wings just above either eye come into clearer focus.

Her eyes, heavily made up with black liner and shadow, only add to her wildly exotic look.

Her beauty is as startling as her sudden presence in the room, and leaves him breathless and uncertain. There is something at once alluring and frightening about this woman, something not quite... right...about her.

Voices...so many swirling around him at various volumes. Human voices, yet they sound robotic and monotone, as if they're reading from a previously prepared text. One male voice in particular is the loudest. It sounds as if the man has swallowed crushed glass or hot coals, his words too grumbled and distorted to understand. The voice circles him, as if from everywhere and nowhere, blending with the others…

At the very edge of his hearing, the gurgling voice becomes clear enough for him to finally understand, albeit only in short spurts.

"Sexual abuse is paramount, as it breaks the subject down and brings about the compartmentalization. Once programmed to forget such abuses, subjects can be more easily programmed to forget other things as well…"

And then he's running. He's running as hard and as fast as he can across an open field, the sun on his back and dark clouds gathering up ahead, just above the trees in the distance. Free of the strange, dark room and the woman, he can smell the air and feel the warmth of the sun, the scratching of the grass as it brushes against his legs. There appears to be nothing chasing him, but he runs as if there is.

"What we're talking about is a type of structural dissociation where the occult is assimilated into the equation in order to bring about compartmentalization of the brain. During this process, satanic rituals must be performed so that specific demons may be attached to the subjects and alters as well."

By the time he reaches the trees, the sunshine is a memory, back there in the field. Here, just beyond the tree line, it is darker and colder and frightening, because these are not friendly woods. These are deadly woods, haunted woods like in the fairy tales his mother used to read to him.

"The shattering of a personality brings about compartmentalization of memory, of trauma too horrifying to grasp or process. The result is dissociative identity disorder."

Disoriented and alone, he stumbles about between the trees.

"All it's about—all it's ever been about—is harnessing the power of darkness."

Where are the voices coming from?

"Our darkness…and theirs…"

And then it is quiet…too quiet for any of this to be real.

A forest is never this quiet.

Unless there is a predator nearby…

Horrible screams shatter the silence. Cries—the cries of children— send him running again, deeper into the forest until his foot catches on something and he vaults forward, free of the earth and soaring through the air, the forest around him rushing by in a blur as the screams fade, swallowed again by eerie silence.

He lands hard, on his stomach and chest, knocking the air out of him. As he lies on the ground, writhing about for breath, he sees the others standing between the trees up ahead.

Lonnie. Sal. Dorsey. Standing in a line, staring at him with blank expressions. A fourth person, partially obscured by the trees, is there too.

They're nude—all of them, nude—but why?

He crawls toward them, but the forest falls away. Like a painting rinsed from canvas in the rain, it all slides off into oblivion and becomes a long, narrow alley, dark and filthy and dangerous. Water drips from somewhere overhead—from rusty fire escapes and battered drainpipes—mixing with a steady downpour of dirty rain.

As the others walk away, through the alley, he follows, crawling on his belly.

The alley empties into a long street, dark and filthy, with fires burning in the night from barrels, spraying sparks to reveal condemned buildings falling apart all around him. A war zone, *he thinks,* an apocalyptic warzone.

To his right is a large lot surrounded by chain-link fence, but he cannot see beyond it in any detail. Something moves behind it, but he can't quite make out what.

There are others, more children scattered about the street and lots, all of them terribly filthy and neglected, dressed in grubby rags and looking as if they've lived under these horrible conditions for a very long time.

Sitting in a diseased puddle, the rain falling all around her, a sad little girl he doesn't recognize paws dirt and rainwater from her face with equally wet and dirty little hands. "No one will ever come, will they?" she asks, her big brown eyes blinking slowly at him, eyes that were once innocent and adorable.

He keeps crawling, and though he wants to stand, he can't. He barely has the strength to drag himself across the slick and slimy cement running with rainwater and trash and debris.

"No one's even looking," says the little waif. "Are they?"

"What am I doing here?" he gasps. "What are any of us doing here?"

The little girl places a hand over her left eye, then presses the index finger of the other to her mouth. "Shhh."

He crawls through another puddle as the rain continues to pummel him. Such filthy water everywhere. To his right, someone or something grabs hold of a length of chain-link fence, shakes it violently and lets out a guttural growl.

Light from a nearby fire reveals more hopeless children huddled in the darkness, watching him. There is a particular kind of evil in this horrid place.

And it is pleased.

More screams of agony echo through the darkness and rain.

The others—his friends—are still there and still nude, but they stand at the end of the street now, wearing intricate and frightening headpieces depicting odd hybrids of animals and demonic faces.

They're all covered in blood.

From somewhere behind him, a voice whispers a single word.

"Rebirth..."

Joel saw him well before he'd reached the car. Fleeing the grave and whatever was watching from the forest, he was halfway down the hill when he noticed an aged and rugged-looking Jeep Wrangler parked behind his car. A thin man in a long black duster, boots and a black knit hat leaned against it, arms folded over his chest, dark clothing standing out against the sea of white.

Joel was still several feet away when the man raised his head.

Trent.

Gone were the Mohawk, piercings and punk fashion, but the face and sad blue eyes were the same, only older and harder. His skin exhibited the tan and leathery look of someone who spent inordinate amounts of time in the sun, and the lines in his face were deeper and plentiful, the pain in him more profound and obvious than in his youth. Sprigs of hair protruding from the bottom and sides of his hat had turned mostly silver.

"We don't have a lot of time," he said in the same soft-spoken voice Joel remembered.

"I'm beginning to wonder if we ever did."

"How's the shoulder?"

"Hurts." Joel moved closer. "That was you?"

Trent looked past him at the hill.

"You were the one who saved me in the rain?"

"I kept my distance until then, but they would've killed you."

"You some kind of a badass now?"

Trent pushed away from his Jeep and, without a word, wrapped his arms around Joel and pulled him in close. It took Joel by surprise, but he went with it, hugging his old friend in return. There was nothing else to do.

"Why didn't you come to me sooner?" Joel asked.

"Time had to be right." Trent released him and resumed his watch of the hill. "You weren't ready for me."

"What are those things up there?"

"Fuck you think they are?" He started for his Jeep. "Come on."

"What about my car?"

"Leave it."

"But—"

"*Leave it.*" He looked back, expression stoic. "We have to move. Now."

"Where are we going?"

"Right now."

"My apologies if I'm not in the most trusting mood," Joel said, shaking from the cold, or perhaps something more. "But I just had a conversation with a woman that died two years ago."

If this information fazed him, Trent gave no indication.

"So I'll ask again. Where are we going?"

"Little deeper down the rabbit hole."

"Straight on to Wonderland, huh?"

"Not exactly our first trip," Trent said, "but you need to know what I know."

"And then?"

"The Devil needs killing."

Joel searched Trent's face for some sign of irony, but came up empty. Without response, he walked around to the other side of the Jeep, pulled open the passenger side door and climbed in.

They left the cemetery, Trent driving as fast and erratically as Joel imagined he might. The ride was anything but smooth, the old Jeep bouncing them both around and reigniting the pain in Joel's shoulder. The interior was bare bones, hadn't been cleaned in ages and smelled like stale fast food and booze. Whatever was behind the seats was covered in a dark wool blanket.

"Heaters broke," Trent mumbled, eyes manically alternating between the windshield, rearview and side mirrors. "Sorry."

"That explains why we can still see our breath."

The Jeep rocketed through the city, which had fully awakened now, and despite the snowfall, the streets were becoming more congested. Trent said nothing else as he drove into the south end.

Joel's gut tightened. "Trent, where are we going?"

"It's okay," he answered, pulling onto a desolate road near the water.

But Joel knew exactly where they were. The deserted side street littered with abandoned old factories and mills, the road that led to Tuser Industries. "Trent—"

"We're not going to the same place they took you. Relax."

"You were there?"

"I was nearby and watching what went down."

"Why didn't you do something then? They could've killed me."

"If they'd wanted to kill you at that point, you'd have already been dead."

"Barney…"

Trent glanced at him. "The homeless guy?"

Joel nodded.

"Collateral damage. Nothing I could do."

"You could've stopped it. You could've saved that old man's life."

"I told you, the time had to be right. I had to show myself to you when you were ready to see me, ready to believe what I have to tell you." He pulled into the weed-infested lot in front of an old mill, and then drove around back, traversing the rugged terrain until he'd found a spot sufficiently hidden from the road. "Let's go." He shut the Jeep off and hopped out.

Joel followed him through a blown-out door at the rear of the building and into a shadowy hallway that smelled like vomit and urine. Shielding his nose, he and Trent climbed a battered staircase to the second floor and into a large room with a row of mostly broken windows along the wall that faced the street. A few old pieces of furniture lay about amid the debris and trash, and Joel noticed a bedroll and pile of personal items he assumed belonged to Trent. Along with a gas-operated hotplate and other camping gear, the items appeared as if he'd been here for some time.

Without explanation, Trent crouched down and began rummaging around in an old knapsack on the floor. He removed a bottle of water, a tin and two metal mugs, and then, using a small cylinder of propane, fired up his hotplate.

"Jesus," Joel said, his voice echoing in the vast, empty space, "you've been living here?"

"Lived in worse."

"How long have you been here?"

"Since right before they killed Lonnie." Trent put coffee from the tin into each mug, then filled them with water, stirred them and placed them on the hotplate. "I tried to help him, but…"

"Why'd you come back?"

"Same as you, I didn't have much choice. They only make it look that way."

"You ran away years ago."

"Same can be said of you, my friend."

"I got married, moved to Maine."

"Only it wasn't that simple, was it?"

"I was trying my best to live my life, Trent, to forget—"

"But you never really did. Neither did the rest of us." He returned the water bottle and coffee tin to his knapsack, then stood up and wiped his hands on his duster. "I tried the same thing. Got married, did the regular life bit, but I couldn't shake the rest of it. The dreams, the…nightmares…the memories and the fear."

Joel turned to the windows, watched the snowfall and the lonely road beyond.

"I got as far away from here as I could. Wound up on the other side of the country. I needed to know what happened to us, and why. Fell in with some other people, more victims like us. They've done it to more than you know. And it's getting worse; they've been ratcheting it up for years. Everything was underground back in the day: hard to find, harder to decipher and even harder to prove. Then the Internet came into existence and everything changed. Information, and the exchange of information, became so much easier and readily available. I did my research and followed that rabbit right down the goddamn hole. There really is a Wonderland, Joel. It's covered in fire, and we've been burning in it for years, but it's there."

"I've talked to Sal and Dorsey."

"I know."

"They're both a mess."

"Why shouldn't they be?"

"Why didn't you let them know you were here?"

"It's never really been that much about them. Or even Lonnie, really."

Joel turned back to him. "I don't understand."

"It involved all of us, because to one degree or another, we were all able to do what they wanted. But it wasn't Lonnie, Sal and Dorsey that really mattered to them in the end. They weren't their star pupils." Trent grimaced. "You and I were."

CHAPTER TWENTY-FOUR

They stood in the silence of the abandoned building.

"You want me to take a look at that shoulder?" Trent asked.

"Are you a doctor too?"

"When you go deep underground like I have, you learn to do a lot of things for yourself." He motioned casually to another knapsack a few feet away. "I've got medical supplies."

Before Joel could answer, the rattling of the tin cups distracted them both. Trent turned the propane off, then grabbed both mugs. "No cream or sugar, hope you don't mind it black." He held one out for Joel.

"You realize that's not how you make instant coffee, right? You want to boil the water first, then add it to the coffee."

"Thanks, Mrs. Olsen. You want one or not?"

Joel took it. At least it warmed his hands. "Let's worry about my shoulder later," he said. "You said I needed to know what you know. I'm listening."

"Little background history. Up until the end of World War II, the Office of Strategic Services, known as the OSS, handled the intelligence and espionage duties for the government. After the war, when the Cold War began, along came the National Security Act of 1947, and the Central Intelligence Agency was born. The idea was for the CIA to expand and improve upon what the OSS had begun, and to establish an official organization that could supervise and manage all of the covert espionage and intelligence-gathering operations on a worldwide scale."

Joel sipped the coffee. It was horrid. "I'm familiar with all that."

Trent continued, unfazed. "One of the first things the CIA did was to delve into something called *behavioral engineering*. Mind control, and all the satellites thereof. As far as anyone knows, this started in the early 1950s. MKUltra was the name they gave the project. It would *officially* continue for the next twenty years. Numerous test subjects—primarily American citizens—were unknowingly experimented on with drugs, sensory deprivation and various forms of torture and abuse. This was sanctioned largely because of what had come before it. During World War II, US intelligence officers and former Nazi scientists first conducted these kinds of experiments. It was known as Project Paperclip. They experimented with mind control and the use of torture to achieve it, and while it didn't work as well as they'd hoped, it opened the door for bigger and more involved experiments down the road. Projects like MKUltra."

Joel sat on a nearby overturned crate.

"Everything was done in secret, of course, but it wasn't just government facilities that were used. We're talking numerous pharmaceutical companies, universities, hospitals, prisons and private companies—all paid by and used as fronts for the CIA to conduct these heinous experiments on unsuspecting human beings. In some cases it went so deep and was so secretive that the people doing the research didn't know who they were working for, and even some of the CIA operatives knew nothing beyond their own individual projects."

"This was all about influencing the mind so information could be extracted during interrogation, right?" Joel asked. "I've done some basic reading and research on it and—"

"Originally, yes. It was mainly about that and also to check the feasibility of creating a Manchurian Candidate, an assassin or operative who could be turned on and off to perform certain tasks without their knowledge or memory. In theory, they'd also be capable of being given secret information without fear of divulging it—even under interrogation or torture by the enemy—because they'd have no idea they were in possession of it in the first place. The result would be, arguably, the perfect assassin, the perfect spy, the perfect soldier, as it were, in their covert war. But it went much deeper than that. Those were only the starter projects. When they started using LSD, things got stranger. It had been around since 1938, but even by the 1950s nobody really knew that much about it. They wanted people with low levels of resistance for subjects, so they began with patients in nursing homes and mental hospitals, inmates in prisons and the like. Many of the victims were children with psychological or physical ailments. *Children*, Joel."

"Like us."

"They needed subjects who wouldn't talk, or who'd never be taken seriously if they did. Who's going to believe a child, a sick child at that, with wild stories that sound like nightmares? Who's going to believe a drug addict or hopeless alcoholic, a homeless person, a prisoner, a prostitute or someone with a history of mental illness? Nobody. They tested with other drugs too: mescaline, sodium pentothal, even weed. But LSD was the star. In one study they gave it to a subject every day for 174 days. Think about that for a minute. There wasn't much left of that poor bastard's mind when they were through with it. And that's nothing compared to what they did to some people." Trent sipped his coffee. "Later, in the 1990s, although most of the records were supposedly long destroyed, the government admitted to these atrocities—many, though certainly not all—and told the American people and the world that these programs had ceased and were abandoned years ago. In 1973, they said, but of course that was just a cover, and many of the projects continued. Many continue to this day."

Joel forced another swallow of coffee down. It was awful, but he was freezing. He tried to find some shred of the punk rocker Trent had once been, some small piece of the kid he'd known, but that version of him was long gone. This was a devastated middle-aged man just like the others, a nervous and brooding soul who had seen the darkness up close. He'd lived it.

"In addition to the espionage angle," Trent went on, "there were other avenues as well. One was to study control, the ability to create subservient and easily controlled human beings that could be utilized in espionage if necessary, but also in other ways, including as sexual slaves. The third was to study those who might have abilities beyond the norm when put in these situations and under such conditions."

"Abilities?" Joel asked.

"In one program in particular, test subjects were given LSD, but in massive amounts that were slowly increased over a short period of time. They also wouldn't allow them to sleep—sometimes for days at a clip—and of course the subjects began to lose their minds. They started to hallucinate, but they were in such terrible shape by then they could no longer distinguish between their hallucinations and reality. Lack of sleep and the LSD, combined with constant barrages of strange sounds and images, broke them down even further. After several days of this, one by one, the subjects began reporting that they were seeing entities. Not surprising, until the doctors realized the subjects were independently describing *identical* entities. Initially, they thought it might just be a consistent hallucination, because the test subjects had all been exposed to the exact same things." Trent stopped a moment, ran a hand across the stubble on his chin. "Until doctors and staff started seeing them too."

"The same entities we've seen?" Joel asked.

Trent nodded. "Supposedly the program was scrapped at that point, the subjects were sent back to their prisons and hospitals, and that was that. Whatever the hell they'd tapped into, they wanted no part of it. That was the official story, anyway. In reality, the powers that be were fascinated. It was a possible link to the occult, to another world or another level of consciousness. Whatever these things were, they needed to know if they were friendly or malevolent. Where did they come from? What, exactly, were they? Could they be used in some way to benefit or further the government's needs and desires? Did they have military applications?"

"What are they, Trent?"

"Not hallucinations, I can promise you that."

"What then? What are they *really*?"

"Evil incarnate."

"Demons?" Joel asked, his voice suddenly reduced to a loud whisper.

"What people don't understand is that the MK-Ultra project was ultimately based on nothing but the occult. Our entire nation was founded on it. Every great empire in the history of man has been. There are deep black ops and covert military intelligence groups that have been delving into these things for years. Every major power, before the Nazis and after, has studied the occult and tried to harness the power of its dark side. What does that tell you? Does that tell you it *doesn't* exist? That it's a bunch of fairy tales and nonsense? No one chases those things, Joel, spends millions of dollars and dedicates enormous amounts of manpower and resources on bedtime stories for the simple-minded. They chase it, try to learn about it and control it because it's real." He took another sip of coffee. "Most people have no clue about the real history of this country, much less this world. They know what they've been taught and believe what they've been told. Or they hold on tight to bullshit they've made up themselves from scraps of other truths. Problem is, you've got two basic sides, the true believers and the skeptics. One believes everything, the other believes nothing, and they're both falsely smug because they're both wrong. The reality is that evil is very real. It may be subjective in a sense, but it exists and it rules this world of ours, always has. Doesn't mean there isn't good; there's plenty of it. My God, there's so much beauty and love in this world sometimes it's hard to comprehend it. But neither of those things is the dominant force in our universe. Those who seek power above all else seek evil, because that's where the greatest concentration of power is. Be it short-lived or even false, for however long that candle burns, it burns strong and bright. And who really knows what lies beyond this world? Nobody. Not the atheists, not the religious fanatics. Nobody. But there's definitely something. Space dust, the pearly gates or something else, it all comes down to what." He stood before the windows and watched the snowfall. "You know Area 51, right?"

"Sure," Joel said. "Groom Lake. It's in Nevada, a base where they test top secret and experimental aircraft. Some say even alien technology."

GREG F. GIFUNE

"You know what else they call it?" Trent looked back over his shoulder at him. "*Dreamland.*"

"There are supposedly all sorts of strange experiments going on out there."

"Right. Now stay with me. Ever heard of Aleister Crowley?"

"He was a famous British occultist."

"Called himself the Beast, 666. The father, to some, of modern black magic, what he called sex magic, and founder of his own occult order, the Ordo Templi Orientis." Trent looked back to the snow. "Okay, so there was a guy named Jack Parsons, a rocket scientist, engineer and a chemist, a pioneer in those areas, actually, someone who ought to be very famous and well-known, but isn't because of his occult ties and black magic practices. Due to that, he's been largely forgotten in history and in some instances purposely written out of it. Truth is, he was an occultist and an avid follower of Crowley's OTO, but as a scientist his contributions to rocket propulsion and design are legendary. He's one of the more important figures in the history of our country. His inventions led to NASA sending astronauts to the moon in 1969, and even today, the solid-fuel rocket boosters used for the Space Shuttle were based on Parsons' innovations. There's actually a crater on the moon named for him. Every year, on Halloween if you can believe it, NASA's Jet Propulsion Laboratory holds a memorial for Parsons. They call it 'Nativity Day'. Yet very few people outside of the jet propulsion community even know who he is."

"What does any of this have to do with us?"

"Stay with me," he said again. "As an occultist, Parsons is credited with being most responsible for spreading Crowley's religion across North America. One of Parsons' closest associates was the man he would eventually lose his then-girlfriend to and the man who would go on to found Scientology, L. Ron Hubbard. Together, in the deserts of Nevada, they and others performed what were known as the Babalon Working, a series of occult rituals designed to bring forth an entity, the literal incarnation of a divine feminine archetype they worshiped, known as Babalon. During this period Crowley was in contact with Parsons and warned him about the potential for error. He warned them not to overreact to what they were attempting to conjure, but also

221

not to underestimate the danger of it either, because the idea was to open a literal interdimensional gateway that would allow passage. Problem was, there was no telling what might come through. For many years, in certain circles, it's been well known that Parsons was successful in his occult and black magic sex rituals out in the desert. He tore a hole in space-time, and something crossed over into our reality, but not in the way he had hoped. He hadn't conjured Babalon at all, but something much more horrific, evil and enormously powerful. This caused other authorities to get involved, the same authorities that operated in the shadows of the government and conducted their own rituals. Because through these satanic rituals in the desert, contact was established with what they referred to as 'the Old Ones.' *Demons*, Joel. Later, on the site of the rituals where the portal was opened, a top-secret military base was constructed." Trent turned from the windows. "That base is known today as Area 51."

A chill danced along Joel's spine. He drank more coffee. "I'm aware of the evil in this world, Trent. I wrote a book about it, remember?"

"I'm trying to tell you it goes much deeper than a bunch of clowns out in the woods sacrificing animals to Satan."

"I know that too, and frankly, your oversimplification of what I wrote about and dealt with, what some people died for, is pretty goddamn infuriating." Joel stood up. "So how about we cut through all the bullshit and secret agent man crap and you tell me what you know about why Lonnie was killed and what happened to all of us that day with the black car?"

"Okay." Trent smiled, but there was so much condescension in it, there was no room for humor. "Let's do that."

"Dorsey said that day in the field wasn't the first time they took us, that it had happened many times before and even after that."

"He's right." Trent paced over by the window. "It started when we were very young. I don't know the exact time and age, but we were little. We were selected, and it went on for years."

"Why us?"

"Bunch of kids from a working-class neighborhood. None of us with big families or lots of ties, nobody that watched us that closely." He shrugged. "In the end, who knows why they settled on us specifically—or anyone else. They must've seen something in us. Potential, maybe."

"Why don't we remember?"

"We do, some of us more than others, but in pieces."

"Some of those pieces are missing."

"Yeah. But they're coming back, aren't they?"

Joel put the coffee aside. "Keep talking."

"They like to use kids," he said softly. "Because they're easier to break, and if they can get to them early enough, they can mold them the way they want. They use a lot of different methods."

Despite the cold, Joel found himself perspiring and nervous. He suddenly couldn't sit still. "What kind of methods?"

A woman, a nurse, holds a baby, humming lullabies to it. She is drawn and serious looking, almost angry, but not quite. The baby looks at him too, such innocence in its eyes. They haven't taken that yet, ripped it away like wild dogs tearing at bloody flesh...

"It starts with sexual abuse," Trent told him, his tone less intense, more reflective. He struggled to get the words out, and his expression and body language showed it. "Only it's not a bunch of guys wearing raincoats in alleyways or creeps pulling up in vans. It's doctors in lab coats and nurses in caps, it's motherfuckers in suits and ties—pedophile senators and the like—having their fun and getting the job done for them. What we remember are the satanic rituals that come before and after—sometimes even during—like something out of a bad horror movie. Only for us, that horror movie is real."

The woman with the jewelry on her face...

"The abuse is so horrific children can't handle it, so they shut down. Their minds compartmentalize the experiences, tuck them away in a safe place, and they move on. And so the process begins. Their minds—our minds—are prepared for the next phase, because once the mind is fractured—some might say the soul—they introduce the drugs and the sensory and sleep deprivation."

An older table fan, the metal blades spinning, twirling...a telephone rings with the old kind of bell, ringing and ringing. No one answers...no one ever answers...

Trembling, his eyes moist, Joel asked, "Why did they do this to us?"

A stern, older man looks down at him, holds out his hand...

223

"We were one of the groups that saw the entities, Joel."

He takes the man's hand even though he doesn't want to.

"All of us saw them."

He watches the fan, concentrates on the fan as he goes away to somewhere else...somewhere safe and quiet where no one is hurting him and there are no screams, where little boys can run and play and ride their bikes in the sunshine...

"But you and me, we were special because we did more than see them," Trent told him. "We could conjure them."

Angrily wiping away his tears, Joel said, "I don't understand."

"Sal, Dorsey, and Lonnie saw these things too. For them, it was the result of what was being done to them. For you and me, we did more than see them in the corners of our eyes and in the shadows. We were able to bring them through. From there...to here..."

"How?"

"I don't know, but where others could only see them, we could make them real. Some subjects had special abilities, like I said. Subjects like you and me."

"Why can't I remember?"

"They've configured your mind not to." Trent sighed. "Problem is, that only works for so long. Slowly, gradually, those walls they worked so hard to construct in our shattered minds begin to fall away, and the truth behind them comes back to us, piece by piece, brick by brick. We're all in the same corridor, Joel. I'm just farther down the hallway than you. They figured out long ago that there are doors, and behind those doors are other realities. They learned how to open them back in Parsons' day. The rituals start here." He pointed to his temple. "So they knew if they could get the right subjects, break us down and control us, wipe our minds clean and replace them with whatever they wanted and needed to make these things happen, they could open more gateways and bring through more evil."

"Why would anyone want to do that?"

"Power. Destiny. Insanity. Makes their tiny cocks hard. Take your pick."

"But it stopped. They let us go."

"On a leash, so they could pull us back in whenever they wanted to. That time you spent in the nuthouse, it was just a tune-up, a reprogramming."

"Why are they trying to kill us? Why now, after all this time? And wouldn't it be easier to just take us out one by one? They could've just come to Maine and—"

"They already killed Lonnie," he said. "And tried to kill you."

"Dorsey and Sal, we have to tell them, we—"

"This is about us now, not them."

"What are you talking about? They're as much a part of this as we are."

"We can't save them, Joel. I'm not even sure we can save ourselves."

Joel watched him a moment. "Are you holding back on me?" he asked.

"It's all just too impossible to believe, right? Sounds crazy. Know why? Because it is, it's off-the-fucking-reservation nuts. The truth usually is. That's why they keep it from us, why they never tell people anything even close to it. Easier to tell them what makes them happy, what keeps them in line, distracted and thinking they're so smart nothing could ever be pulled over their eyes." He turned and looked out at the road. "Well, guess what? Think again. Never underestimate the power of ego and arrogance. Convince someone they're too intellectually superior to believe something, and you'd be surprised what they'll ignore and explain away or excuse rather than let go of that make-believe brilliance they've been convinced they possess. And why wouldn't they? Look at the dolts on the other side of the fence. In the end, they have an army of unknowing advocates and enablers. They don't have to hide things and claim they aren't true. Add as much misdirection and misinformation as they can get away with, and an entire generation of people step in and do it for them, thoroughly basking in how brilliant and informed they all think they are. Meanwhile, the fires burn right in front of them. They don't feel the heat, don't hear the screams, because to them, none of it's real."

Joel continued to pace, shaking his head as if to dislodge the traces of memories slowly slinking back. "Why did they kill Lonnie?"

"People die and disappear all the time. They've got plenty of ways to make you go away, weapons that can kill you and make it look like a heart attack or stroke. Fast-acting cancers and diseases they put in your veins that kill you in days but look like freak infections. They don't have to gun people down in the street."

"Yet that's exactly what they did to Lonnie."

Trent returned to the windows and looked out at the road below. A few cars were passing by through the snow, headed out of the area. "Everything they do has a purpose. None of it's random; it's only meant to look that way. They did Lonnie to bring you back. Now they're bringing me back too, both of us, out of the shadows."

"And now that we're here?"

"They want hell so bad, I say we bring it to them."

"Apparently we're pretty good at it."

"Storm's closing things up early from the looks," Trent said. "Employees are leaving Tuser Industries, have to go right by. It's why this is the perfect outpost."

Joel joined him at the windows. "Jerry Simpson…"

"The rest is on him. He knows the answers because he's behind what happened to us. He was directly involved, then and now. I think there's a good chance he was Lonnie's handler."

"What the hell is a handler?"

"Someone who helps control us out in the real world," Trent explained. "They influence and guide us without our realizing their connection to all this."

"And this Simpson sonofabitch, he was Lonnie's?"

"I believe so. We all have one. They come to us at various points in our lives, often beginning in childhood, but not always. They're particularly influential in our lives during times of trauma, fear, sadness and confusion. They give us just enough of a nudge to send us in whatever specific direction we're meant to go in during those times. From what I've been able to find out over the years about Simpson, he's in this up to his neck." Trent pointed to a black Mercedes-Benz slowly passing by in the mounting snow. "And that's his car."

The terror and tears were gone. Rage had taken their place. "You said the Devil needs killing," Joel reminded him.

Trent nodded. "That I did."

"Then let's go kill us the Devil."

CHAPTER TWENTY-FIVE

In a small town on Cape Cod, behind a large wrought-iron gate, the house sat more than a hundred yards back from the road, atop a long ridge surrounded by forest. The driveway, which was longer than many streets in town, carved through a patch of woods and wound along to the top of that ridge, The grounds encompassed nearly fifty acres; much of it meticulously landscaped and expensively maintained open lawn. At the rear of the property, well behind the house, a second building, a cottage, sat off by itself. Beyond the cottage was a boathouse, then a stretch of private beach, a dock, and the Atlantic Ocean.

Joel and Trent had barely spoken on the ride there, following Simpson's Mercedes from New Bedford toward Cape Cod, then finally crossing the giant Sagamore Bridge onto the cape. Going on the Cape Cod Highway was treacherous, as the snow had gotten worse and begun to accumulate—there were already a good three or four inches on the ground—but the slow speeds also made it easier to hang back and safely follow their prey. All the while, Joel's mind raced with possibilities and memories. Or were they only remnants of bad dreams? He could no longer be sure. Of anything.

"Looks like Mr. Simpson's done pretty well for himself," Joel said as Trent drove past the property, then turned around on a nearby dirt road.

Rather than answer, Trent pulled over to the side of the road but kept the wipers moving against the snow spattering on the windshield.

"Sal and Dorsey should be here," Joel said.

"They are." Trent looked at him. "We're always together, all of us, in a way."

"They deserve to be here for real."

Trent reached behind his seat and pulled free one of his knapsacks. He opened the flap and pulled out a gun, a .45. "I don't know what's waiting for us in there," he said, "but I'm not taking any chances with this fuck."

The gun made it real. The manner in which Trent handled it with such ease and familiarity made it disturbing. The moment he saw it, Joel felt like every muscle in his body had constricted in unison.

Trent tucked it inside his duster, pulled a second gun from the knapsack, a 9mm, checked it over, then held it out for Joel. "Take it."

"I've never fired a gun in my life."

"Here's the safety," he said. "Make sure it's off. Aim and shoot. Don't aim unless you intend to shoot. Don't shoot unless you intend to kill."

"What happened to you?" Reluctantly, Joel took the gun and put it in his coat pocket. "What happened to us?"

"We survived."

"All those years ago," Joel said, the words catching in his throat. "We were happy and carefree once, weren't we? Just kids. Playing, laughing…"

"Once upon a time."

A burst of cold wind cut through the Jeep.

"We don't have much time," Trent said. "They'll be coming."

Joel nodded, but he was focused on the flakes silently falling all around them. "It's beautiful, isn't it? The snow."

"I prefer the desert. I like the heat. At night it gets cool, even cold sometimes, but the heat, it's never far. And it's alive, the desert, hot or cold, day or night, alive. Always alive." A slight smile creased his weathered face. "I wish I could show it to you, man."

"You will."

The smile drifted away as Trent's sad blue eyes turned steely and cold. "We need to move. Rich little town like this, we're gonna stand out. Ready?"

"No, but what choice do we have?"

"None. Never did."

Together, they stepped from the Jeep and started up the road toward the gate. Moving through the falling snow, two dark smudges in a sea of white, they approached the gate, then stood there a while, watching the house in the distance.

Who was this Simpson? Joel wondered. Did he have a wife, a family, people he loved? Did he do these horrible things, then come home to them and pretend that all was right with the world? Did he rationalize his atrocities in his own mind, drape them in patriotism or some faux greater good? Or was he well aware of the master he served, the havoc he'd wreaked and the pain he'd administered? Did he revel in his accomplishments or hide in the darkness of his own black soul?

When they reached the gate, Trent began searching for a release. Simpson had utilized a remote device to open and close the gate, but there appeared to be no external manual controls. While he fiddled with the mechanism, Joel looked through the rails at the long driveway ahead. A Lexus sedan, Cadillac Escalade and Simpson's Mercedes-Benz were parked in a circular brick area in front of the house. The doors of the three-stall garage attached to the house stood closed.

"Why aren't the cars in the garage?" Joel asked.

"Who knows? People have garages all the time and don't use them."

"Seems strange, especially in this weather. Maybe the Lexus and the Escalade belong to people that don't live here. Maybe Simpson doesn't plan to be home long."

"Maybe you're overthinking it."

Trent removed something that looked like a screwdriver from his duster pocket and was about to force the tip into the gate lock when it simply opened with a loud click. With a baffled look at Joel, he returned the tool to his pocket, then casually opened the gate and walked through. "Wasn't even locked."

Joel followed him through and closed the gate behind them. "Something's not right. It can't be this easy."

"I know." Trent pulled the .45 from his duster, held it down against his leg, then started up the long drive. "Come on."

"We walk right in? Just like that?"

"What'd you think we were going to do, parachute in?" He kept walking, stepping in the fresh tire tracks Simpson's vehicle had left behind. "Act like you belong here, and no matter what happens, keep moving."

Joel trailed behind as they moved along the snow-covered driveway.

As they walked, silence engulfed them. Their breath swirled liked clouds and the temperature was harsh, but they continued on, waiting to be seen, for someone to appear and confront them. But nothing happened, and they soon reached the house, feet from a chipped stone path leading to ornate double front doors.

Lights filled a few of the downstairs windows, giving the home a warm and inviting look in the storm.

Trent approached the front doors. He tried the handle on the left-hand door. It opened without resistance.

"Like I said, too easy."

With a quick look back at Joel, Trent stepped inside.

A foyer, modest in size but outfitted with an expensive tile floor, a carpeted hallway to the left, a large living room to the right and a staircase straight ahead. The warmth was immediate, washing over them in waves. Closing the door behind them, they slowly moved a bit deeper into the foyer.

In the living room, an older woman Joel assumed was Simpson's wife sat in a comfortable chair, watching an animated version of Alice in Wonderland on an enormous flat screen, the sound muted. Dressed in a flannel muumuu, she was a plump, haggard woman well into her sixties, with hair styled like a football helmet. She stared blankly at the silent television, as if medicated to the point of no longer being cognizant of where she was. She seemed not to notice them.

They passed by a spacious kitchen and a set of French doors leading to a patio that was closed for the winter but featured extravagant fire pits and grills.

The entire house seemed preternaturally quiet.

Another room farther down the hallway appeared to be some sort of spa, with a large Jacuzzi, massive walk-in showers, a sunken bathtub and a variety of high-priced exercise equipment.

At the end of the long hallway stood a single door. Closed, it had no markings and gave no indication of what lay behind it.

As they approached, Trent held up his free hand, signaling Joel to stop. He listened a moment, then tried the door. It opened to reveal a large study, the walls lined with floor-to-ceiling bookcases, the floor covered in an expensive Persian rug. At the rear of the room were a desk and chair positioned in front of three large windows overlooking the back of the property, the second building in the distance. In the center of the room sat a pool table, and along the far wall, an extensive and fully stocked bar.

An older man stood behind the desk, his back to them. Gazing out the large windows, he calmly smoked a fat cigar, apparently transfixed by something outside.

Trent leveled the .45, holding it with both hands now as he stepped deeper into the study. Joel reached into his coat pocket and gripped the 9mm, but kept it in his pocket.

"Come in, children," the man said in a deep, raspy voice. "Father's been waiting for you."

Joel knew that voice. It had spoken to him countless times in his nightmares. It struck him like a hammer. He shook like the frightened child he'd suddenly been reduced to.

"Turn around," Trent demanded, remaining in his shooting stance.

Simpson did as he'd asked. Thick-necked and broad-shouldered, he was under six feet tall but built like a professional wrestler. Age had robbed him of what was probably once a powerful body and had left him pudgy and soft around the middle, but money had allowed him, among other things, a year-round tan, a bright capped-tooth smile and a watch and pinky ring that cost more than most cars. With a slow and plodding gait, Simpson came out from behind the desk. In one hand he held his cigar; in the other, a glass of brown liquor. He motioned vaguely to the bar. "Something to drink, children? Some vintage Scotch, perhaps?"

"Stop calling us that," Trent snapped.

"We're not children," Joel said. "Not anymore."

Simpson watched them a moment, his beady eyes dark and intense and looking mildly amused. Bald but for a ring of closely cropped white hair, the man possessed a presence and arrogance those in positions of power often wielded. He took a tug on his cigar, then exhaled a stream of smoke toward the ceiling. "You'll always be my children," he said, plucking the cigar from his thick lips. "Always."

"Are we alone in the house?" Trent asked. When no answer came, he stepped closer, the gun aimed at Simpson's face. "Answer me, you piece of shit."

"For Christ's sake," Joel said. "Answer him. Are we alone in the house?"

"My wife is in the other room, but she's of no consequence."

Simpson's pig eyes found Joel. It felt like they'd gone right through him, stabbed directly into his soul. He knew this man and yet he didn't.

"It's almost like meeting God for you, isn't it?"

"You're no god," Joel told him.

"I'm *your* god, boy." With bored indifference he drifted across the room to the bar. Selecting one glass decanter from a row of them, Simpson poured more Scotch into his glass, swirled it around a moment, then took a long sip. "Are you sure you wouldn't like a drink, children?"

Trent joined him at the bar, this time pressing the .45 against the man's temple. "Last time I'm asking."

"Is there anyone else in the house?" Joel said.

"No," Simpson replied evenly.

"Awful lot of vehicles out there for only two people."

Simpson raised his glass. "You always were the smartest one."

"Close the door, Joel," Trent said, lowering the gun.

He did.

"Anybody comes through it, shoot them."

Joel nodded. "You killed Lonnie to bring me back," he said, "and you brought me back to bring Trent out into the open. Well, here we are, Simpson. After all these years, here we are."

"You're the only one that ever really counted," Simpson said. "The other four, well, they had their purposes, of course, but you were always my *special* boy, Joel."

"Is that why you tried to have me killed?"

"Everyone has an expiration date, son. Even you. Even me." He shrugged as if there was nothing else to do. "Sooner or later we all become irrelevant. Bees in a greater hive is all, serving the queen, the master, for a greater purpose."

"What about Lonnie? Was he irrelevant too?"

"Now here I call you the smart one and you ask a silly question like that."

"Kidnapping us as children—abusing us, experimenting on us, *destroying* us, ripping our minds to shreds—that wasn't enough?" Joel tightened his grip on the 9mm but kept it in his pocket. "Why did Lonnie have to die? Why do any of us?"

Simpson considered him the way one might an addle-brained preschooler. "Not only were you the smartest, you were the best of them, weren't you, Joel? Are you worried about Sal and Dorsey? Don't be. We have no use for a broken-down alcoholic greaseball and a drug-addicted old nigger. They present no threat to us or anyone else. Frightened mice scarcely worth the time, much less the bullets."

"You're not worth the price of a bullet either," Trent said, raising the gun again. "But I don't mind wasting one long as it goes through your skull."

Simpson ignored him and sucked on his cigar. "They're ghosts now, Joel. Gone from you, as if they were never really there at all."

"Why was Lonnie branded?"

"It was necessary and he was our property. We own you. You're our slaves."

"He was a human being, with a daughter."

"You think you're gonna reach this garbage?" Trent asked. "You think you can reason with evil like this?"

Joel shook his head. "I just need to understand."

"Rebirth," Simpson said flatly. "There are many portals. We open them."

"With no regard for what comes through?"

"We know exactly what comes through. And so do you."

"Why then?"

"The master we serve, Joel. We serve him, you serve us."

"We were able to conjure entities," Joel said. "Trent and I."

Simpson smoked his cigar a while before answering. "Others glimpsed them. You made them real."

"What did I tell you?" Trent said.

"So many doors," Simpson said, laughing lightly. "You already know everything you've come here to ask me. It's all about opening the right doors, isn't it, Joel? Unlocking them to reveal the right answers."

Trent, the .45 still aimed at him, said, "You're gonna give us those right answers, Simpson, or I'll put your brains all over this nice rug."

"Who are you?" Joel asked.

"Just a man," Simpson said. "A scientist. Some might say a pioneer."

"A devil."

"Some might say that too."

"And they wouldn't be wrong."

"I suppose not."

"We're part of the Monarch Program," Trent said. "Aren't we?"

Simpson sipped his Scotch but didn't answer.

"Monarch," Joel said. "Like the butterfly."

The swarm of butterflies flying from Trent's mouth…

"What is the Monarch Program?" Joel pressed.

"In simple terms, trauma-based mind control."

The voices…the swirling voices moving all around him…human voices from everywhere and nowhere…

"Trauma," Joel repeated, as if involuntarily

One lone gurgling voice finally becomes clear enough to understand.

Simpson grinned. "Mmmm."

This voice. His voice.

And then he knew. He remembered. Joel put a hand to his mouth.

Sexual abuse is paramount, as it breaks the subject down and brings about the compartmentalization…

"We teach the brain to disassociate," Simpson said, slowly pushing the cigar between his fat lips with a suggestive widening of his black eyes. "And the result is a mind-controlled subject that has no idea he or she is being controlled."

Once programmed to forget such abuses, subjects can be more easily programmed to forget other things as well…

"The result, Joel…is you."

A stern, older man looks down at him, holds out his hand.

Joel focused on Simpson's hands. "You," he said through a hard swallow. "It was you."

He takes the man's hand even though he doesn't want to.

"Do you remember the fan, Joel?" Simpson asked.

The old table fan, the metal blades spinning, twirling…

"No, I—you son of a bitch, I—"

The ringing phone no one ever answers…

"Don't listen to him," Trent said, leveling the gun at Simpson again. "I'm gonna shoot this motherfucker. I'm gonna shoot him in his fat fucking mouth."

"There are so many," Simpson said, unfazed by the threat. "Slowly, gradually, we've taken you. One by one, and readied you for what's coming."

What we're talking about is a type of structural dissociation where the occult is assimilated into the equation in order to bring about compartmentalization of the brain…

"Do you think your descent into the occult, into the satanism running rampant all those years ago, was a mistake? Do you think it happened by chance?"

During this process, satanic rituals must be performed so that specific demons may be attached to the subjects and alters as well…

"Nothing happens by chance, Joel."

The shattering of a personality brings about compartmentalization of memory…

"The assassins, the sex slaves, the spies."

Of trauma too horrifying to grasp or process…

"None of them mean anything without the special ones."

The result is dissociative identity disorder…

"The ones like you, Joel, because you helped us usher them in."

The wiping clean, the death of one mind…and the birth of others…

"First come the children. Then the master."

"You're sick."

"*Diseased,*" he said, grinning again. "Wonderfully, eternally diseased."

Trent's gun hand began to shake so violently he dropped it back down to his side and took a few steps away. "Christ. Christ,

I—I don't know what to do, I…"

Simpson chomped his cigar with a disturbing slurping sound. "Do you know what happens to a child's mind when it shatters, Joel?"

Please—stop—help me—I—I can't move…

Joel looked away, his emotions raw and surging through him. He felt sick, like he might vomit or pass out at any moment.

"When something so horrible happens to their sweet, pure, innocent little minds?"

Simpson rolled the cigar back and forth along his bottom lip, the leaf damp with saliva. "Do you know what happens, Joel?"

"Shut up," he said through gritted teeth. "Just—just shut up."

"When the trauma is so extreme, the child's mind protects itself. Do you know how it achieves that, Joel? Do you remember?"

"Shut your mouth." Joel staggered over toward the desk, swung at a glass lamp on the corner and knocked it to the floor. It shattered at his feet. "Shut your fucking mouth!"

Trent looked at him, horror and panic in his eyes.

"The most severe torture," Simpson said, licking his lips as he pulled the cigar away. "The most delectable rape. It creates MPD. Do you know what that is, Joel? Multiple personality disorder."

His head, held in place…locked in place…held by some strange metal contraption that holds his head still…his eyes pinned open so he cannot blink, cannot close them…cannot look away from the things moving through the walls…

Joel's eyes locked on Trent, who looked as if he were about to explode as well. Please, his eyes seemed to say, let me kill him. Let me end this. Now.

"Do you know what an *alter* is, Joel?" Simpson asked. "Would you like Father to tell you? Those created when the mind breaks, yes? From chaos and pain, from horror and violence, comes birth. Messy and covered in blood, it comes, and in the same manner they must die, systematically destroyed, one by one. That's what we're doing, you and I. We're killing off those alters."

"You're lying."

"Or are *you* the alter, Joel? It's so hard to know for sure, isn't it? So hard to be completely sure of who is who and what is what in a world of deception…"

"You're a liar." Joel moved toward him.

236

"I serve the King of Lies. As do you. You haven't come here for answers. You've come for vengeance. You've come because I've sent for you, son."

"I'm not your son."

Simpson smiled, then winced in apparent ecstasy, rolling the cigar back between his lips. "You're my little boy, Joel, my special little boy. Father's missed you so very much."

Before he realized what he'd done, Joel had pulled the 9mm from his coat, closed on Simpson and hit him across the side of the head with it.

Simpson staggered toward his desk, dropped his drink but remained upright, a slow trickle of blood running from the fresh wound on the side of his forehead. Still clutching his cigar, he raised his other hand to the bloody gash and let out a slow moan. "We're in the final stages," he said. "You can't stop it. No one can."

"You're insane."

"No, my precious," Simpson said, smiling through his pain. "You are."

Trent paced maniacally over by the windows, mumbling to himself.

"The whole world is a lie, Joel." Simpson leaned back against the desk. "It's the world *behind* the world that matters, and the one who controls it all from the world we cannot see. Not yet. It's not what anything thinks it is. Not the pipe dreams of the non-believers, not the hooves and pitchforks the Jesus freaks piss on and on about, fearing their alleged savior and his tormentor both, frightened little children huddled in their ridiculous churches to nothing. Not any of the madness disguised as religions a bunch of savages dreamed up in their simple and stupid, superstitious minds while wandering in their deserts, as frightened of themselves as the world in which they found themselves. Weak, all of them, weak, with their rules and laws and prayers to a void that doesn't even know they exist, much less care. Not even the fools who think they've harnessed and worship darkness have it right, with their television rituals and music industry nonsense, their movies and award shows and their silly little cabals. Even the precious scientists, even we were wrong about more than we had right. It's all a magic trick. It's all a lie. And it's all the truth.

Every last bit of it, because everything is possible in the abyss. Everything and nothing..."

The horrible screams...

"It's time to come home, Joel. Don't you see? I've brought you home. It's time to quiet all those storms in your pretty little head, boy."

"You made those storms."

The horror and darkness...

"Yes, and now Father can quiet them." He dropped the cigar into a glass ashtray on the desk but kept his other hand pressed against his head wound, though it did little to curb the flow of blood. "Just like your pain and fear, Joel, do you remember?"

The agony...the shame...

"Father can bring pain...or Father can take pain away."

"Kill this fuck," Trent muttered, still pacing back and forth in front of the windows. "Kill him. Just kill him, just—just kill him."

Joel kept the gun at his side. "Tell me about the numbers stations," he said, motioning to the windows and the second building beyond. "That's one, isn't it?"

"They're all over the world," Simpson said. "Speaking to those who can hear them, to those who don't realize they can, and to those who have no idea they even exist. It's all part of a bigger plan, Joel, a bigger hive. Bringing the world to slavery slowly and quietly, while using our greatest gift against us. Our minds. Listen to the broadcasts, Joel. I know you hear them even in your sleep. Hypnotic, aren't they? Nearly as wondrous as the growls and whispers you hear at the very back of your mind while you're awake. It's beautiful. Beautiful slavery, child, *beautiful* slavery..."

"Kill him," Trent said again, suddenly more focused. "Or I will."

"All these years of magic," Simpson said. "All this time. The Devil's not a sprinter, Joel. He's a stroll on a hot summer day. He's a gentle breeze slipping through the trees. He's a drop of rain slowly gliding across a pane of glass, dew hanging from the petals of the most delicate flower. He's a butterfly emerging from its chrysalis in all its exquisite glory. He's everything you think he's not...and everything you fear him to be. Magic is real, Joel. Reality is built on it."

The door suddenly opened, and in one motion, a man stepped

into the office, a shotgun leveled in his hands. By the time it registered, he'd already fired.

Trent vaulted backward, into the windows, as a huge wound exploded across his midsection and a deafening boom shook the house to the chorus of shattering glass and splitting wood.

Reflexively, Joel raised his 9mm and fired several times.

The first two shots missed, tearing into the doorframe behind the man. The third struck him in the shoulder and spun him around. The fourth hit his side and dropped him to his knees as he cried out in pain.

In shock, Joel stood in the center of the office, the gun still aimed at the man he now recognized as Novak. Simpson remained where he was, a ridiculous grin on his face. Trent was collapsed and caught in the destroyed windows, half his body hanging outside, the other half still in the office and covered in blood.

Snow and cold air blew through the newly formed portal.

Novak, grunting and groaning in agony, reached for the shotgun he'd dropped when he fell to his knees.

Joel aimed and fired, blowing several of Novak's fingers from his hand in a spray of blood and bone.

Screaming, Novak slumped forward. "Motherfucker!"

Music...I hear music...sad...strange music...piano...a sad and lonely piano...

Stepping closer, and with a skill and calm Joel had no idea he possessed, he placed the 9mm under Novak's chin and fired.

The body flopped over onto its side, the top of Novak's head a bloody and mangled mess of brain and tissue. The body convulsed several times, then lay still.

Blinking Novak's blood from his eyes, Joel turned back to Simpson.

The son of a bitch was still smiling. His free hand reached down to his crotch and gleefully rubbed the erection pressing against his slacks.

Those eyes...dark and horrific...looking down at him...inside him as a piano plays in the distance...

"The things I've seen, Joel, the things I've shown you through skies torn open like wounds in Heaven," Simpson said, his speech slurred from the blood trickling into his mouth. "Fires burning and alive in the ruined minds of geniuses and fools, starving children and bloated kings on thrones of pride and lust. Liars and prophets, slaughter, slavery and exterminations on scales unimaginable, blood running in the streets, butchers loose in the West, the killers of children unleashed in the East, the rise of night, the fall of light. Each and every glorious moment, every unanswered prayer, every tear, every breath. I remember them all."

What do you remember, Joel?

"I remember you," Joel said. "You, Father. I remember you."

"As above, so below." Simpson began to laugh as he opened his arms in welcome. "Come, child. Fulfill your destiny. Send me through the door. Open it wide for all that needs to come through."

Joel shot him in the throat.

Simpson slumped to the floor, a gurgling, bloody mass writhing about on the rug. Straddling him, Joel began to hit him with the butt of the 9mm. Again and again, until he had no strength left and there was little more to the man's skull than a frothy mess.

As if in a trance, Joel stumbled over to the windows.

Drenched in blood, Trent lay on his back in the destroyed window frames, his upper body bent back and dangling out in the storm.

Carefully, Joel pried him free of the jagged glass, pulled him inside, and together, they slid to the floor.

"Trent," he whispered, holding him in his arms. But he was already gone.

Images drifted through his mind, disjointed and muddled, yet comforting somehow. Trent, much younger, his Mohawk spiked and defiant, his *Dead Boys* T-shirt torn and a cigarette dangling from his mouth as he smiled that rebel grin of his. And it was that grin Joel thought of most. So alive and maybe even happy, with no idea what it would all lead to.

Children...all of us...children...

Joel began to cry, and once he started, it felt as if he'd never stop, that nothing would ever be all right again.

Some time later, Joel let Trent go, gently laying the body down beneath the broken windows. When he stood up, he saw

Simpson's wife standing in the doorway to the office.

She stared at him with dead eyes, her wrists freshly slashed and dripping blood. "Resut," she said softly.

To come awake…awakening…from a dream…

"Magic is real," she muttered. "Forward or backward, makes no difference." She looked around at the carnage before her, completely unaffected, then turned and shuffled off down the hallway. "Time is a palindrome."

Before she'd reached the end of the hallway, she collapsed.

Covered in blood himself, Joel grabbed Novak's shotgun and moved back through the house, numb and as if in a dream. His mind could take no more, and yet, it somehow was managing just that. He wanted to sit in a corner and die, to close his eyes and forget all this, to make it stop. He wanted Taylor. He wanted peace. But that was not possible. Not now. Not yet.

Outside, he moved through the snow and cold wind blowing in off the choppy Atlantic, and trudged across the yard and what was now five inches or more of accumulation. When he got to the back building, the door was open.

The small shortwave radio station was outfitted with an array of automated broadcasting equipment. On a slowly moving reel, an artificial female voice repeated number sequences and phrases in monotone, interspersed with strange sound waves and brief clips of music.

In the boathouse near the dock, Joel found containers of gasoline.

Later, he stood outside the gates and watched it all burn a while, the flames oddly beautiful in an otherwise snow-covered world.

By the time authorities arrived, Joel was gone.

Like he'd never been there at all.

CHAPTER TWENTY-SIX

Music echoes through the forest. A piano sits alone amid the trees. No one plays it, none of the black or white keys move, yet there is music, beautiful music, peaceful and magical, as nearby other sounds drift from the darker parts of the forest. Screams of those dying and long dead…and those being born…

Something hangs from a tree. Large and bulbous, a cocoon of sorts, it is slick and wet and dripping a thick mucus. Something within it writhes and fights to break free, struggling against its prison to be born into this forest of lies and darkness.

Above, an impossibly black rainbow cuts the gray sky.

Joel stands at the very edge of the strange woods, watching and listening and trying to understand. He is afraid but he does not run. There is no point because it is he that is trapped within that giant cocoon. The thing struggling so fiercely to free itself is as much a piece of him as the little boy watching it all unfold.

A single feather falls from the treetops, floating and dancing on the breeze as it descends to earth. When it lands, Joel recognizes it for what it is: a piece of a larger whole, a headdress perhaps, sacred and forgotten. He crouches to pick it up, but it is covered in the blood and misery of ghosts.

It is then, as he stands and backs away from the strange feather, that he sees blood pouring from the sides of the piano onto the forest floor, covering the piles of scorched human bones scattered about at its legs.

The piano continues to play, unabated, its beautiful music unaware or full of callous disregard for what is happening all around it.

"Genocide," the forest whispers. "That which was before, is now, and shall be forever and ever."

Joel closes his eyes, sees Lonnie dying in the street...

Trent dead on the office carpet...

Dorsey in his bed in a pool of vomit and blood, dead from an overdose, an empty bottle of booze lying on the floor just beyond his outstretched hand...

Sal killed in a car accident, his body thrown and dead on the side of the road, eyes open but seeing nothing, the car wrapped around a nearby tree, mangled and twisted, smoking metal and shattered plastic...

One by one...

Every life, every story moves on. Forward or back, makes no difference.

When Joel opens his eyes, the music has stopped and the piano is gone, replaced instead with a small black-and-white television. A dated commercial plays, something with a stereotypical 1950s housewife flitting about a kitchen in her heels and pearls...

Forward or back, makes no difference.

And then he's pedaling his bicycle... Faster and faster, he pedals along the edge of the forest, the big black car not far behind in pursuit...

Time is a palindrome.

A screech of tires, a struggle, and his bike is left in the middle of the street, the rear tire still spinning as he watches from the backseat of the car...watches it all fade into the distance...watches himself fade into the distance...

Blood...so much blood...spraying and splashing everywhere...

The cocoon has broken; the butterflies are free, exploding from it in a cloud of wings and crimson motion...like a horrific dream turned loose...

Before the silence, the awful silence that skulks toward him in that horrible room, the world turns blindingly white as the screams come.

The screams of little boys and girls lost, orphans all, huddled in the shadows of Wonderland.

He came awake in unfamiliar surroundings and immediately bolted upright in bed, thrashing about in the darkness despite the pain savaging his shoulder.

"It's all right," Taylor said, grabbing and holding him close. "Baby, it's okay." When Joel felt her soft, warm hands on him and remembered where he was, he felt himself begin to decompress and calm down. Slowly, he lay back into the pillows and sighed. "Sorry, I…"

Billy had done exactly as he'd asked and taken Taylor to his cabin in the woods of northern Maine. Joel had found them there just hours before, and while Billy stood watch out in the kitchen, his shotgun at the ready, Taylor had recleaned and re-dressed his wound, then convinced him to lie down with her for a while on the bed to get some rest. She'd wanted explanations, but he had none to offer yet. Instead, he'd collapsed onto the bed in Taylor's arms and slipped into a deep sleep for the last several hours.

"What time is it?" he asked, staring up at the ceiling.

"Late," she said. "After two."

He reached over and stroked the side of her face. He'd stripped down to a pair of boxers, and she wore only an oversized T-shirt. The rest of their clothes lay in a pile on the floor just inside the door, yet he was burning up and drenched in sweat.

"Why is it so hot in here?"

"Billy has the woodstove cranking," she explained.

Joel looked immediately to the nightstand where he'd left his gun. "The 9mm—"

"It's in the drawer," Taylor said. "I didn't want it out in the open. You know I don't like guns, Joel. And since when do you? You don't even have a license to be in possession of a gun; you could get in a lot of trouble."

"I'll take my chances." He rolled over, swung his legs around onto the floor and yanked open the drawer to reveal the gun. He took it out, placed it on top of the nightstand, then closed the drawer.

"You have to tell me what's happening," she said, crawling

closer and wrapping her arms around his back. "Please, Joel. You owe Billy an explanation too. We're frightened and confused and sitting up here like criminals hiding in the storm, waiting for you to make some sense of what's going on. We can't stay here forever. No one even knows we're here, not my family or friends or even anyone from my job—no one—but sooner or later people are going to start wondering."

"It's been quiet since you've been here?"

"Yes, it's been just the two of us, and it's been positively boring."

He nodded but didn't look back at her.

"Please, Joel, tell me what's going on."

"I need time," he said softly, watching the dark windows on the far wall and the traces of black forest beyond the clearing in which the cabin had been built.

"Time for what?"

"To figure out what to do next. I don't know if this is over, Taylor. It may never be."

"*What* may never be over?" she pressed. "For God's sake, you won't even let us take you to a doctor and you've got a serious wound. Who did that to you?"

Joel rose to his feet, pulling free of her even though he didn't want to. He drifted around the foot of the bed to the windows on the other side of the room and looked out at the forest there.

"Are you expecting someone?" Taylor asked from behind him.

"Just being sure no one's out there."

"Joel, we're in the middle of nowhere. No one's out here but us."

Maybe she's right, he thought. *Maybe it's over in a way, or as close as it ever can be.* Maybe it ended when Simpson took his last breath and died with his secrets and magic spells. Maybe now it was about moving forward and trying to forget, surviving in a world gone mad.

He remembered shoveling snow at the house—that seemed like a lifetime ago—and wondered if he and Taylor would ever return to their home.

Could things ever be same?

Life is a palindrome, a story told forward or backward, makes no difference.

"Joel, why don't we leave in the morning, all right?" Taylor rolled over onto her back, her hands behind her head and her legs stretched out before her. "You have to see a doctor, sweetie."

"My shoulder's fine for now."

"I'm not talking about your shoulder. You need to see a doctor. Like before."

He turned and looked back at her. "You think I'm crazy."

Taylor wouldn't make eye contact.

"I can't blame you," he said. "Maybe I am."

"You just need some help," she said quietly. "This isn't...normal, Joel. Your behavior isn't...it's not..."

He moved closer to the bed and gently stroked her hair. "I'll explain best as I can in the morning, all right? You need to know what I've been through and what's happening out there."

She looked at him, baffled. "Out *where?*"

"Try to get some rest. We'll talk in the morning."

"What are you going to do?"

"I told Billy to keep watch. It's been hours; he's probably exhausted. I'm going to relieve him for a while so he can get some rest too."

"What is he keeping watch for, Joel?"

He kissed her forehead. "We'll talk in the morning."

"Joel—"

"I love you."

Taylor sighed, stroked his arm. "I love you too."

Joel brought her hand to his lips and kissed it, and then started toward the nightstand to retrieve the 9mm.

"You don't need the gun," she said, rolling toward it. "I'll put it in the drawer, okay? I really don't like all these guns around. They're scaring the shit out of me."

"Taylor—"

"How did you even get Lonnie's gun in the first place?" she asked, opening the drawer.

"What?"

"How did you get it?" She reached for her eyeglasses and slid them on. "Did his daughter give it to you?"

Something deep within him tightened, clamping down on his gut. "How do you know that's Lonnie's gun?"

"Huh?"

"How do you know that's Lonnie's gun, Taylor?"

She looked back at him and made a face. "You told me it was."

"No, I didn't."

"Yes, sweetie, you did."

"I couldn't have, because I didn't know it was Lonnie's gun until just now."

"This is ridiculous, I—I don't know what you're talking about."

His eyes dropped to her ankle and the tattoo there. A tattoo he'd once found beautiful. A monarch butterfly in all its glory, burned into her flesh.

Shaking, he slowly looked back at the freestanding mirror in the corner.

A triskele had been branded into the back of his shoulder.

I got married, moved to Maine.

"No," he whispered, backing away.

Only it wasn't that simple, was it?

Taylor moved away from the gun and rolled over onto her back. "You need help."

I think there's a good chance he was Lonnie's handler.

"That's where you come in, isn't it, Taylor?"

What the hell is a handler?

"This isn't about me." She sighed, folding her arms across her chest. "This is about you and your problems. I want to help, but if you're going to get—"

"Who the hell are you?"

Someone who helps control us out in the real world. They influence and guide us without our realizing their connection to all this.

"I'm your wife. What the hell kind of question is that?"

We all have one. They come to us at various points in our lives, often beginning in childhood, but not always.

"Who are you really?"

They're particularly influential in our lives during times of trauma, fear, sadness and confusion.

"I met you right after my mother got sick," he said, the vision of the only woman he'd ever loved blurring through his tears.

They give us just enough of a nudge to send us in whatever specific direction we're meant to go in during those times.

Taylor stared at him. "And?"

Joel turned and ran from the room, pushing through the door

and into the kitchen, where he'd left Billy sitting at the kitchen table hours before.

His shotgun lay on the table alongside a mug of coffee, but Billy was gone.

He spun toward the large glass slider. Just beyond the deck, Joel saw him in the moonlight.

Upside down, stripped naked, gutted and crucified to a tree.

Joel lunged for the shotgun just as the entities appeared in the darkness, hundreds of them hobbling out from between the trees in a single wave, closing on the cottage and surrounding it.

A ring of fire suddenly burst to life, encircling the cottage, and behind him, in the bedroom doorway, Taylor began to laugh.

CHAPTER TWENTY-SEVEN

There was something wrong.

A sudden burst of light filled the sky overhead, and the little boy realized then that he'd opened his eyes. Lying in the field, everything was so quiet. Even the breeze blowing through the trees and across the grass, it was all so different from the bad dreams, so soft and peaceful. Yet the crippling fear remained.

All he could remember was the big black car and the bad dreams, always the bad dreams about things he couldn't understand, barely remembered and didn't want to think about.

With a deep breath, the little boy got to his feet and brushed himself off.

He looked to the road. Nothing. No one. He was alone.

Nearby, his bicycle lay in the grass, the back wheel spinning. He'd best get home before dark. It made him feel better to think his parents were likely worried about him, though he knew they probably didn't even know he was gone. Still, he grabbed his bike by the handlebars, pulled it upright, then climbed on. It was easier to believe what made him feel safe and secure than it was to face those things that frightened him so.

Besides, he thought, *maybe it's just a game. Maybe I was lying in the grass, pretending to be asleep.*

Far away, on the horizon, black storm clouds were gathering, threatening to ruin an otherwise beautiful day.

Horrible images flashed in his mind, but in all the terror and hopelessness, the little boy thought that maybe, just maybe, if he could survive this, he could survive anything. That maybe hope was the only thing that would survive, that could survive, because if the night could rise and light could fall, then the opposite was also true. If there was hope even when it appeared there should be none. If there was love even when it appeared such a thing no longer existed. Maybe if, even in the face of pure evil, there was no hatred, violence, anger or judgment, but only love beyond anything that evil could imagine, then the dark would not— could not—be quite so dark and hopeless after all.

And maybe, just maybe, it was not the night that triumphed at all, but the day, because it wasn't really true darkness at all, only a shadow hiding from the sun.

His fear fading, the little boy took one last look back at the storm clouds.

Then pedaled for home.

AUTHOR'S NOTE

Although *Orphans of Wonderland* is of course a work of fiction, MKUltra, as well as many other mind control programs, were (and some would argue still are) quite real. Number Stations also exist, and while there are many theories regarding their purpose, some more generally accepted by the mainstream than others, they remain largely a mystery. The topics explored in this novel have always intrigued and troubled me on a deeply personal level, for a number of reasons, due in part to some as yet not fully explained or resolved aspects of my own childhood history, and while writing *Orphans* proved to be an emotionally draining experience on a number of levels, I'm glad to have finally had the opportunity to explore these themes in my fiction. Thank you to everyone at Journalstone for giving me the opportunity to get this novel back in print, particularly Chris Payne and Jess Landry for their belief in me and my work, and for all their support. Finally, thank you to all the readers and fans across the globe for the continued enthusiasm and unwavering support. My deepest and sincere appreciation goes out to each and every one of you. I hope you enjoy *Orphans of Wonderland*.

Greg F. Gifune is a best-selling, internationally-published author of several acclaimed novels, novellas, and two short story collections. Working predominantly in the horror and crime genres, Greg has been called "the best writer of horror and thrillers at work today" by *New York Times* best-selling author Christopher Rice, "one of the best writers of his generation" by both *The Roswell Literary Review* and horror grandmaster Brian Keene, and "among the finest dark suspense writers of our time" by legendary best-selling author Ed Gorman. Greg's work has been published all over the world, translated into several languages, received starred reviews from *Publishers Weekly*, *Library Journal*, *Kirkus* and others, is consistently praised by readers and critics alike, and has garnered attention from Hollywood. Two of his short stories, "Hoax" and "First Impressions," have been adapted to film. His novel, *Children of Chaos*, is currently under a development deal to be made into a television series.

His novel, *The Bleeding Season*, originally published in 2003, has been hailed as a classic in the horror genre and is considered to be one of the best horror/thriller novels of the decade.

Greg resides in Massachusetts with his wife, Carol, a few cats, and a dog named Dozer. He can be reached online at gfgauthor@verizon.net or on Facebook and Twitter.

www.ingramcontent.com/pod-product-compliance
Lightning Source LLC
Chambersburg PA
CBHW020828260626
47169CB00003B/887